I0738016

FERTILE GROUND

FERTILE GROUND:

A NOVEL

PENN STEWART

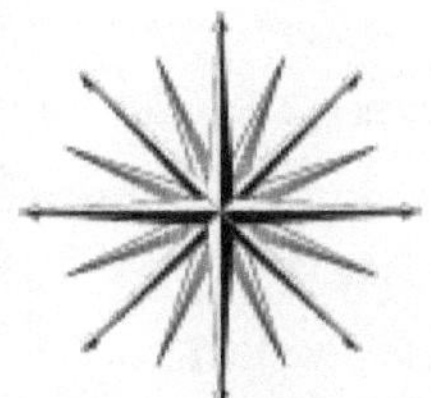

Wandering Aengus Press
Eastsound, WA

Second Edition published by Wandering Aengus Press
Fiction
ISBN: 978-0-578-63285-8
Library of Congress Cataloguing-in-Publication Data available.
Cover Image: Away by Marlene Bitzer, Pixabay 820298
Author Photo: David Taub

Wandering Aengus Press
PO Box 334 Eastsound, WA 98245
wanderingaenguspress.com

Wandering Aengus Press is dedicated to publishing works to enrich lives and make the world a better place.

First Edition published by Knox Robinson Publishing
34 New House, 67-68 Hatton Garden, London, ECIN 8JY
Copyright © 2014

Acknowledgments

A considerable amount of time and energy was spent researching this novel. While the characters are fictitious, and any resemblance to any person living or dead is purely coincidental, the events depicted represent a very real and often overlooked aspect of American History.

This book would not have been possible without contributions from the following exhibits, texts, people, entities, and organizations. Many thanks to the following:

"Snow Country Prison: Interned in North Dakota," organized by North Dakota Museum of Art and the United Tribes Technical College, curated by Laurel Reuter, with assistance from John Christgau, author of *Enemies: World War II Alien Internment*, 2001.
United Tribes Technical College, Bismarck, North Dakota
Lucy Schulze, author of *Lucy and Hans: Who Were They?*
Stephen Fox, author of *Fear Itself: The Past as Prologue*
Rod Gragg, author of *From Foxholes and Flight Decks: Letters Home from World War II*
The Oxford Companion to World War II by I. C. B. Dear
Ned R. McWherter Library at the University of Memphis
National Geographic
University of Buffalo
"Memories and Words from Snow Country Prison," by Dan Gunderson *MPR*
Western New York Heritage Press
Sherman Registry of Steel Foundries
New York State Police
Department of the Navy—Naval Historical Center in Washington, DC.
U.S. Department of Justice
Federal Bureau of Investigation

I would also like to thank and acknowledge the contributions of individuals who helped me in the completion and publication of the novel. Dennis J. Nuemann, Public Information Director of the United Tribes Technical College in Bismarck, North Dakota; Professor Jonis Agee, my mentor; Professors Fran Kaye, Gerry Shapiro, Judith Slater, and Hendrik van den Berg; John Sibley Williams, Susan Kim Campbell; numerous colleagues at the University of Memphis and the University of Nebraska-Lincoln who read and commented on early drafts; and lastly, I'd like to thank my wife Rajean, who was very supportive of this project throughout the years it's taken to complete.

I dedicate this novel to my wife and daughters.

In the end, family is all that matters.

Chapter 1

By the time she was fifteen, Lucy had helped deliver three still-born siblings. Her father, as though he had some seer's sense about such things, allowed obligations to draw him away from his wife in the time of greatest need. As the oldest child, Lucy shouldered responsibilities beyond her years. She buried the children in unmarked graves on the edge of their property as her mother lay in bed under the weight of grief. Lucy imagined names for the little ones who were lost before they had a chance to begin, and with those names she imagined the stories of lives not lived, sketching out constellations for each one so that they may shine against the canvas of night. As each child was raised to the sky, Lucy's mother fell deeper into solitude, bereft by the vacancy and the stillness of time. When Lucy became a woman, married for love, bore two healthy sons, and lived much of her life without the heartache her mother had suffered, her years sped by, little more than a shining moment of a dream.

She and her husband Hans owned a small farm outside the town of Friedberg, roughly ten miles southeast of Buffalo. In late March of 1942, the wind whistled through the eaves of the old farmhouse and the rain pelted the picture window behind Hans as he sat in his favorite chair listening to a German news report on his short-wave radio. His fingers drummed his chin as he stared into the middle distance. The battle reports and patriotic musical interludes blared with maniacal enthusiasm. Lucy bought the radio four years ago as a Christmas present. It was expensive, but at the time she thought the expenditure worthwhile if it meant an end to Hans' countless newspapers. The papers arrived weeks after their post dates, but Hans read every word. Sometimes four or five sat in his lap, and he'd move from one to the other, like trying to put puzzle shapes together that didn't quite fit. The radio didn't replace any of the newspapers, and it brought its own ills. Something in the way Hans sat hypnotized by the distant voices crackling amidst the static, not looking at anything—but searching—hit a nerve in Lucy. The feeling snuck up on her, dug its teeth into her, and held tight before she could dismiss it as the typical annoyance one must endure in a marriage.

She stood in front of the pantry, trying to decide what to prepare for the evening meal when she heard a gasp. She peeked around the corner of the kitchen doorway. Hans shook his head in disbelief and rubbed his forehead, as though trying to smooth out the creases that had recently deepened. Her husband had changed over the last few days. He responded to her with curt replies and issued terse commands. She felt the shift suddenly, like the click of a locked door, and now, the way he sat listening to endless broadcasts worried her. It made her anxious because he never talked about any of the stories he heard. At some point or another, she felt, all those reports and stories would come spilling out of him in a tirade that she didn't have the energy to endure or deflect. She knew it would be a mess and more than likely she would be the one to clean it up.

She decided a moment of distraction might be in order. "*Mein Lieb?*"

Hans looked up. "What is it?"

Lucy crossed her arms and arched her eyebrows. "Please pardon the interruption, *Herr Müller*, but would you prefer rutabagas or parsnips with supper?"

Hans sat back in his chair, reached over and turned off the radio. "I apologize. Rutabagas will be fine."

She walked toward him, leaned over, and planted a kiss on his forehead. "You mustn't fret so much. I know you're worried about Carla and Oscar and the others, but there's nothing you can do."

"*Ja.* I know."

She walked across the room to the bookshelf, pulled a book, handed it to him, and said, "Why don't you read something good. It'll take your mind off the war."

Hans looked at the title. "The Count of Monte Cristo." He said it as though it were a question.

"It's one of my favorites," Lucy remarked as she returned to the kitchen to begin supper. She stood at the sink, washing the soil from the vegetables when something outside the window moved. She looked but didn't see anything. Her sons, Robert and Richard, were upstairs. Maybe a deer, she thought. They were crazy with spring fever this time of year and romped through the fields and across roads without a care or thought of a farmer's rifle. She wondered how something could be so graceful, full of life, and at the same time oblivious to the danger that surrounded it. She heard the familiar click of the radio and a moment later a faraway voice laced with static floated into the kitchen. She turned to walk back into the sitting room when something caught her attention. She peered out the window and blinked twice to make sure her eyes hadn't fabricated an hallucination. A New York State Policeman in a heavy overcoat scurried across the backyard.

Three rapid knocks on the front door rattled one of the loose glass panes. Lucy jumped a bit. She glanced at the policeman in the backyard and then walked with urgency to the front door, wiping her hands on her apron. She opened the door to two men standing on the covered porch. The rain dripped from the brims of their hats and their open overcoats hung loosely. One was short, with a clean-shaven round face and a paunch that pushed against the brown suit he wore. He listed under the weight of a large black satchel in his right hand. The other man was tall, had dark brown eyes, and wore a gray suit. He had an easy smile as he displayed a wallet with a golden badge.

"FBI, ma'am." He gestured with his thumb to the man in the brown suit. "He's an investigator with the State Attorney's Office."

Hans rose from his chair and walked to the front door.

"We just have a few questions, ma'am." Looking beyond her, he asked, "Is this your husband?"

"Yes." Lucy said, unable to move. "What's the matter?"

"Please excuse my wife's manners," Hans said. "Come in from the weather."

"Yes, please. Sorry." Lucy stood aside. "Let me take your hats and coats."

The men walked through the door but made no attempt at removing their wet coats. Water dripped onto the floor and small puddles formed around their feet. The four of them stood in the foyer for a moment. Hans and Lucy smiled at the men and then looked at one another. The agents stood in place, cocking their heads just a bit, listening to the low sounds of the radio. Lucy began smoothing out imaginary wrinkles on her apron. "I'll get some coffee started," she said.

Hans followed Lucy's lead. "Come sit. What an awful day to be working." He led the men into the sitting room and gestured to a small sofa. He walked over to the radio and turned it off. Lucy filled the percolator with water and grounds and then took up her post at the kitchen door and watched things unfold. From her vantage point, she was able to see the policeman on the back porch and the G-Men in the sitting room.

The two men settled into their seats, their wet overcoats splayed around them. The agent with the gray suit gave Hans an enigmatic smile. His mouth turned up at either end, and his teeth showed, but no mirth touched his eyes. The shorter agent in the brown suit dug through his leather case, searching for something. He couldn't seem to find what he was looking for and kept starting his search over again. He cleared his throat and glanced around the room. Gray Suit's smile tightened as he looked at the other man's briefcase. Lucy wondered how much longer Agent Gray Suit could maintain the rehearsed smirk. She imagined him practicing in a mirror, attempting to replicate sincerity and endearment, but never managing to bleach out the irony.

"Ah," Brown Suit finally said and pulled an accordion folder tied shut with a flat brown string. As he unwound the latching, he looked around the small room. "You have a nice little home here, Mr. Müller."

Hans nodded.

"Is that a short-wave radio?" Agent Gray Suit pointed to the low table littered with newspapers and magazines.

"Yes, a gift from my wife."

Gray Suit stood and crossed the room and loomed over Hans. He ran his hand over the top of the Westinghouse radio as if it were a specimen. "Wow, that's a beauty. Marine Band, too. That must've set you back a pretty nickel."

"I really don't know," Hans said. "It was for Christmas."

He turned the knob and the dial light glowed. After a momentary hum as the tubes warmed and a blast of crackling static, a thousand voices chanted *Sieg Heil! Sieg Heil! Sieg Heil!*

The agent jerked as if he'd been burned and turned the knob to silence the radio. Brown Suit looked at his partner with his mouth agape. After a moment, he realized his frozen expression and he pulled three or four papers out of the folder. He produced a pair of glasses from his inner pocket and set them on the end of his nose.

"Hans Joachim Müller? From Meuselwitz, Germany. Born May 4, 1906?"

Hans nodded.

"Married a citizen on November 11, 1930?" Brown Suit asked.

"You mean Lucy. What is this about?" He looked from one man to the other. "If you don't mind me asking."

"Just trying to make sure we have our facts straight, Mr. Müller. There's nothing to be concerned about." Agent Gray Suit moved over to the mantle and held a photograph. "And who is this?"

"My brother, Oscar." Hans pointed. "The one next to it is of my parents, who are both deceased, and the other one is of my Aunt Carla. If you'd like, I have a family photo album I could show you."

"You have two sons, Richard and Robert, both born of your wife," Brown Suit said from the settee.

"No. We found them in the cabbage patch outside."

"Mr. Müller," Agent Gray Suit walked over and rested his hand on Hans' shoulder. "There is no need for sarcasm."

"I don't understand all these questions. You seem to have all the answers stowed away in that briefcase of yours, and yet you keep asking me questions. Ask me something you don't know."

"Did you apply for citizenship in 1933 under an alias?"

Lucy walked in carrying a serving tray with three cups of coffee and set it down on the table in front of the small sofa. "I'm sorry, but all we have is goat's milk." She smiled at the visitors, but they kept their eyes on Hans.

Once again, silence settled into the room and it made Lucy nervous. "But in the coffee you probably can't tell."

Brown Suit looked up at Lucy. "Black's fine," he said as he leaned forward and picked up his cup. He peered over the rim at Hans as he sipped. Lucy stood for a moment. She turned to Agent Gray Suit. "Would you care for anything else? I have some cookies. Han's mother's recipe. You look like you could use a little—"

"Lucy? I think these gentlemen are fine with the coffee," Hans said.

"Do you think the officer on our back porch would care for some coffee?"

All three men turned abruptly. Lucy presented a pleasant smile as she smoothed out her apron.

The ceiling thundered with the sound of children and all eyes looked skyward.

"Lucy, will you get those boys to settle down before they collapse the house?" Hans looked at the two men and smiled. "Do you two have children?"

Lucy walked through the sitting room, ascended the stairs, and hushed the boys. She came back down but stopped before she reached the landing.

Agent Gray Suit moved in closer, towering over Hans and crossed his arms against his chest. "Are you a member of the *Frohsin Bund?*"

"Yes. Well, I was. It's been some time since I've been to an event."

"Event? So that is what you call them? So, *it's been some time since you've associated with known Nazi sympathizers.*"

"Excuse me?"

"Do you know this man?" Brown Suit passed Hans a grainy black and white photo that looked like it had been taken from a passport.

"Yes, I've seen this man before."

"So you do know him," Agent Gray Suit said.

"We talked once at a picnic."

"A picnic. How delightful." Brown suit put the picture back into the file. "What'd you talk about?"

"I—" Hans shifted in his seat. "I don't remember what we talked about. I talked to so many people that day. I couldn't tell you half of what I said."

Brown Suit looked at Hans and took another sip of coffee. He swished it around in his mouth and for a moment looked like he was about to spit it out. After he swallowed he looked at Agent Gray Suit, who nodded. "I think we have all we need. Thank you, Mr. Müller. And tell your wife thank you for the coffee."

Brown Suit collected his papers and they disappeared into his briefcase while Agent Gray Suit walked over to Hans' radio. "So you like to listen to the German news." He put his hands in his trouser pockets and seemed content to leave them there. "Interesting."

"I listen to the BBC, too. I like to have a broad perspective," Hans said.

Agent Gray Suit looked at Hans; his false smile had faded a bit and now it looked more openly sardonic. Brown Suit arose from the settee. "Com'on, Roger." The two made their way to the entrance of the house. Lucy descended the last few steps of the stairs and opened the front door for them. A strong gust blew and swept the rain onto the porch. Lucy and Hans watched as the men pulled their coats shut. Lucy moved into Hans and put her arm around his waist.

"I wonder if it'll let up."

"Not any time soon," Agent Gray Suit said.

The two men left the shelter of the porch and dashed across the yard. In the drive sat a dull green Chevy with US Government stenciled on the door. Behind it, a State Police car sat parked. Lucy could just see the outline of a man sitting behind the wheel of the second car and could only imagine how cold and wet he may be. Agent Gray Suit splashed through a muddy puddle, stumbled, and righted himself. They got into their car and it rumbled to life. The car turned around in a tight circle and sped away, the State Police car directly behind.

"What did they want, Hans?"

"I don't know." He shut the door against the wind and rain.

Lucy wanted to press her husband, but he walked over to his chair and picked up the newspaper he had been reading before the visit from the G-men and didn't say a word. For the moment, Lucy decided to let it go. She left the front door and walked into the kitchen. And as she did, she heard the distinct click of the radio knob, and a moment later the familiar hum and static. As she heard the cheers of a vast and foreign crowd, she felt a quiver in her stomach. She walked into the front room, picked up the coffee cups, and placed them on the tray. Hans didn't say a word to her as he continued reading and listening. She noticed the novel he had set aside and put it back in its place on the bookshelf and then carried the tray to the kitchen and sat down at the small table in the family used for breakfast. She poured herself a cup of coffee and gave it a splash of goat's milk. She watched as the white liquid swirled in the black and turned it a dark caramel color. Gazing out the window, she watched the rain fall. She was worried the temperature would drop and the rain would turn to sleet or snow. Early spring snows were normally a good sign for the upcoming year, a good indicator that rain would be plentiful during the growing season and the crops would prosper. But it didn't feel that way. There was no optimism in her bones. She took a sip of the coffee; it was tepid and had gone bitter. She set the cup down and put her mind to supper but couldn't focus on the task at hand. She kept coming back to the image of the agent stepping in the puddle, the muddy water splashing. As much as she tried, it wouldn't go away.

The family sat down to supper later that evening. Lucy prepared potatoes with sliced rutabaga mixed in. The aroma of the onions and garlic wafted through the house and when she called the boys and Hans their appetites brought them quickly to the table; Hans patted his stomach as he walked in from the sitting room.

Lucy displayed a smile and dished out servings for the two boys as a secret tussle under the table ensued between them. "If you two don't settle down you can go to bed without your supper." She paused and an iron stare ended their shenanigans. The two boys sat with their heads bowed and hands in their laps as she moved on to her husband's plate.

"What do you have for us tonight?" He leaned over and inhaled deeply. "Ahh. *Ja,Das ist gut.*"

Lucy dished out her plate last and sat. "Shall we say grace?"

The family bowed their heads as Hans said the prayer. "*Alle guten Gaben, alles was wir haben, kommt, o Gott, von dir. Wir danken dir dafür.*"

Hans and the boys ate without conversation. She was pleased they were enjoying themselves, but she couldn't wrest the feeling of dread she felt from her consciousness. The façade that FBI man played across his face reminded her of the way a butcher would gently walk up to an animal with soothing words, a reassuring pat on its haunches, and then a hidden blade revealed just before slicing its way across the neck, dropping the animal instantly.

Lucy did little more than move food around on her plate as Hans and the boys ate theirs and asked for seconds. She obliged in a perfunctory way, careful not to let her feelings flash across her face.

"Richard," Hans began, and then took another bite from his plate. "Be sure to come home directly from school tomorrow. We need to clear the fields and it will be much easier when the soil is still damp from the rain."

"But I- I- I have to—"

"*I- I- I-*" Hans shook his head. "Do as you're told."

The thirteen-year-old boy hung his head as his younger brother Robert seemed to stretch his neck upward, surveying the table. Richard's face grew flush; the muscles in his temples rippled with tension.

"What is it you need to do after school, Richard?" Lucy asked.

"Don't coddle the boy. He's needed here." Hans took another bite of his food.

"I'll come straight home, too," Robert said.

Lucy nodded toward her youngest and then looked back at Richard. The rest of the meal was completed with only the sounds of chewing and silverware clinking against the plates.

Afterwards, Lucy cleared the table and washed the dishes, trying to find comfort by keeping her hands busy. But moments, like the State Policeman in her backyard with his gun drawn, struck suddenly and froze her movements as though she had just gazed upon hideous Medusa. Eventually, the kitchen was clean and there was nothing left to do but prepare for bed.

As the couple lay together, Lucy could tell from his breathing her husband was awake. "Hans," she said. "We should talk about what happened this afternoon."

Hans coughed. "Tomorrow. We'll talk about it tomorrow. Now go to sleep."

Lucy turned on her side, away from Hans and tried to close her eyes. The storm had abated, but distant lightening flashed, casting shadows across the wall. Lucy knew it was simply the apple tree just outside their bedroom window, but its form seemed distorted.

At some point, she drifted off to sleep. Vague shadowy notions dashed across her slumbering mind, too amorphous to be called dreams or nightmares. She rolled over and her eyes opened before she realized the absence of her husband. She imagined Hans had gotten up to listen to another broadcast. She put on her robe and walked through the dark house only to find the sitting room empty. She ventured into the kitchen for a glass of water and through the window could see the glow of a lantern coming from the open door of the barn. Long ago, Hans had spent evenings in the barn birthing a foal or calf, but the last cow had been sold before winter and the horse had been replaced with a tractor. The chickens were in their coop and weather of any kind didn't seem to bother the goats. She noticed her boots by the backdoor, their tongues and laces loose, and thought briefly about putting them on in order to investigate, but before the thought could coalesce into action she saw Hans emerge from the barn, hunched over, dressed in a heavy coat and hat and holding a lantern aloft. She took a step back when she saw him, feeling as though she'd been caught, but then leaned forward and watched her husband disappear into the night on the far side of the barn, the side where he had built a tractor shed. The impulse to investigate slipped away. Although curious, something, possibly prudence, pulled her back to her bedroom and back into her bed. She lay there, straining to hear the backdoor open and close, footfalls in the hallway, or the creak the floorboards made on his side of the bed. She drifted off to sleep without hearing any of the things she'd hoped for but awoke the next morning to her husband sleeping next to her.

Chapter 2

The morning after the FBI visit, the air stood cool and damp. During breakfast, Hans' brushed aside his promise to discuss the visit with Lucy. His newspapers and chores took precedent over any kind of meaningful exchange. While this perturbed her, she wasn't at all surprised. She decided that she'd make Hans' favorite lunch and broach the subject when his mouth was full. Lucy rode her bicycle into town to the butcher.

They had settled in Friedberg, New York shortly after they married. It had the charm of any upstate New York burg and the land on the outskirts was inexpensive. At the center of the small town was a square. In one corner of the square, surrounded by a horseshoe of shrubs, stood a flagpole with a plaque commemorating service members from Friedberg who had served and died in the Great War. Two churches faced the square, one Lutheran and the other Catholic. They were on opposite ends of the town center, like prizefighters, their respective bells calling the faithful to service on Sunday morning. Since both services began precisely at 9 a.m. their bells often overlapped fifteen minutes prior to worship, creating a jerky rhythm. As awkward as it was, this solution had been settled upon following a scheduling adjustment that had the Catholic bell tolling in the middle of the Lutheran homily. Things had gotten contentious as church schedules began changing from week to week and the parishioners became so annoyed with their respective clergy that they threatened to convert. Pastor Peterson and Father Moffat eventually came to terms. Some say an apology was made. Regardless, they agreed on a common schedule as a remedy and Sunday mornings resumed with their traditional arrivals and departures at the houses of worship.

Main Street was the heart of commerce in the town, lined with shops fronted with awnings, display windows decorated with sale notices, and large hand-painted signs: Bangstrom's Grocery, Dillard's Drugs, Smith's Millinery, and Miller's Emporium. Bangstrom, Dillard, Smith, and Miller were the names of the people who mattered most in the town, or at least they acted as if such a statement were true. They were the folks who, for all intents and purposes, ran the town, both in a commercial and political sense. Although they felt themselves special, they were simply the latest representatives of a long line of small-town politics.

The town had a rich history dating back to before the Revolutionary War. As is often the case, streets were named to honor its past, even if that past was rather murky to begin with and further muddied by time. Church Street was a good example. Many folks were taken by the irony that there were no churches on Church Street. But these folks were unaware that it had been named for Sergeant Elijah Churchill, a Revolutionary War hero who attacked the British at Fort George on Long Island with whaling boats and captured 300 prisoners. He had passed through the small town after receiving the Badge of Military Merit from George Washington and the townsfolk were so excited about his visit that they named a street in his honor. Somehow, his name was shortened on the sign and the story was soon forgotten, except by a few of the residents.

Lucy parked her bicycle in front of Kocher's, the butcher shop. She hoped to find a few links of knackwurst for her husband's midday meal. She realized her efforts would be painfully transparent, but she also knew they would ultimately have the desired effect. There was something happening with her husband. As much as he tried to hide those changes since the beginning of the war, they had become apparent. It wasn't simply his mood, something else stirred deep within his mind and it worried her. As she rode back from the butcher shop, the wurst wrapped in brown butcher paper secured in the basket between the handlebars, she let her mind wander among the possibilities. She wanted to believe his inability to contact or help his family back in Germany caused his short temper, but deep down it seemed to be something else. The fear and apprehension that one might feel for a loved-one in harm's way was one thing, but Hans' actions and temperament were caused by a different sort of pressure. Pressure that showed in the operation of the farm.

Hans had always been diligent and pragmatic when it came to farming matters. As he had gotten a bit older, plowing the fields with a horse became impractical. They had decided upon a used tractor and implements that would serve the function of the horse, and thus made the horse, Philomena, obsolete. He'd always been of the mind that an animal's worth correlated to the value it could bring: goats provided milk and cheese, chickens provided eggs and the occasional fricassee. Once Philomena's duties were carried out by a machine, her disposal should've been a foregone conclusion. But Hans kept her for weeks after the tractor purchase, an impractical move that caused friction within Hans and it bubbled out of him with spats of sarcasm and criticism of others. The horse was old and of little purpose to anyone aside from the glue factory. The years of coaxing the horse along the rows in the fields had created a bond between them, one Hans loathed to admit but was obvious to everyone else. Eventually, over a month after the purchase of the tractor, a horse trailer arrived on the farm and Philomena was loaded and hauled away. Hans spent the rest of the day in the fields and missed supper while he busied himself with repairing implements stored in the barn. Days passed before his general mood resembled normalcy.

What she saw in her husband presently reminded her of that internal struggle he endured, the sense of knowing what must be done but having feelings that run counter to that end. The newspapers and the broadcasts had something to do with it, and maybe there were other clues she hadn't discovered yet, but she felt certain if she could simply get him to open up, to begin talking to her, things would come flooding out. In that moment, she both sought and feared the truth.

When he came in for the lunch, Hans' eyes widen as they took in the plate of wurst and sauerkraut. He ate with delight and purpose, but no conversation came forth. Lucy could see in his eyes that he knew what she was up to, but kept his focus on his plate and ignored the way her actions implored him for an answer. The rest of the week didn't bring anything to the surface, and Lucy felt the tension begin to ebb. Hans and the boys had worked hard to clear the fields and as the time to plow approached, an issue arose with the tractor. At the end of the week, Hans emerged from the tractor shed, his hands black with grease and a look of exasperation on his face. He glanced at the empty paddock and she knew the memory of Philomena had poked its way into his mind. All the horse ever needed was a bucket of oats, a field of grass, a trough of water, and a warm blanket for winter nights. The machinery of the tractor had stumped Hans.

Chapter 3

Later that week, winter, unwilling to give way to spring, uttered its last gasp and blew in an arctic torrent. Sleet and frozen rain pelted the house throughout the night. Lucy and Hans slept amidst the fury, until a banging awoke them. "I thought you fixed that shutter," Lucy said.

"Go back to sleep," he said. Hans got out of bed, wrapped himself in a robe, and put on his slippers. "I don't think it's the shutter. It sounds like the front door."

Lucy rolled over and watched as her husband disappeared down the hall. As she listened, she realized he was right. He turned on a small lamp and the hallway glowed in soft amber, the banging stopped. She wondered who would be out this late and in this awful weather. It occurred to her that perhaps there had been an accident on the highway and their house was the closest refuge. This thought pushed her out of bed. She cinched the belt of her robe, walked through the hall, and turned the corner just as Hans reached for the doorknob. She saw two silhouettes through the opaque glass panes of the door and knew a car was parked facing the front of the house, its headlights beaming. The figures shuffled impatiently. One was wearing a hat like a policeman, or perhaps a military officer.

As soon as he opened the door, two men pushed through like a storm. Hans stumbled back and sat with a thump on the bottom stair. Both men wore long overcoats shedding water onto the floor. Lucy recognized the agent who had worn the gray suit while questioning Hans. The other, a shorter man in a blue raincoat that looked like a uniform had a sharp chin and darting eyes. He looked around the darkened room with his flashlight held out at arm's length.

"Hans Müller," the agent said. "You will have to come with us."

"Are you insane?" he asked.

The man in the uniform hurried through the living room, following the beam of his flashlight. He flung newspapers and magazines about.

"What are you looking for?" Hans asked.

The policeman stopped for a moment and looked at Hans. It was an odd look, like he was trying to decipher the words that were spoken.

Hans stood up from the bottom stair and began again. "If you could just—"

The agent grabbed his arm, pulled it up behind his back, and pushed him over onto the floor. He landed with a thud. The sound made Lucy feel ill. The agent pulled handcuffs from a secret pocket on his belt and cuffed her husband as he lay face down on the floor. Her legs moved her toward the commotion. "What is this?" she said. "Hans, what have you done?"

The beam stopped searching the room and blinded her. She lifted her hand to block the light from her eyes and someone grabbed her arm from behind and pulled her into his body. She felt the dampness of the rain from his overcoat soak through her nightclothes and the smell of stale cigarettes on his breath that heaved on her bare neck. He held her tightly against his body and as she struggled, felt an all too familiar stirring in his trousers. At that moment, with her two sons sleeping in the attic room, panicked thoughts leapt through her mind. She expected the agent to produce another set of cuffs, but instead he walked her over to the settee and sat her down. "Sit there and do not get in our way."

The agent didn't wait for an answer. Hans looked up at her. "Lucy, I—"

"Shut up, you," the policeman said. He pointed at Hans with his flashlight, making Lucy's husband squint. The policeman's voice wavered a bit, the anger and tension in it fighting with his sense of duty. The agent walked over to the table next to Hans' chair and turned on the lamp. Lucy looked up to the top of the stairs, wondering when and if her sons were going to walk in on this scene. She didn't want them to see their father face down on the floor and these two men treating him like a criminal. The agent bent down and unplugged the radio. He picked it up and wrapped the cord around it. "I've got the radio," he said and walked over to where Hans lay. "Pick up those papers," the agent directed.

"This crap?" the policeman said, holding up a copy of *Le Figaro*.

"Gather all of them," the agent said.

The policeman gave him a brief look, as if to ask if he was serious. "All of them."

"They're just newspapers," Hans said.

"What is it my husband has done to justify all of this?" Lucy looked at the agent, then the policeman, and finally at her husband. Each man met her eyes, but none were forthcoming with an answer for her. "You come into our house in the middle of the night, throw my husband on the floor, and take our things," she said as she gestured toward the radio with her chin. "And you can't tell me why? There is something wrong here."

"Mrs. Müller," the agent said. "Your husband is a suspect and we have to take him into custody. I can assure you we are following the letter of the law here."

"Do you have a warrant?"

"I don't need one." He held Lucy's eyes for a moment, and then the agent nodded to the policeman, who set the newspapers down and pulled Hans to his feet.

"Where are you taking him?"

The agent handed her a folded piece of paper. "You can send correspondence to this address. Be sure to use his full name and today's date."

"This isn't right." Lucy's hand reached for the paper out of instinct. It felt foreign in her hands, cold, stiff. "I'll write a letter to the editor. Everyone will know what you're doing." Lucy stood arms akimbo.

"Look, you tell whoever you want to tell. See how your neighbors react. We'd like to keep it quiet, in case your husband has been working with someone. That's why we use the troopers. To keep the locals out of it." The policeman pushed Hans toward the front door and Lucy ran towards him. The agent put his arm out and blocked her, as the trooper pushed her husband through the door.

"Lucy," was all she heard before the agent closed the door and pressed his back against it, blocking her. She moved towards him and he towered over her. The radio was under one arm and with his free hand, he gripped her by the wrist. She could feel his heat, knew he'd been drinking coffee within the last hour, and that he'd probably had steak for dinner. She imagined him at some hotel, in the restaurant, laughing with his pals over a meal, lusting after the big raid that had been authorized. It seemed so absurd to her that the government would be interested in a farmer. Someone who grew turnips should not be arrested by the FBI. Yet, on some level, Hans' obsessive following of the war news, his wandering silences, and his ill temper as of late made her believe that there was a possibility that perhaps he'd done something. After all, the government doesn't go around arresting innocent people. She glanced up the stairs and then looked at the agent. He let go of her and she took a half step back.

"I'm sure this is difficult, Mrs. Müller. But I can assure you we would not be here without cause."

"Where are you taking him?"

"Just send your letters to the address I gave you." The agent reached into his breast pocket and pulled out a business card. "Take this. If you have troubles." She looked at it, but didn't read it because the moment her eyes left him he was halfway through the door.

"Wait," she said, but the man walked out into the rain and sleet, his right arm raised above his head, making a circular motion. Two cars in their driveway came to life and the agent got into the passenger seat of the same car that he'd come in earlier in the week. The other car, a black and white Ford Sedan with *State Police* painted on the door, turned around and led the way down the drive. Lucy held the business card in her hand tightly as the cold wind blew rain and sleet into her face. She finally looked at it after she saw the red taillights of the cars turn onto Newton Avenue and head toward a place Agent Roger Jordon was unwilling to name.

"Mom?"

Lucy turned and Bob, her youngest son, was standing on the last stair in his nightclothes, his hair mussed. She closed the door and then picked her boy up. "What are you doing out of bed?"

"Where's papa going?"

The state trooper pushed him from behind as he tried to turn to talk to Lucy. The car door opened and he was in the backseat with the door slammed shut before he had a chance to say or do anything. The trooper got in behind the wheel. Lightning flashed and a crack of thunder rolled through his bones. He sat in the backseat, shivering, his nightclothes, and slippers soaked by the weather. "Where are you taking me?" he asked. The trooper ignored the question. After a few moments the other man, the agent who had come days before, ran from the porch through the pebbles of sleet and rain and placed Hans' radio and newspapers in the trunk of the sedan, and then sat in the passenger seat. It was all a smooth operation that took only a few minutes before they were driving down a wet and muddy Newton Avenue. Lightning flashed again through the sky and Hans saw the two men in the front seat as ghostly blue silhouettes.

"Where are we going?" Hans asked.

Neither man said a word.

Hans tuned to look back at his house and was blinded by the headlights of the car following them. The wind blew hard and sheets of rain overwhelmed the windshield wipers as the trooper struggled to keep the car on the road. They drove deeper into the night in silence, the sound of the engine droning, the wipers' cadence counting the seconds, the tires splashing though puddles. Hans fell back into the seat, his teeth chattering, resigned to a fate that was not totally unexpected.

Lucy busied herself in the kitchen the next morning feeding the boys breakfast; she hadn't slept at all and the only way she could keep from falling into complete panic was to keep moving. Someone knocked on the front door and her heart rattled. She wiped her hands on the dishtowel and set it down on the counter. "You two stay put and finish your breakfast," she said. The boys nodded. So far this morning she had been able to deflect questions about their father, but she knew eventually she'd have to tell them something. She walked to the door and recognized the shape of the head before she opened it. Martin Adder stood on the porch, holding a large red toolbox that tilted the man's posture.

"Morning, Lucy. Is Hans about?"

There it was, the question she didn't have a good answer for, on her front porch, first thing in the morning. "I'm afraid you just missed him, Martin."

He set his toolbox down, tipped his hat back, and then scratched his temple. "He told me to meet him here this morning."

"Oh, that's right," Lucy said. "He did mention something about that." She left it at that, hoping Martin would fill in the blanks for her. Hans had said nothing about his plans for the day—nothing unusual about that—but at the moment it put her in a pickle.

Martin shifted between his feet and put his hands on his hips. "So does he or doesn't he need any work done on the tractor?"

"Well of course he does. You know where it is, Martin. Go ahead and see to it."

Martin nodded but didn't move from his spot on the porch. He turned and looked behind himself, as though someone called his name, then turned back to Lucy. "Well—"

"What is it, Martin?"

"We also needed to fix a price for the work," he said. Martin shuffled a bit and seemed disinclined to make eye contact with her. She had noticed before how uncomfortable farm men were when the subject of money arose, especially so when they had to have the discussion with a woman.

"When'll he be back?"

"He had to leave rather suddenly last night," she said. That sounded good to her. She didn't have to lie, or give anything away. "What do you think it'll cost?"

Martin looked like a schoolboy being quizzed after forgetting to bring in his homework. "I'll have to take a look see." Martin had a pained expression on his face. "Why don't I come back when Hans is here and we can work things out."

"But we need the tractor fixed. I'm sorry Hans isn't here right now, but I'm sure he'd want you to get to work on it." Lucy could see something processing in Martin's head and she knew he just needed a little push to make the right decision, just like most men. "You've come all this way," she said. "I'd hate for you to have wasted your time." Something in what she said struck a note and she could read his response before he said anything.

"Well I suppose..."

"Absolutely," Lucy pointed to the tractor shed next to the barn. "You know where we keep it. You do what needs to be done and then come talk to me when you're all done and we'll settle up."

Martin picked up his toolbox and made his way to the barn. He glanced back at Lucy and gave her a half wave. She shut the door and stood there for a moment. She exhaled, and for a second she wondered if she'd be able to breathe again. The feeling passed and she walked back into the kitchen. "Time to go, boys. You don't want to be late for school."

Chapter 4

They left from Newark. That much he knew for sure. Where they were to land remained a mystery. The train was similar to what Hans had experienced when he took the train from Penn Station to Rochester when he'd first come to this country, a Pullman car with paired rows of seats that faced one another, but there were some distinct differences. During the trip the detainees, or internees—which he was, Hans was unsure—were guarded by young soldiers with stern faces and grease guns. They looked too young. During the long trip, they often wavered on their feet. Hans glanced around at his fellow travelers and felt the simmering panic rooted in uncertainty that had settled in. The other difference in this Pullman car was that the sash and the curtains were drawn on all the windows. Hans remembered being introduced to upstate New York through a picture window like this. Being able to see the rolling hills of farmland, silos, haystacks, and livestock grazing in the fields gave Hans a reassurance that he had needed at that moment. Perhaps the comfort of that memory made him peek through the heavy fabric to assess their progress.

"Hey!" One of the young soldiers leveled his weapon at him. The black hole of the barrel of the gun fell upon him. Hans' arms flew up in surrender, and the two men's eyes locked for a long moment. The soldier couldn't be more than seventeen, Hans thought.

"Touch that curtain again and you'll be one sorry fellow."

"I apologize. I didn't mean to—" Hans stopped because he didn't want to articulate possible reasons for his actions. Best to let him simply think what he is already thinking, Hans surmised. The soldier kept the gun trained on him for another moment and then let the leather strap slide across his shoulder until the barrel pointed to the floor. Hans nodded and slowly lowered his hands. He didn't know he'd been holding his breath until the soldier broke his gaze. His heart thumped in his chest.

"Maybe you shouldn't do that again," a slight, gray-haired man sitting next to Hans offered in a thick German accent. "I don't think he liked it very much." The old man's expressionless face softened in a flash as he winked at Hans. He tried to smile in response, but it took a few minutes for Hans to calm down. When he had tried to look out the window, he realized they had painted it black, nothing in or out, good for air raids and keeping passengers in the dark. He should have known this before he even thought about touching the curtain, but his life had been turned upside down over the last month and the need to have some kind of certainty outweighed any common sense at that moment.

"I'm Werner, by the way." The man held his hand out to him. "So where are you from?"

Hans looked over at the old man sitting next to him and took him in. His wispy gray hair sparsely covered his balding head. The man's eyes were sunken deep into their cavities, as though they had decided to back away from the things they had witnessed over a lifetime. His nose was typical of an old man: a feature asserting its dominance over its owner's face as everything else faded and withdrew. The old man's body looked like a grotesque child, one that had jumped from 12 to 72 without ever having become an adult in stature. Hans shook the man's hand and introduced himself. "I'm from Friedberg, in New York."

"No, where in Germany are you from? Not Bavaria, no. Saxony?"

"*Ja*, Meuselwitz."

"I can hear it, even in your English."

The young soldier kept his eyes on the two men as they spoke, and they in turn didn't let the soldier escape their attention for more than the obligatory glance required for polite conversation. The men traded stories of their trips to America, their families here and abroad, and the circumstances that led to their meeting on the train. Werner was a tailor by trade, and as soon as he mentioned this Hans could picture him with a measuring tape draped around his neck and straight pins delicately secured between pursed lips.

"They must think I'll sew *Fallschirms* for Hitler. Imagine New York City under siege by German paratroopers, landing softly in Central Park under their silk umbrellas. All thanks to one old tailor." Werner nodded as though the thought and premise were not only possible but a bona fide reason for his sudden incarceration. He ran his index finger back and forth over his callused thumb. "Paperwork," he finally added. "It always boils down to paperwork whenever you deal with governments."

Hans nodded in sympathy. "America shouldn't even be involved."

"Twenty years in this country I've lived." Werner's voice rose more than he expected and it garnered renewed attention by the young soldier with the grease gun. Werner rubbed his forehead as though he was trying to remove some insignia or invisible mark laid upon him, something that had set him apart from everyone else. Hans patted him on the arm and nodded to the young soldier, trying to communicate with him with a simple look, one that said, *forgive his frustration; he will not cause any real trouble*. The young soldier didn't acknowledge the look with anything that could be mistaken for sympathy, but his gaze wandered away from the two men to other passengers on the train.

The train rolled on through the night. Occasional horn blasts by the engineer and crossing bell alarms punctuated the quiet of the Pullman car. No berths on this trip, each man slept in his seat. Hans closed his eyes and tried to let the rocking of the train take him into the land of slumber, with little success. Soldiers changed guard shifts, conductors passed through the car, making their rounds more out of ritual than need, and the collective snoring in the car caused just enough of a disturbance to keep Hans from finding that place within that allows one to slip into sleep.

Hans let his thoughts carry him back to his home on Newton Avenue where he and Lucy moved in shortly after Robert was born. She had come down with the flu and the doctor gave strict orders for her not to be in contact with the baby. Robert was colicky and did not sleep well. Before Hans arranged for help with the baby, he had suffered through several nights of Robert's distress. Neither holding, nor rocking or bouncing would alleviate the baby's discomfort. He cried with such force Hans wondered how anyone else in the house could sleep. He was not expecting any help from Richard, but he half-expected Lucy to ignore the doctor's orders, and her own misery, and arrive with the assurance of an experienced mother and relieve him, but she never did. Robert eventually accepted his father as a surrogate and calmed down. At the end of a long night, the sun began to peek over the horizon and Hans knew the cows would need milking. At his wit's end, he put on his coveralls and his brown wool coat. He fastened the bottom button, placed Robert against his chest, and buttoned the baby into the coat. Robert protested at first, but as Hans walked out into the frosty morning and made his way to the barn, the baby seemed to find comfort in the motion of his father's body. He located the pail and three-legged stool and began his work. The cows softly lowed. He pulled the lapel back that he had folded over his son's head. Two little eyes looked up at Hans with a sparkle of fear, but Hans saw something more akin to anticipation, the desire for an adventure. Perhaps this early memory was colored by the way Robert had turned out, fearless, adventurous to a fault, qualities Hans admired in his youngest son and traits he believed he had passed on to him. His infant son settled into his father's breast under the warmth of the coat and slept soundly for the first time in days. The extra weight around his waist did not feel foreign, and the warmth of the small body next to his translated into something more than heat. After the chore, he simply sat for a moment feeling the pulse of his son's body. Occasional gusts of wind stirred the dusty floor and gave substance to the beams of sunlight slipping through the gaps in the slats. He felt as much as heard the gentle breathing of his son. Hans brought Robert back into the house and placed him in his crib, pausing before closing the door.

A train whistle blew and Hans' thoughts returned to the present. Werner had dozed off, his head hanging forward and to one side, his shoulders and torso swaying to the rhythm of the train as it tracked its way through the night. The young soldier who had pointed his weapon at Hans had been replaced with another fresh-faced youth. He wished to be back in the barn, to reclaim that feeling of home, the warmth of his son against his body, and the feeling of freedom that he'd somehow taken for granted. There was no rest that night as darker memories began to creep into his mind, recollections of decisions and deeds that had placed him in this train car, far away from his home and family.

More than a month had passed since the night of Hans' arrest. The boys were unsettled by their father's sudden absence but managed to get along with relative normalcy. She had told them that their father was working for the government, in the war effort.

"Like a spy?" Richard had offered.

She balked at the word. "In a way." She asked herself if her response constituted a lie but pushed the question away before an answer formed. She had sworn both boys to secrecy about their father, but she knew as hard as they might try, such a secret could not be held for long. She also knew that in the absence of definite information, rumors were a small town's natural response. Curiosity would lead to speculation, which always led to conjecture. She decided it best to become involved in any activity that supported the war effort. Her family had to be above reproach. Lucy laid the groundwork in earnest. She and Bob pulled his wagon from house to house on tin drives. Richard and Bob collected pop bottles for their deposits. Lucy urged her boys to wear their Cub Scout and Boy Scout uniforms whenever they went to Bangstrom's Grocery or Dillard's Drugs to return the bottles they collected, and instructed them to bring their pennies to the bank. Each haul garnered at least one 10¢ savings stamp, which the teller affixed to the small booklet that tracked their progress toward their first war bond.

For Lucy's part, she became involved with the Ladies Auxiliary. Lucy had never been overly involved in the social spider web of Friedberg prior to the war, which many of the other farm wives could also say. The age-old tension between town and country persisted despite the larger issues at hand. While always polite to the Dillards, the Millers, Mayor Brown and his wife, they simply did not move in the same social circles. Now that she'd crossed the boundaries all parties seemed content to abide by, an underlying uneasiness poked its head up at the meetings. Glances at her worn shoes or her faded dresses were quickly followed with hand-guarded whispers. Perhaps, Lucy thought, it was merely her sensitivity that made her perceive looks or comments in a way not intended by these well-meaning folks, but as soon as she began to talk herself out of such perceptions, something would happen to reinforce the initial impression. This became taxing over time, but she persevered.

The Ladies Auxiliary busied themselves in the war effort and arranged monthly bake sales at the VFW. Lucy knew she had to make an appearance. It would be expected. She had, after all, attended each one since Hans' departure. Lucy sat at the table, pulled the recipe for Butter Knots, and began her shopping list. When completed, she wheeled her bicycle out of the garage and rode into town.

After finding everything on her list, Lucy pulled the ration book from her purse and handed it to Mr. Bangstrom. The grocer, his glasses resting low on his nose, looked for the appropriate signatures and stamps, and then flipped it open. He carefully removed one flour, two coffee, and the last remaining sugar coupons from the book.

"Someone has a sweet tooth," he said without humor.

"I'm making something for the Ladies Auxiliary bake sale," Lucy said.

Mr. Bangstrom nodded slightly and tallied the rest of the groceries. "Would you like that on account?"

Lucy nodded. "And could you have your boy deliver the order tomorrow? I'm in a bit of a rush, just now."

Lucy left Bangstrom's, the aroma of spice and vinegar still hovering in her nose, a smell that conjured childhood memories of her grand-mere's store. Hers had been the only store for miles around. She ordered items from the Sears Roebuck catalogue, sent and received telegrams, and even on occasion acted as a matchmaker. On a daily basis she performed duties as the postmistress, portioned out beans and rice by the sack, and baked her own confectionary delights. Lucy, as it turns out, was the one who had the sweet tooth; her grand-mere had cultivated it. She would sit atop the pickle barrel in her maternal grandmother's store, watching the transactions and listening to myriad voices and accents as her grand-mere conducted business and traded stories about the people in the community. Some might say it was gossip. *Plus ça change, plus c'est la même chose,* Lucy thought. Then she recalled the look Mr. Bangstrom had given her and its similarity to the one her grand-mere would shoot at customers who inadvertently revealed too much about personal information through their purchases. The customer, of course, never realized those moments became fodder for conversations with other customers for the rest of the day. Lucy imagined Mr. Bangstrom telling his next customer how she had already spent all her sugar rations for the next three months and that he was going to keep an eye on her. *Think about the boys over there,* she could hear him say.

She had spent all her sugar rations, but her accounting of her stores was less than scrupulous when they first issued the ration books. The questionnaire she filled out had the War Office stamp. As she measured she fully intended on being honest, but a nagging voice in her mind exuded such anxiety that she understood caution as the only course of action. So she lied. It was not as hard as she thought.

Lucy and Hans had met just after she turned seventeen. As the oldest of eight children, she played the role of a second mother to her siblings. It was a rare occasion when she was allowed a day off. She and her classmate Eloise were sharing a soda at a drugstore when she first saw Hans. He walked up and down Main Street in Buffalo, stopping in every store. This caught her eye. That, and his bare head. While all the other men on the street walked with purpose and wore hats, this lone, hatless and sad looking man, plodded from store to store. After seeing him come out of two or three different shops and continue on to the next, she began to anticipate his exit. He stayed inside each store less than a few minutes, would exit, and then enter the next one. It didn't matter what type of store, a bakery, a cobbler, a dress shop, he would pop in and then out like a bee looking for the right blossom to pollinate. His methodical nature struck a note deep within her. She assumed, after the fifth or sixth shop that he was looking for work. With each exit she imagined each rejection, but his shoulders never fell, and his pace, although not quick in the first place, never slowed.

Eloise nudged her. "Is that your new boyfriend?"

Lucy straightened up from the straw. "He seems so strange. Doesn't he?"

Eloise shrugged and returned to the soda. "Where's his hat?"

Lucy lost sight of him as he crossed the street at the end of the block and he would've been lost to her memory altogether if he had not entered the drugstore ten minutes later. The bell over the front door rang as he entered and walked directly over to the soda jerk, a young man no older than Lucy, and handed him a worn slip of paper. The soda jerk scratched his head as he read the note. "Mr. Peterson," he called to the druggist. "This fellow needs a job but he don't speak a lick of English."

"Who's that?" Mr. Peterson said as he stepped behind the counter. "Here, let me see that." Mr. Peterson put on his glasses and stretched his arm out as he read the note. The man before him, in a threadbare, pale green suit, seemed to shuffle from one foot to the other as the druggist read the note, looking back and forth between the man and the paper. "So you don't speak English, huh?"

The man merely shrugged, not knowing how to answer.

"*Sprechen Sie Englisch?*" Lucy offered.

The man turned to her, his face lifted, his pale blue eyes alit. "*Nein, Ich spreche kein Englisch.*"

"Sorry, Mr. Peterson. He says he doesn't speak any English," Lucy said.

Peterson looked at the soda jerk and then over at Lucy. "Well, what can he do?"

Before Lucy could ask the man the question he began to mime the action of sweeping and wiping the counter top, and then he dashed over to the large plate glass window and moved his hand in a circular motion.

"I thought you said he couldn't speak English," Peterson said.

"Maybe he understands it a little bit but just can't speak it too well."

Lucy said.

The man nodded emphatically. "Little bit, little bit English."

"Well, I got Billy here who does most of the sweeping and mopping. Tell him to go check with Abrahams' Hardware. I know Harry had a deaf and dumb boy working for him until last week when the state took him away. I suppose this fellow would be just as good." Peterson handed the well-worn note back to Billy and walked back behind his own counter where he mixed the prescriptions. Billy looked at Lucy and then at the man.

"Gee, Eloise. I don't know the German word for work."

"Don't look at me."

Billy and the man looked at one another. Then the man looked at Lucy and put his hands out, palms up.

"No work here," Billy said rather loudly, and then handed the note back to him.

He nodded and then gave a slight bow as he turned and headed out the door.

"Wait," Lucy said.

The man stopped and turned toward her.

"I'll be right back, Eloise."

Lucy slipped out of her seat and motioned for the man to follow her. She stood outside and pointed to the hardware store just down the street, pantomiming the action of a saw and then a hammer. He looked a bit confused. Lucy grabbed him by the arm and escorted him down the street toward Abrahams' Hardware store, smiling over her shoulder at Eloise.

After leaving Bangstrom's, Lucy rode down the street to the post office and parked her bicycle. In her purse, she touched the letter she intended to mail. She had lost count of how many she'd already mailed from home over the last month, but this one felt like a secret thing, and she held onto it as if it were likely to be snatched away. She knew this was childish, but she couldn't dismiss the feeling. Her real concern was the postal clerk noticing the address and then talking about it to... She didn't know who and that was the problem.

She entered the post office and placed the letter on the counter along with a nickel for the 3-cent postage.

"Morning," said the clerk with a smile.

Lucy smiled.

As the clerk picked up the letter he hesitated a moment. "Oh," he said.

That moment made her feel transparent and exposed. The clerk affixed the stamp and seemed to mouth the letters INS just before he tossed the letter into a large canvas sack. He looked up and past her. "Next in line," he said.

"Thank you," Lucy said, and the clerk nodded. She walked out of the post office and sighed. Since the night the FBI had whisked her husband away, each day she felt less certain than the one before. Some people she and Hans had known for years pretended not to recognize her on the street. They would simply pass her by, heads bowed as though in prayer. Try as she might to protect her sons by cultivating a patriotic image for the family, she still worried about her boys. Richard's stammer had gotten worse, so he rarely spoke at all. Bob seemed to be taking things in stride. His popularity amongst his classmates before that night had changed little since. Lucy still felt as though their existence as a family was in continual peril. She had read in *Life* about entire Japanese families secreted away by the War Relocation Authority, and she was thankful that there was some semblance of normalcy in her and her boys' lives. She also wondered if it would not have been better if she and her sons had been taken with their father and the family kept together. None of the letters she had sent to the address Agent Jordon had given her had garnered a single response. As Lucy walked to where she parked her bicycle and rode home, thoughts coursed through her mind. Her legs pumped the pedals with purpose as her teeth clinched her bottom lip.

Wispy clouds like pulled cotton stretched across the powder blue sky. She felt the fading coolness of late April. There would be good rain this year, she thought. Some people needed the almanac to know the weather, but Lucy always sensed such things; she felt it in her bones with such certainty that she never doubted her predictions. As she rode the bicycle along the dirt road, she thought how strange it was that she could be so certain about something as nebulous as the weather, but at the same time be overwhelmed with the sense she was walking through a dark room, unsure of the location of furniture or walls. She retreated into the circular motion of the pedals, the turning of the tires and the passing of distance.

She entered the home on Newton Avenue, the first house she and Hans had ever owned. It had been a welcome change from the apartment in town that they had rented while he worked and she raised the Richard. Although the house was several miles from the center of town, it was what he wanted. It had fifteen acres of land, an old barn, and a garage. *Soil*, he had said. *I need to put my hands in this fine soil and grow something.* In her mind's eye, she could still see him squatting on the edge of the small field, more concerned with the dirt under his feet than with the house. Since his arrest, Lucy maintained things as well as she could. The ground had thawed and she and the boys had finished clearing the fields of rocks and turned the soil over in one field. Fresh darkness had risen to the top. The earthy musk reminded her of her husband. She was ready to plant tomatoes and melons, which would come in during the summer. In the fall, there would be potatoes, squash, carrots, and fennel. As the coming seasons ran through her mind something rose through her body like she was on a roller coaster at Coney Island, and what was left in its wake was a sense that it was too late, as though something had passed her by, that she'd been left behind.

Lucy walked to the kitchen and put the kettle on for tea. Her boys would be home from school soon. She sat and thought about the letter that she had just sent her husband. She poured herself into her letters, as much as she could, even though she knew that someone before her husband would read everything she wrote. While it was easy to keep things general in the first few letters, it had become increasingly difficult for her. She wanted to ask Hans the hard question. *Why had this happened to them?* She knew he would not be able to answer, at least not to her satisfaction. She wondered if he ever would be able to explain adequately to her how all this came about. Initially, she was able to blame the INS, the FBI, and the War Department, but the longer Hans remained in custody, the more her unanswered questions about her husband began to gnaw at her. There had to be a reason they singled him out.

She spooned loose tealeaves into her grand-mere's teapot and poured the hot water over them. As the tea steeped, Lucy looked through the back window and at the field where they harvested potatoes last fall. It all seemed so far away. She felt pride in her ability to continue on, keeping things somewhat normal in the face of the unimaginable, but she also felt a tinge of bitterness. Hans' internment had placed her in her own prison. Thoughts began skating up to the edge of her consciousness. She pushed back the dark and shadowy images she could not bring herself to face. Hans was her husband and she must continue to support him, especially in his absence.

She poured a cup of tea and held it just below her chin, letting the steam rise over her lips and nose. She inhaled deeply. The warmth of the steam spread through her and began to loosen knots that she had not been aware of in her shoulders and neck. At that moment, Lucy settled into a peace because the reality of the world, the turmoil that had engulfed her life, had slipped out of her conscious mind. There were no whispers behind her back, no innuendos spoken to her face, no harsh words said to her sons by their classmates, and no averted eyes on the street. She felt strength enough to let the storm pass, to endure for another day.

Chapter 6

Lucy stooped over in one of the fields, finishing the weeding as the boys ambled down the road. Bob's book strap hung over his shoulder and his books banged against his back with each step. Even from a distance, she could see a mischievous notion flash across his face. Bob screamed a battle cry, ran, and swung his strapped books at Richard. The older brother deftly dodged the assault and slapped his brother in the back of his head as Bob's momentum carried him past his target. Lucy brushed the dirt from her hands and shaded her eyes. As she looked at her two sons something at the base of her sternum twisted a bit and made breathing difficult. She turned the feeling over in her mind, like examining some strange rock pulled from the field. Their faces reminded her of Hans. Richard's broad forehead and rounded jaw gave his face a blunt, honest look that made it seem like nothing could get past him without his noticing, and in Bob, she could see the shimmering blue eyes of her husband in a nine-year-old face. They seemed so carefree, so lucky that the weight of the world had yet to descend upon their shoulders.

Lucy sank her hands into the pockets of the denim coveralls she wore when working in the fields. They belonged to Hans and hung loosely on her slight frame. She watched the two boys as they slowly made progress up the drive. In her right pocket, she felt the button she had found while weeding. It had just been sitting there between the rows, as if dropped minutes before. But it hadn't. It was a large brown button from Hans' work coat, the warm wool one that hung on a nail in the barn, the one he put on whenever he worked the fields in the early spring or late fall. Lucy thought of how much rain had fallen since he last wore the coat and it puzzled her how this button could look so clean. The fingernail of her forefinger ran along the hard edge of the button as she pushed it against her thumb.

"Stop it!" Richard said to his brother.

Bob was a full head shorter than Richard, but he had the temperament of a bulldog. He thoroughly enjoyed rattling his older brother and would push and push until someone put a stop to it. There was a softness to Richard that Lucy knew would not serve him well in life. Someone, she was sure, would take advantage of such a soul. Although she knew that he would eventually have to learn to stand up for himself, she intervened.

"Bob, if you don't stop annoying your brother—"

She wanted to add a threat, but at that moment, nothing was coming to her. Bob, with his silver blue eyes, stood there, books swaying at the end of their strap, waiting for the rest. Since nothing came to her, Lucy turned to Richard. "How was school today?"

Richard shrugged, seeming more interested in the cuffs of his trousers than with the question at hand.

"Well?" Lucy pressed.

Richard shrugged again and then Bob chimed in.

"Some of the big kids were picking on him because—"

"Shut up!"

"They were—"

"Bob, why don't you let Richard tell me what happened," Lucy said.

Richard did not meet her eyes, and then she noticed a tear in his shirt at the shoulder. Fortunately, it was at the seam and she could mend it.

"They called him a Nazi," Bob said.

Although she felt a jolt at the word, the epithet did not surprise her. In their father's absence, assumptions would be made, and sins—even assumed ones—of the father would be visited upon his sons as the gossip spread from adult to parent to child. Lucy wanted to be outraged, to storm into the principal's office with indignation alight, and demand something be done. She wanted to ask her son, *Who called you a Nazi?* But she held these impulses inside and reached out to hug her son. Richard turned away from her offered embrace and ran across the field behind the house, dirt splashing up with each stride.

"They said Papa was a spy for the Nazis and that's why no one has seen him," Bob said, looking at his mother with a sense of complete confidence in what he was saying. At the same time there seemed to be something underlying his tone, as if he was asking if it were true.

"Horse feathers," Lucy said. "Now go inside and get your homework done."

She turned. Richard stood in the middle of the field, kicking at a clump of dirt. She felt helpless. People were so vicious with their gossip that it made her want to kick something too. She wanted to wash all his pain away, to take her son in her arms and comfort him, but he had obviously grown beyond such consolation. Richard had reached the crossroads of child and man. Although he had much to learn about how to cope with his anger and frustration, he had already moved away from her security. While painful, it was the very step Richard needed to take to toughen up, the very thing needed to wash away his softness and ease of spirit that made Richard such a gentle child. So she left her son alone in the field, without a word of solace or admonishment, allowing the incident at school to begin building a callus on her oldest child's sensitivity.

Lucy walked inside the house where Bob sat at the table, books splayed open, and his pencil filling his tablet with notes.

"So how was your day, Bob?"

"Fine."

Lucy did not expect much more of an answer. Bob, although always willing to share the trials of others, rarely felt the desire to share his own adversities. In many ways, he seemed so much older than his brother, but there were times, just like when he chased his brother down the road, that it was obvious he was only a nine-year old boy.

"Would you like some milk while you study?"

"Sure," He flipped the pages in his geography book.

Lucy poured a glass of goat's milk for her son and asked, "What are you studying?"

"I have to do a report on Timbuktu."

Lucy wasn't sure if her son was pulling her leg or if this was an actual assignment.

　　　　　　　　　　　　　　　　Fertile Ground

"Why on earth would Miss Wilson assign you such a thing?"

Bob shrugged. "She said the world is changing, and the more we know about how things were the better we can understand how things are now."

Lucy took a breath, ready to question her son further, but noticed a delivery boy pulling up on a bicycle with a large basket affixed to the handlebars; it was filled with her groceries. She opened the side door for the young man and peered around the corner of the house, hoping to catch sight of Richard. The delivery boy was older than most of the boys Bangstrom hired. He stood as tall as a man and had broad shoulders. His red hair and scattered freckles across his nose and cheeks were the only things that made him look like a boy. He carried the sacks in and stood for a moment, waiting for instructions.

"You can set them over there on the counter," Lucy said.

The boy nodded and set the bags down without a word. Something about him seemed to indicate discomfort inside their house. He glanced over at Bob but didn't say anything to him or act as though he recognized him. Instead of the typical courtesy of an immediate departure, something all of Mr. Bangstrom's delivery boys adhered to as a matter of course, this young man stood for a long moment, as though he had something to say but was unsure how to form the words.

"Is there something else?"

"Ma'am," the boy said. He reached into his back pocket and handed a folded letter to Lucy. "Mr. Bangstrom wanted me to give this to you."

The boy tipped his cap as soon as the letter left his hand and quit the kitchen. Lucy watched the boy scurry off on his bicycle, legs pumping with unusual fervor. At the edge of the property, the boy gave a quick glance over his shoulder as he hurried down the road. She'd never seen the delivery boy before, which was odd. Bangstrom always hired local boys and Lucy and Hans had been in the community long enough that they knew just about everyone.

"Do you know that boy, Bob?"

"That was Caleb Brewster, one of the guys who picked on Richard."

Chapter 7

Lucy watched the boy disappear around the corner at the end of the driveway and let his name settle on her lips, Caleb Brewster.

"You said there were others, Bob?"

Her son nodded. "Johnny Adder and Billy Miller."

"And what about you? What did they say to you?"

"Nothing, really. They were all on Richard. I just watched."

The images in Lucy's head made her feel like her legs were water. She could see the three boys taunting her son, circling him as he walked, taking turns with their remarks, hoping to land on the one phrase or word that would spring the trap, giving them a reason to pummel him.

"Get back to work on your report, Bob."

Lucy began to unload the bags of groceries, and every time she passed the window, she couldn't help but look for Richard in his father's field.

When she finished, the envelope from Bangstrom caught her eye. She picked it up and knew that it was the monthly bill from the grocer, but she did not expect the red stamped words across the top of the invoice: Past Due.

It was true. She barely had enough to pay the mortgage and the utilities, and Bangstrom's bill had been set aside. She thought she had been clever when she recognized a look in the grocer's eye that reminded her of her own grand-mere when she had a store. But now, to realize that the look had such a different meaning made her feel thick in the head. She slipped the bill into the pocket of her apron.

Lucy was standing at the sink when Richard walked through the kitchen door.

                                    Fertile Ground

He didn't say anything. He did his best to hide his face from his mother. It was red, his cheeks clammy from tears. He walked stiffly through the kitchen and up the stairs to his bedroom. She leaned against the counter and dried her hands with a dishtowel. The joints in her fingers had begun to ache and she rubbed them; it'll rain again soon, she thought. The soil could certainly use it, and it would make the weeding easier, but a feeling of apprehension married to her weather prediction let her know that something new was on the horizon, something more powerful and enduring than a storm. She thought she should go upstairs to talk to Richard, to see what she could do, but as soon as this thought occurred to her, she heard Hans' voice in her head: *The boy has to learn for himself.*

Things had been difficult for them in their father's absence, but not any worse than her own trials. She pretended everything was all right as a tacit way of surviving the prying of neighbors and townsfolk. While emotionally taxing, it kept her from having to explicitly lie. People believed what they wanted to believe, and they would look to her for confirmation of their assumptions. So, if she could simply ignore the fact that her husband had been taken away by the FBI nearly two months ago, sooner or later the people who saw her on a regular basis would begin to accept the notion that Hans' absence was nothing of concern. Even though this strategy had yet to yield the desired results, she still felt it a sound strategy.

Lucy hung the dishtowel on a hook next to the sink and rubbed her hands on the side of her legs. She retrieved a mixing bowl from a cabinet, walked over to the flour bin, and measured out four cups. She opened a tin she stored the sugar in and measured out a cup. Lastly, she put in a tablespoon of baking powder and a couple pinches of salt. She blended the dry ingredients with her hand as she carried the bowl over to the kitchen table. She had removed the butter and eggs from the ice box before she had gone outside to weed and now they were at room temperature. She cracked two eggs, beat them, added a bit of milk and vanilla, and then beat in the dry ingredients. She turned the mixture with a wooden spoon and then added the softened butter and almonds. The aroma transported her to her grand-mere's kitchen. She floured the table, poured the dough from the bowl, and began to knead. Her fingers dug into the mixture as she rolled it out. She could feel the slight grittiness of the sugar, the oil from the butter cut through the four and made her hands feel smooth. She rolled it out flat and began to cut out cookies.

Over the stove was a shelf, a place where she kept her shortening, salt, and oils. Next to these items was a large box of wooden matches. She turned on the gas, opened the oven door, struck a match, and held it next to a small hole beneath the bottom rack. Blue flames swooshed as the gas ignited. She closed the oven door and walked over to the sink. She ran the water over her hands and worked the dried flour and dough from under her fingernails and cuticles. Outside the window, a front moved in from the west. Lake Erie had a way of stirring things up, just like the town's children. Lucy could only hope that the storm would dissipate before it began, or at least spend itself before she had to leave for the Ladies Auxiliary Bake Sale at the VFW Hall. It was a fundraiser for the USO. The bake sale was not a moneymaking venture for the women who brought their baked goods; it was supposed to be charity, but Lucy thought it reasonable to deduct her expenses from the proceeds. Deep down she felt stirrings about her plan. There would be money collected and it would end up benefiting someone, she told herself. The silent part of her pointed out the fallacy of rationalization. This was not a new feeling. Something inside made her lie on the war ration book application. The OPA requested a full accounting of how much sugar the family had in its stores. At the time, she did not see it as being unpatriotic, but there was nagging sense of uncertainty that made her withhold the truth. She debated whether to ask Hans about her feelings. She knew he would simply call it women's intuition and dismiss it the way he normally did. On one hand, she could agree that the vague feeling would be lucky to rise to the level of intuition, but on the other hand, she also felt his reaction would trivialize something deep inside her that she trusted. In hindsight, it was a survival instinct, one that helped hold her family together.

Lucy dried her hands and pulled a sheet pan from below the oven. She dipped her fingers in the open can of shortening and smeared the grease on the pan, and then set it down next to the bowl on the kitchen table. She took the raw cut dough and placed the cookies on the greased pan. Once she

　　　　　　　　　　　　　　　　　Fertile Ground

had filled the pan, she took a fork and gently pressed the tines into the dough, creating a crosshatch patterned. She placed the sheet in the hot oven and sighed. She always felt good when her hands were busy. Whether she was planting seeds, pruning a bush, weeding, sewing, or making the recipes her grand-mere had taught her, there was something comforting about the action. But in that moment of completion, rather than focusing on the accomplishment, there was a feeling of emptiness that came rushing in; it was almost unbearable.

The aroma of the cookies began to waft through the house. It would not be long before she would have to fend off the boys. She knew she was to blame for their insatiable sweet tooth, but at the same time, she also knew that the more treats she could sell the better off the family would be. Of course, trying to explain the advantages of delayed gratification to two young boys whose noses are filled with sweet aromas is by no means easy. Lucy understood cruelty was a part of life and the sooner her sons learned how to cope with it the better off they would be, but it seemed needlessly cruel to deny them a little treat. So, she would play act by purposely mangling a cookie or two when removing them from the pan sheet. "Clearly," she would say. "No one in their right mind would pay for this. It seems such a waste." She would overplay her part and the boys would magnanimously offer to do extra chores in exchange for the broken cookies. Lucy knew her boys understood the ruse, but they were willing to accept it and play their part for a treat.

Almost on cue, Bob descended the stairs as the first pan emerged from the oven. Lucy expertly removed each and every cookie from the pan as her youngest son watched. He did his best to hide it, but his shoulders sagged just a bit as she lifted the last one off the sheet without injury. Lucy smiled to herself, but Richard's absence made the slight grin disappear as quickly as it arrived.

"Where's your brother?" Lucy asked Bob.

"Upstairs," he said, looking at the cookies rather than his mother.

Chapter 8

After the cookies were packed in a basket and ready for the bake sale, Lucy climbed the stairs to the boys' room. The narrow stairway led to an attic bedroom with walls that tilted in after rising vertically just four feet. Lucy never liked this room. She'd always had the sense that the walls were falling in on her, but for two young boys it was more than adequate. It was long and narrow, running nearly the length of the house. At the far end of the room, opposite of the stairs, there was a dormer. On either side of the dormer sat two beds, Bob's on the right and Richard's on the left. She found Richard in his bed, rolled up like a doodlebug, trying so hard to be invisible.

Lucy walked over and sat on the edge of the bed; it creaked. Richard's breathing was steady, but Lucy knew he wasn't asleep.

"Son?" She waited.

"Richard," she said. "Tell me what happened today."

The words made him flinch and tighten up even more. She reached out and stroked his hair.

"Honey," she said.

Richard rolled over, looked at her, and then began picking at his nails the way his father often did.

"What happened?"

"Th-th-th- there were th— boys cornered me. Th-they- said dad was—"

She pulled her son into her arms. Richard began to stutter around the age of four, and after much effort, he had nearly erased the stammers and pauses from his speech, but it seemed the war had washed away all progress. She held her son to her chest and began to rock ever so slightly. Richard told her about the three boys, Caleb Brewster being the ringleader, how they surrounded him, called him Kraut, Fritz, Adolph. That was nothing new, but this time they brought his father into it. The boys said that they had heard about him. How he had derailed a train that was helping the war effort just outside of Buffalo. How he had been seen on the shores of Lake Erie in the middle of the night, sending messages with a naval signal lamp to a u-boat. They had learned the word "saboteur" from the newsreels about the French Resistance, and now they applied it to Hans.

"Why can't we tell th-th—"

"Hush, honey," she said. "You know why we can't tell anyone where your father is."

"But—"

"Richard, we can't. Don't you think I know you want to tell them how brave your father is being? How special he is? God. I want to climb this roof and shout it as loud as I can, but I know, and you know, we can't. It would only make it more dangerous than it already is."

Richard sighed. Lucy held him at arm's length and looked into his eyes. "Promise me," she said. "We have to keep this to ourselves."

Richard nodded and fell into his mother's chest. Lucy could feel the warm tears soak through her blouse. She held her son and promised him everything would turn out all right, and when his father returned home after the war, he could tell everyone all about his father's exploits behind enemy lines. "Perhaps you could even write a book about it someday," she added. They stayed like that for a few moments and then Lucy held her son by the shoulders.

"Now I need you to stand up, collect yourself, and do something for me." Lucy looked her boy in the eye. "I have to go out this evening, to a bake sale. I need you to feed supper to your brother, clean up the kitchen, and make sure that Bob goes to bed on time. Can you do that for me?"

Richard nodded. He stood, removed a handkerchief from his pocket, wiped his eyes, and blew his nose. He took a deep breath and said, "Okay."

Mother and son walked down the stairs and into the kitchen. Bob was nowhere to be found. Lucy looked over at the basket and wondered if the folds of the cloth covering the cookies were still the way they had been when she went upstairs. It was not so much as the physical evidence as it was her knowledge of her youngest son, and a tinge of intuition, that allowed her to picture her youngest, outside, next to the far wall of the garage, crouched behind the car, eating what he had stolen. She could imagine the way he would look down at his hands and shirt, dusting off any incriminating crumbs. And then he walked through the back door, nonchalantly, and she noticed crumbs clinging to the corners of his mouth.

"I have to go out," Lucy said to him. "Your brother is in charge, young man. Don't give him any grief."

Lucy picked up the basket, paused, and opened the folded cloth that covered the cookies and reached in and retrieved one. She turned to Richard and handed it to him. "That is for dessert, and not before," she said. She covered them back up and walked towards the door.

"Is that for us to split?" Bob asked.

"No, it isn't," she said.

"Don't I get one?" He wore a smile that was seemingly genuine, but also tinged with panic.

She could see it in his eyes. Lucy stood there a moment. Wondering how he could be so good at being bad at such a young age. "Another one? No, one each," she said. "Now listen to your brother and be good."

"But—" he began.

"By the way, Robert," she said. "Wipe your mouth." She closed the door and walked into the garage. She rolled her bicycle out, checked the pressure in the tires, and then put the tin of butter knots cookies in the basket. As she peddled, the coolness of the evening wrapped itself around her and she regretted not having brought a sweater along. It reminded her of another time. Hans would go hours without saying a word to her during an evening, she'd suddenly feel a chill and decide she needed a sweater but before she had a chance to actually make a move towards anything, Hans would be there, sweater in hand. "Put this on," he would say. "It's getting chilly." Even now, she imagined him stepping out from behind a tree or building, sweater in hand. This thought kept her warm until she arrived at the VFW hall.

Chapter 9

The pale sun hung low in the western sky, hardly a match for the whims of blustery winds. Behind her, the courthouse chimes began to strike the five o'clock hour. Lucy pedaled a bit faster. Audrey Smith, the milliner's wife, ran the bake sale and was very persnickety about everyone having their goods in place on time. Lucy could already imagine the pursed lips and forced sigh in response to her late arrival. As this image solidified in Lucy's mind, her legs stopped. The resentment bubbled up in her mind, and she just let the bicycle coast. The imagined admonishment from Audrey made her feel like a child who had misbehaved, and Lucy decided she would not tolerate that. She began pedaling again, but at a slower, more deliberate pace. The clock struck its last chime of the hour as Lucy steered her bicycle into the parking lot.

People strolled into the hall, chatting and laughing. Bicycles leaned against the side of the building, and only a few cars were parked in the lot. One of them, a Hudson, belonged to Audrey. The other was a blue Ford Coupe Lucy had never seen before. She lifted the tin of butter knots from the bicycle basket and walked inside.

The VFW Hall was not large, but with the tables pushed against the back wall, the room opened up. Each table had red, white, and blue bunting, and American flags stood at either end of the long row of tables. Lucy saw Audrey and made her way through the crowd.

"Hello, Audrey," Lucy said.

"Oh." Audrey blinked with her mouth slightly open. "I don't know if we have any space left." Her head turned with the suddenness of a chicken, her finger planted on her chin as she scanned each table. "I do wish you could've gotten here a bit sooner."

"I suppose I could've driven the car, Mrs. Smith, but—"

"There's a spot for you. Right next to Mrs. DiMarco."

Lucy nodded and walked in the direction she had indicated. Liza DiMarco stood next to a table at the far end of the room. She and Liza had been paired before and aside from being a bit gossipy, Lucy thought she was a pleasant woman. Liza was plump and short, dressed in a pale blue smock dress, a tortoise comb pulling her black hair back. Her eyes were such a dark brown that they appeared black. She stood straight, her fingers interlocked with one another in front, but something in her face made her seem tired. Her husband, a plumber, was serving in the Navy.

"Good evening, Mrs. DiMarco," Lucy said, doing an exaggerated impersonation of Audrey Smith.

"Why hello, Mrs. Müller. And how are you?" Liza rejoined.

"Positively splendid. And you, my dear?"

Lucy and Liza giggled at their haughty tone and quickly stifled their laughter for fear of Audrey overhearing them. Seeing Liza smile and joke around made Lucy feel good, better than she had in weeks.

"So what'd you bring tonight, Liza?"

"Oh just a little something my grandmother used to make for me when I was little. It's called zaletti."

"Oh. They do look marvelous, my dear."

"Hush, you."

"Well," Lucy said. "I guess I should put these out if I expect anyone to buy them." She arranged the butter knots on a plate with a lace doily she had tatted. She set the goodies in a circular pattern, letting one overlap another. Once she was satisfied with the presentation of her wares, she stepped to the side, smoothed out her skirt, and took in the room. Friedberg's elite were all making their presence felt in the room. The Browns and Wrights attended. Dora Brown, the Mayor's wife, walked by each table scrutinizing each offering as if she were a general inspecting her troops. A raised eyebrow was enough to intimidate and effect a change in the display. Marjorie Wright, the president of the Ladies Auxiliary, was her shadow.

When the tandem reached Lucy and Liza's table, they slowed. Lucy straightened, her shoulders back, and she imagined herself in formation and found it difficult to keep from smiling. The two women whispered to one another and then moved on without comment. Lucy relaxed her posture and looked over at Liza, pretending to wipe the sweat from her brow. Liza smiled.

"Thank you all so much for coming," Marjorie announced. The room quieted down as she continued. "As you know the proceeds from tonight's sale will be donated to the USO. So don't worry too much about those waistlines; it's for a good cause. I also want to thank all the ladies who are donating their time, effort, and precious commodities to this cause. Let's give them a big round of applause."

The room clapped politely. "And now I want everyone to wander about and spend as much money as you can." Marjorie's smile looked painted on. People began to mingle and converse again. Lucy removed an envelope from her skirt pocket and placed it on the table next to her plate. There were no set prices and each person simply gave what they thought the item was worth, or simply gave what they could afford. It was up to each baker to collect the money and give it to Laura Adder, the treasurer for the Ladies Auxiliary, at the end of the sale. A friendly rivalry amongst the participants had been born, and each woman strove to be the one with the largest donation. Public recognition at the meetings and a nice mention in the local paper accompanied the accomplishment. As much as Lucy's competitive spirit made her want to contend with the rest of the women, she knew how much she had to hold back in order to make ends meet this month. Every third dime she earned found its way into her pocket. Lucy was careful to make sure her envelope was never the thinnest. While people enjoyed her cookies, and did not mind parting with some change to enjoy her baking, hers were not the crowd favorite. On some level, this bothered her, but she knew that if they were, then Audrey's and everyone else's expectations for her donation would rise. Better to be in the middle of the pack, she thought. Either extreme would bring unwanted attention.

"Marjorie sure has her hands full tonight," Lucy said.

"You know she wouldn't have it any other way," Liza responded.

"Have you ever noticed we always seem to be the caboose?"

The two women leaned forward and looked down the line of tables and noticed Mrs. Bangstrom and Mrs. Dillard were the first two. "Can't say

I'm surprised," Liza said with a bit of a smirk on her face.

"Liza, do you know anything about a new family in town? I think their name is Brewster. Their boy does deliveries for Bangstrom's."

"Yes, I do. They just moved up from Virginia, I believe. I was in Miller's the other day and I overheard something about them." Liza paused to make a sale and then continued. "It's just a boy and his mother. I think the father is in the Army, but I'm not positive. That bell over the door kept ringing and I couldn't hear what was being said. I do know that boy is almost seventeen and is still in ninth grade."

"He delivered some groceries to me today, and I did think he was rather odd."

Liza nodded. "I talked to him and you'd think I was speaking Chinese the way he looked at me."

"Why on earth do you think Bangstrom hired him? I mean, he has to know how odd he is."

"No telling."

The women paused their conversation as they sold more confections from their plates. Lucy wondered what could motivate a woman to up and move to a town where she didn't know anyone. "Do you know where they're living?"

"Actually, out by you, on Newton."

Lucy straightened the rest of the cookies on her plate and looked around the room. People were milling about and gossiping. Laughs, gasps, and empathic nods of the head. Lucy heard "krauts" and "Fritz" float above the other words that swam through the air. She wanted to think that none of it was directed toward her or her family, but she felt a pang in her chest every time one of those words landed in her ears. As she looked out into the crowd, she did her best not to focus on anyone directly, but rather to take in the entire crowd. These people had been her and Hans' neighbors and friends for years before the war started, but now there was a distance. It may have been real or simply perceived, but either way it created the same feeling inside her gut.

"Have you heard?" Liza asked.

This caught Lucy off guard a bit and Liza read her expression.

"They want to change the name of the town."

"What? Change the name of Friedberg? Are you serious? To what?"

Liza nodded. "Our esteemed leader, Mayor Brown, thinks it'd be a great way to show our patriotism. He wants to call it Freedom Town or some such nonsense. To tell you the truth, I think he's just trying get his name in the Buffalo paper again."

"And how are people reacting?"

"What do *you* think?"

Lucy could not imagine anyone coming out against the idea, even though it seemed petty. What would changing the name of the town actually do? It would make a good story for a couple of days, and at best it might end up in a newsreel, but in the long run it wouldn't really do anything to help the people who lived in the town. If anything, it would make some of the residents consider doing the same thing with their names. Changing Schmidt to Smith or Müller to Miller would be easy enough, but—

"Oh, did you hear about Laura Adder?"

Lucy shook her head and smiled. "Don't tell me she was caught embezzling."

Liza's face grew grave. "Her oldest son is missing. She got a telegram the other day."

"That's awful."

"He was in the Atlantic, escorting cargo ships when they were attacked by a U-boat."

"I was wondering why I hadn't seen her tonight. She must be devastated."

The town was full of half-empty households. Sons, husbands, and fathers were absent from the places where they would normally be. Those left behind did their best to live their lives as normally as possible, to keep busy, not to think too much about where their men were, and to place the prospect that they would never return as far away from their consciousness as possible. But then telegrams would arrive and everyone would hold their collective breath, hoping the young man on the bicycle would not turn down their street, and if he did, would continue on past their house, but he always had to stop somewhere.

Lucy could see the telegraph boy on the Adder's porch, with his head down, doing his best not to make eye contact. Laura reaching out, more from reflex than from any desire to see the news the yellow paper held for her. Her oldest boy, Jay Adder, could be injured, captured, missing, or dead. It was like a dreadful lottery with no winners, just varying degrees of despair awaiting the recipient.

"Poor thing," Lucy said.

Liza nodded and sighed in trepidation. Lucy knew Liza's husband had been assigned to a ship, somewhere. Somewhere in the Pacific, she hoped.

"Have you heard anything from Joe?" Lucy asked Liza.

"I got a letter the other day, but it looked like Swiss cheese."

"Well at least you know he's okay and thinking about you."

Liza nodded and sighed again, looking down at the plate she had brought. "I hope they don't give him any grief about it. I know they've been told what they can't write about, but he doesn't seem to be listening."

"I'm sure it'll be okay, Liza."

Pastor Peterson and Father Moffat walked up to Lucy and Liza. The two men often appeared together at secular events, despite their differences; *God's envoys* they had been called more than once. Father Moffat's face was an unnatural shade of red. It was as if the fires of hell that were so often the topic of his sermons burned deep within him. His hair was thick and shockingly white, which made his red skin, particularly during service, even more captivating. Father Moffat's piercing blue eyes seemed as though they could easily pry into one's soul, an apt characteristic for a priest. "Good evening," he said to Liza. "And what do we have here?" he asked as he examined the plate in front of her.

Liza reflexively smiled and fingered the little silver cross she wore around her neck. "Hello, Father Moffat." She reached down, picked up the plate, and held it out to the man, like an offering. "These are zaletti. It's a polenta and raisin cookie my grandmother taught me how to bake," she said. "Please, help yourself."

Father Moffat obliged and bit into one of the cookies, his cheeks instantly broadening in a smile. "Absolutely delicious, Liza."

Pastor Peterson, meanwhile, stood in front of Lucy. "We've missed you and Hans the last few Sundays. I hope everyone is well."

Lucy felt her face blush. There was an urge to make some kind of movement so she would not have to look the pastor in the eyes. "Please have a butter knot," she said holding the plate up for the man.

"Thank you," he said. "Don't mind if I do." Pastor Peterson was relatively new to the area, having only moved there four years ago. He was a tall man with an imposing presence. Not fat, but his height and broad shoulders brought to mind the physique of a Viking. It was only his thin wire-framed glasses that softened his appearance. They looked so delicate on his face that one wondered how such a man could take them off without damaging them. He took a cookie and bit into it, looking into Lucy's eyes before she had a chance to look away.

"Hans was called out of town. A family matter in Rochester," she said. Once again, she felt blood rush to her face and the beginnings of perspiration at her temples.

"Everyone is all right, I hope," he said.

"Oh yes, everyone is fine. It's just with Hans gone the boys and I have been so busy on the farm."

Pastor Peterson nodded. "Well, please let me know if there is anything I can do to help, Lucy." He smiled at her and glanced over at Father Moffat. As if choreographed, the two men bid the women a good night and moved on and into the crowd, both neglecting to place any change in the bowls next to the plates of cookies each woman had baked.

The two women stood there for a moment, an awkward silence created a distance between them. Liza looked around the room. "Seems like things are beginning to thin out."

Lucy nodded and waited for Liza to ask about Hans. Various scenarios ran through her head as possible answers to the unknown question, but the question never came and that troubled Lucy more than if she had asked a question. Perhaps she had already heard the rumors floating around town and thought they were true. Maybe she did not want to put Lucy in an awkward position by asking. Lucy tugged at the knot holding her apron on. "Well, I guess we're about done then. How'd you do?"

Liza counted the change she had collected during the sale. "Nearly five dollars."

"Goodness. Maybe you should open a bakery. I didn't make half that."

Lucy's face blushed as she felt the weight of the dimes against her leg, the ones she had pocketed during the sale. She estimated it was close to three dollars' worth and hoped that they wouldn't jingle too much and give her away. On cue, Audrey arrived at their table with her clipboard and gingham sack she collected the money in.

"I do love to see empty platters at the end of the night," she said to Liza. Lucy hung her head as she looked at the number of butter knots that remained on her plate. Audrey's eyebrows arched in surprise and delight as Liza counted out the dimes to her. "Splendid," she said and then repeated it to herself as much as to Liza. Audrey's gaze fell upon Lucy, with a hopeful expression. An emptiness inside Lucy seemed to widen, and made her feel as though she were on the precipice of a great chasm. Despite this, she counted out the dimes she had in front of her. When she was done, Audrey stood there for a moment not picking them up or noting the amount on her clipboard. Lucy put a smile on her face, one she felt was eerily similar to the one Bob had on his face as he tried to finagle an extra cookie from her before she left.

"I suppose that'll have to do, Mrs. Müller." Audrey turned and walked away, leaving both women standing in silence. Lucy turned to Liza, her eyebrows raised. Liza resisted looking at her, but when she did, Lucy rolled her eyes.

"Such a warm soul," Liza said.

"I don't think I've ever felt so bad about baking before."

The two women collected their plates and doilies and prepared to leave when they noticed Audrey and Marjorie having an animated, albeit a hushed conversation. Marjorie darted glances over toward Lucy and Liza and soon her balled fists were resting on her hips.

"I'm not sure what's going on over there." Lucy pointed with her chin at the two women, "but I think we'd better scoot."

Lucy did not wait for a response from Liza and headed toward the door. She walked with purpose and resolve across the room, hearing snippets of conversations. Words her brain did not want to process seemed to climb into her head and rattle around like a blind bee. Did she hear "treason"? Or was it simply "reason." Did she hear "kraut"? Or was it "stout," "about," or "without"? She could turn and face the source, put on a face that would not belie the earnestness she wanted everyone to see. She could slide into the conversation as easily as a warm bed and read the expressions on those women's faces, but she was tired and too much had already happened this day. Instead, she kept walking, doing her best not to hear anything. Just as she was about to push the door open, on the edge of freedom from the eyes and opinions of the old hens, she heard her name. There was a slight hitch in her step as she wrestled with the choice of responding or pushing through the door. When she heard "Mrs. Müller" a second time with such clarity that she was certain everyone in the VFW Hall heard it, she stopped and turned.

Initially, she thought it may have been Audrey, or worse, Marjorie, but as her name echoed in her head she realized that it was neither of those woman who called her, and it was confirmed when someone she didn't know walked toward her.

"Mrs. Muller. I am so glad I caught you before you slipped out. I believe our sons go to school together. I'm Betty Brewster," she said, with a faint southern lilt to her voice.

Lucy introduced herself as the familiar last name rung in her ear.

"We're new to the area, as I'm sure you know, and I just thought it would be nice if Caleb had someone to walk to school with. You know, a buddy of sorts who could introduce him around."

"Is your son working for Bangstrom's?" Lucy asked.

"Why yes. Yes, he is."

"I guess you could say I met him this afternoon," Lucy said. "He delivered my groceries."

"Well that is wonderful. He seems to be finding his way around much better than I thought he would. Caleb is such a bright and gentle boy and can be so shy around people he doesn't know. And what with his father and all—"

Lucy did her best to nod in the affirmative as she recalled the boy's face in her mind's eye and heard Bob's account of what he did to Richard. She waited for more information about the absent Mr. Brewster, but it seemed Betty was not willing, without prodding, to share anymore. "So what brings you and Caleb to Friedberg? It is an awful long way from Virginia."

"Why yes it is. How did you know we were from Virginia?"

Lucy did her best to squelch the blush she felt rushing to her face. "Your accent, of course," she said.

Betty gave a long look.

Lucy smiled. "And I suppose you know that secrets never last very long in a small town."

"Yes, I know that as well as you do."

Lucy nodded, trying to decide what Betty was trying to imply.

"Well," she finally said. "Don't let me keep you. It looks like you're ready to head home. I'll tell Caleb to stop by in the morning so he can walk with your boys."

"I—" was all that came out of Lucy's mouth before Betty had turned and disappeared into the crowd in the VFW Hall. She stood there for a moment, playing the conversation over in her head, certain that she never accepted Betty's proposal. She continued out of the foyer of the hall, mounted her bicycle, and began to pedal home.

Chapter 10

Leftover cookies filled Lucy's bicycle basket. The change she had skimmed from her sales was neatly stowed in a leather purse; she could feel its weight next to her skin. She pumped the pedals, each cycle making a clicking sound as the right-hand crank clipped the chain guard of the bicycle. She could not wait to get home, and was thankful to be away from the awful Mrs. Brewster, or Betty as she insisted Lucy call her. She had almost been free. The more she thought about the encounter with Mrs. Brewster, and her too sweet southern inflection, the more her frustration began to boil up. As she rode, her mind reached back into the past to try to understand how things had gone so wrong.

The secrets Hans kept became apparent for the first time back in the spring of 1941. They were in Orchard Park. The *Frohsin Bund* held their spring picnic in the center of town. It was a jolly time with beer, music, and children running around. Hans had gone to the car to retrieve her sweater and was walking back through the crowd, her cardigan draped over his forearm. Hans saw her looking at him and his boyish grin spread across his face. Out of nowhere, a short man in a dark suit and a black fedora grabbed him by the arm. Lucy remembered how odd it was that he was so formally dressed for such a casual affair. Hans pulled his arm away from the man, but then he stopped resisting. The little man kept asking Hans questions, all the while never letting go of his arm. Hans looked around, as though he were nervous, but kept nodding. The man's eyes peered up at Hans like he was pleading with him. There was something desperate about his look. Then Hans' cousin Walter walked up to the two men and joined in the conversation. Walter smiled and placed his hand on the little man's shoulder, seemingly an advocate for whatever the man was telling Hans. The three of them spoke for just a few minutes and then Hans nodded curtly, and then hung his head as he walked away. Walter and the little man looked at one another and shared a moment of accomplishment. Lucy did not care for Walter. Years before Richard and Robert were born, he had danced with her at another picnic hosted by the *Frohsin Bund*. He told her she was too beautiful for Hans, and as he said this his hand slipped down her to her backside. Hans cut-in at that moment, but seemed oblivious to his timing. Since then, Lucy often felt Walter's leering glances at these functions. Hans returned to her at the blanket and his face had paled.

"Thanks for getting my sweater," she said.

"Where are the boys?" he asked, scanning the park.

Lucy sat up, put on her cardigan, and inclined her head toward the bandstand.

Richard was imitating the dancers. He stood on one foot and slapped the bottom of the other foot, and then tried to switch hop from one foot to another, nearly falling over. Bob just clapped his hands with the dancers and left the fancy footwork to his older brother.

"Richard says he wants a clarinet."

"And I suppose Robert wants a Sousaphone."

Lucy smiled. "Who was that I saw you and Walter talking to?"

"Aaah," he said, as if he had a bad taste in his mouth. "No one." Hans picked at the blades of grass and tore them into little pieces.

"He seemed very intense."

Hans looked out into the crowd of people.

"Was he trying to sell you something?" she had asked.

"Nothing I wanted to buy." Hans picked up the little scraps of grass that had accumulated on the blanket and returned them to the lawn. When he finished he said, "Come, it's time to pack up." He struggled to his feet. "I'll get the boys."

On the way home, he said they were through with the *Frohsin Bund*. This struck her as odd, but she did not share the obvious disappoint he felt despite his declaration. She had tolerated attending the picnics and dances because Hans enjoyed the fellowship of his countrymen so much. Although she did not mind the change, the lack of an explanation troubled her. Her instinct told her Walter had steered her husband away from the *bund*, but it was only a guess because Hans never spoke of it again. After that day, the secrets grew.

Later, in the summer of the same year another strange thing happened. Newton Avenue was not busy by any stretch of the imagination, so when she saw a dark sedan sitting just off the road near their house for three days straight and mentioned it to Hans, he made her feel as if she were crazy. "What is he doing there?" she had asked.

"How should I know?" He dropped his paper and shook his head at her. "I'm sure it's nothing."

"Well go ask."

"You want me to walk up to a stranger and ask him what he's doing on the side of the road in his own car? This is a free country, remember?" He picked his paper back up, but Lucy knew he wasn't reading. She could see him shaking his head in disbelief.

"I will go then." Lucy pulled off her apron and began toward the door.

"Wait," he said and threw down his newspaper. "Don't go poking the hornet's nest. Okay?"

Lucy paused with her hand on the doorknob. "Hornet's nest? A moment ago you said there's nothing to worry about and now this man in his car is a hornet's nest?"

Hans stood and came over to his wife, smiled wanly, and embraced her. "I will take care of it." He released her from the embrace, donned his hat, and as he walked out the door he looked back over his shoulder. "Stay here."

Lucy watched him through the window until he reached the end of the driveway and was out of sight. She wanted so badly to walk after him, to see the conversation occur. She would not be able to hear anything, but if she could see how each man reacted, that would tell the real story.

And now he was being held by the government, somewhere. For the first time in a very long time, she felt rage. She was no longer sure whether she was angrier with Hans for the secrets he kept or at the FBI for taking him away. The raw emotion found an outlet in her legs and she pushed her pedals with such constant force she unexpectedly found herself on Newton Avenue. Once she realized where she was, she knew she had to calm down. Walking into the house in the state she was in would not be good for the boys. She coasted down the road and took a few deep breaths. She noticed the mailbox at the end of the drive and suddenly realized that she had not checked it today. Ever since she had mailed the first letter to Hans, she had looked every day for a response, and each day she had faced a disappointment. She stopped to open the box, already resigned to the idea it would be empty, but to her surprise there it was, a thick letter. She picked it up and recognized her husband's handwriting. She was flush with excitement, giddy even. She started to open it, right there in the middle of the driveway when a commotion up by the house caught her attention. She put the letter in her pocket, pedaled up to the house, and saw Richard leaning out of his window, framed by the golden light from his bedroom. In his hand was Bob's baseball lamp, and he looked as though he were ready to throw it to the ground. "Richard," she said. "What on earth do you think you're doing?"

Richard had prepared the evening meal and he and Bob cleaned up the kitchen. Afterwards, he went upstairs to complete his studies. He sat at his desk, working on his assignments for the next day, but every time he started, something would halt all progress. He had three pages of mathematics, twenty pages to read in History, and a theme paper to compose in which he had no idea whatsoever of what to write. It all seemed so overwhelming that he couldn't even start.

    Thwack.

    He decided the math would be the best place to begin because he could pause after each problem and think about what really mattered to him.

    Thwack.

    He opened the book to the appropriate page and sharpened his pencil. He liked the way the tiny blade peeled the wood of the pencil like skin, curling it into a fragile spiral.

    Thwack.

He looked at the first Algebra problem and copied it down on his paper. 3+5x=28. Easy enough. He wanted to simply write down 5 and move on, but Mrs. Archer never gave full credit without showing the work. "It's fine that you know the answer, Richard, but you also have to know how you know it," she said whenever he tried shortcuts. He began rearranging the numbers, jumping them from one side of the equation to the other until he had his proof.

Thwack.

Richard tossed down his pencil and went to the window. Below, in the driveway, in the waning light, Bob was throwing a ball against the house. "You—you better get your work done before Mom gets home."

Thwack.

Bob threw the ball again and didn't look up at his brother.

"I'm serious. You had better get it done. You know how she gets." Richard was actually more worried about what his mother might say to him, rather than remarks sent his little brother's way. "You're older," she'd say. "I expect more out of you." It was never enough that he took care of his own work; he also had to make sure Bob did the same, but Bob had a different take on this.

Thwack.

"I'm serious, Bob. Mom's going to be ticked, and I'm not going to stand up for you."

At this, Bob finally looked up at the window. He had a puzzled look on his face, as though his brother was a Martian and was speaking some kind of alien tongue.

"You can't even stand up for yourself, Richard."

Thwack.

Richard looked around the room for something to throw at his brother. Books, a chair, a lamp. They all seemed like they could do a fair bit of damage from this height, but his pragmatic side took over. A book would flutter and maybe get torn. A chair would be an excellent projectile, large, heavy, and more than capable of putting a dent in his brother's pointed head, but it would most assuredly break. Money was tight since Papa had left on his mission and he knew his mother would be incredulous at his wanton

                    Fertile Ground

wastefulness. Then he noticed Bob's lamp. It would not do a lot of damage, but it would get his attention. If it broke, Richard could simply say that Bob broke it and then threw it out the window.

Thwack.

"You asked for it." Richard moved away from the window and over to his brother's bedside table. On it, sat a lamp made from a miniature baseball bat with a base shaped like home plate. A white wooden ball with painted red stitches sat on the base, up against the nub of the bat. On the shade were players: one swinging a bat, another sliding into home plate, and one reaching over his head, catching a pop-up. Bob loved the Dodgers, and his favorite player was Leo "The Lip" Durocher. Bob believed it was Leo catching the pop-up. Richard pulled the lampshade off and wrapped the cord around the base. "Let's see him dodge this," he said.

He went back to the window and looked down but didn't see his brother. He stood there, his pale arm cocked and ready to sling Bob's prized lamp down two-stories, already picturing it smashing, and Bob's horror. He reared back ready to throw the lamp when his mother appeared gliding up the driveway on her bicycle, coming to a stop just below the window.

"Richard," she said. "What on earth do you think you're doing?"

He heard footsteps behind him. Bob grabbed hold of the base of the lamp. Richard pulled it away. Bob caught the cord and pulled back, ripping the lamp from Richard's grasp. It fell to the ground and broke. The two boys looked at the pieces on the floor, the smashed glass, the broken base, and the wooden orb painted to resemble a baseball wobbled as it rolled toward a bed.

"Mom!" Bob yelled.

Richard's face grew hot as he heard his mother's footsteps climbing the stairs to their room. He pushed his brother down and kicked what was left of the lamp. As his mother entered the room she saw her youngest son on the floor and her other son's burst of anger.

"Richard! What is wrong with you?"

She walked across the room, grabbed him by the arm, and shook him. "Do you think just because your father's not here you can destroy things in the house and beat up your brother? I thought I could rely on you to take care of things while I was gone. Instead I come home to find you acting like a—" Lucy paused. Something gave way and she slapped his face.

The sound was louder than Richard expected, and his face felt thick and numb before the sting came to the surface. He looked at his mother's eyes. If he hadn't known better, he would've guessed he saw fear, but his mother had never shown fear before so the boy was uncertain what it would look like on her face. Richard turned to Bob, who was still on the floor, sitting up with his legs in front of him and one arm supporting himself. His mouth hung open.

"Y—You—" Richard managed before he ran out of the room. He flew down the stairs, out of the house, and into the field. The dirt felt soft under his feet and every step took more effort than it returned. He ran hard. Each stride made him tremble. He ran until he reached a small grove of trees on the far side of the field. His lungs burned with the cool air and his face was both hot with anger and cold with windswept tears. He reached the grove and stopped, bent over with his hands on his knees, and tried to catch his breath. A large branch had fallen from one of the trees, about three inches thick. Richard picked it up and swung it as hard as he could against the trunk of a tree and screamed as the branch shattered in his hand. Shock waves shot up through his wrists and arms as his voice rang out across the night.

The silence that followed it loomed large as the void his father had left. He dropped the remnants of the branch, collapsed on the leaves and grass, and sobbed. It all spilled out of him. He couldn't stop, even when he thought he should be done. His body kept heaving and had no power over his breathing, so he held his breath. His chest convulsed, refusing to be controlled. After a few moments, he took a measured breath. He leaned up against one of the trunks and slowly regained himself.

Across the field sat the little two-story white farmhouse he had run from. He waited for the back door to open, for his mother or Bob to make their way across the field, but nothing happened. The house stood silent, devoid of all humanity. In the darkness of the night, a light breeze blew and the chill made him shiver.

After Richard ran out of the room and down the stairs, Lucy picked Bob up from the floor and cradled him. "Are you all right?"

Bob nodded and leaned his head into her chest.

"I don't understand what has gotten into Richard. Did he hurt you terribly?"

Bob shook his head and kept it bowed.

"Come, let me see your face." She held Bob's head, a hand on each cheek and looked deeply into his eyes. "Are you sure you're okay?"

"He broke my lamp," he said, looking at the pieces on the floor. "Why'd he do that?"

The lamp had been a source of envy ever since Hans returned from New York City with it as a gift to his youngest son, and neglected to bring anything for his oldest son. As an afterthought, Hans dug into his pocket and pulled out three brass subway tokens, and told the naive boy they were gold. Richard's deflated face came alive as he hugged his father with such might that Hans' careless exaggeration—his word—quickly caused regret. A few months later after Richard had taken the coins to school to prove to his schoolyard chums that he did indeed have gold coins; he came home shrouded in such shame that he did not say a word for three days and only spoke to his father when he absolutely had to. Afterward, the lamp remained a constant reminder of his gullibility, his father's untrustworthiness, and his brother's great pride in being the favored son. All these things lay smashed on the floor.

"What on earth made your brother do this? Were you two arguing?"

Bob did not answer immediately. He did not defend himself with a reflexive response the way he normally did when blame pointed in his direction. Lucy looked down at Bob, trying to get him to meet her eyes, and with a quick glance up at her she knew the reason. "Okay. Pick up these pieces and I'll see what we can do about fixing things." She gave her son a quick hug, stood up and left the room. As she reached the door, she saw Bob's baseball glove, with his baseball in the pocket, on the floor, tossed there carelessly. She glanced over at Richard's desk and saw his books open, as though he had just stepped away from his studies. She took this in and had a reasonably good idea of what happened. Lucy realized at that moment all the anger that had built up inside her over the last few months had been suddenly and without real cause released on the one person who deserved it least.

She walked down the stairs to the dark kitchen and put the kettle on for tea. The flames on the range glowed orange and blue in the shadows of the kitchen. She left the lights off, looked through the kitchen window to the field behind the house, and saw nothing but the night. She wanted to know her son was all right, and she wanted to go and find him, to ask his—

The word stuck in her. She could hardly think it, let alone say it. Forgiveness. There it sat like a dead fish on a plate with a blank stare. She was the parent. How could she, even when wrong, ask for such a thing when she herself couldn't forgive her husband, and, in some sense, herself for not seeing, for not knowing.

Chapter 11

The kettle whistled and she poured the hot water over the tealeaves and let them steep. She turned on the lights in the kitchen and the brightness stung her eyes. She sat at the table awhile, sipping tea and waited for Richard to come home, unsure what she would say to the boy. As difficult as her day had been, she knew his may have been worse. She hated to admit it to herself, but she knew if Hans had been there, she would've let him take the lead in how to deal with the boy. The tea settled her down a bit, but mulling things over brought no resolution; it only seemed to make things worse. When she least expected it, the back door opened and Richard walked into the kitchen. Lucy thought he would try to scurry through without a word, his normal mode of behavior, but instead he stopped and looked at her. Lucy dropped her eyes to her teacup. "Have a seat," she said.

At first he didn't move. He seemed to realize he gained something in that moment, and to obey his mother's command would mean giving it right back.

"Richard," she said. "Sit down and let's talk."

He moved over to the table and pulled out a chair, not taking his eyes off her. His stare began to make her feel uncomfortable and she responded the only way she knew. "Don't look at me that way."

Richard shifted in his seat and looked at the teacup on the table. He focused all his anger on the inanimate object in front of her, and in some part of her mind, she would not have been surprised if the cup and saucer exploded from the intensity of his gaze.

"Look," she said. "I know things have not been easy since your father left. They're not easy for me either." She paused as she measured her words and tried to gauge her son's reaction. "I need your help, Richard." The words hung in the air and she wasn't even sure she'd actually said them, but Richard's face confirmed she had, in fact, asked her son for help. This opened a new dimension to their relationship. She had asked him to look after Bob while she was gone, and to perform other tasks around the house since Hans had departed, but always in ways where Richard could only respond in the affirmative. The requests may have been framed as questions, but they were more commands than anything else. But now, the tone, the phrasing, her posture, all pointed to a plea for help from a fourteen-year old boy. Richard saw through the facade she had kept up for the last two months and he sat up a bit straighter.

In her son, she saw the man he might become. His pale blue eyes searched hers.

"We all have extra weight to pull right now," she said.

Richard nodded. "I can help."

The words were fluid and heartfelt. Lucy felt something surge inside her. Her pulse quickened and despite the coolness of the evening, she felt a bit of perspiration on the small of her back. "Good," she managed. After a quick breath she asked, "Have you completed your studies?"

Richard shook his head slightly.

"Well let's get that out of the way, shall we?"

Richard got up from the table without a word. Lucy watched her boy climb the stairs with a deliberateness that didn't indicate reticence or enthusiasm. Lucy took the last sip of tea. It had grown cold and left a bitter taste in her mouth. She sighed and got up from the table and brought her cup and saucer to the kitchen sink. Standing there, looking into the dark, a tear began to form in the corner of her eye. She wiped it away before another could join it.

After the boys went to bed, Lucy sat at the table and pulled out the letter from Hans. She held it in her hand and looked at it, felt its weight. At the mailbox she wanted to tear the envelope open and read it right away, but after all the turmoil of the evening, doubt had settled in. She wasn't sure she wanted to read it. Wasn't it enough for her to know he was alive and in a place where he could write to her? She turned the letter over in her hand and after a few moments, she knew she had to open it.

30 April 1942

Lucy, my dearest,

You would not believe all I've been through. They interrogated me like a criminal. I didn't even know where I was after they took me away that night. We drove and drove, and then they put a blindfold on me. I couldn't believe it. There were no windows and no one would answer my questions. Afterwards, they moved me to Ellis Island in New York harbor. I could see the Statue of Liberty when they let us out for fresh air. The men were on the main floor and women and children were on the mezzanine level above us. I thought they were going to send me back to Germany. They gave me a hearing. At least that's what they called it. I could not speak in my own defense and I had no lawyer. They think I'm a threat. Can you believe it?

Nearly a month later I've landed in the middle of the ██████████ ████████████████████ of all places. The accommodations are less than desirable. The barracks are drafty, especially so when the wind blows, which it always does. Our lantern flames shudder and so do we. There are about ██ men here. Some are Japanese and the rest are German and such. The Japs are in a separate section of the camp, but we see them all the time. A few of them have started a garden. We were supposed to have a trainload of Italians someone said, but there was a big brouhaha in town about them coming and then they didn't. They ended up going to ██████████████.

I have received your letters, all one hundred and two. How do you have so much time? I hope you and the boys are tending the fields. Talk to Gus at the co-op, he might be able to help you with labor and he'll make sure you get a fair price when you bring things to market. But you know all this. It's just so hard to be away, to not be able to provide for you and the boys. How are Robert and Richard? Good, I hope. I understand why you told them a story; they are young. You make me sound so daring. How could they believe it? They always liked the fairytale.

I miss you, Lucy. I don't understand this cruelty from my country. I have a thought, something I want to share with you, and I turn and remember where I am. It all comes back like a snap. Lucy, I need an attorney. There is one here in town that is willing to help, but I don't trust him. I think he's a Jew. You must go to Rochester and see Walter. He will help you find someone who is good. They say I never filed the proper paperwork after we were married. Lucy, they said I'm an enemy alien, illegally in this country. After the war I'll be sent back to Germany, repatriation they call it. I have a hearing with the INS scheduled for next week. I'll write when I find out what they decide. Of course, it doesn't look like I'll be going anywhere soon. Keep me in your thoughts. You are never far from mine.

    All my love,

        Hans

Chapter 12

Hans' long train journey had ended far from any station. The train cars stopped on a flat, desolate stretch of white land. Nothing of consequence was in sight except the tips of fence posts poking out of the snow along the perimeter of blanketed fields. A small cadre of Army trucks with canvas tarps over the cargo area sat parked near the tracks. The boy soldiers who had guarded them across the country gave way to new soldiers who were bundled in heavy, army green coats, black fur-lined trooper hats with earflaps, and sturdy boots. These men were older, their faces leathery and creased from the cold. They held automatic weapons at the ready as Hans and the other internees were marched off the train, through the snow, and into the back of the trucks. The wind howled and the thin coat that had been given to Hans in New York did little to keep him warm. Werner had trouble climbing the wooden ladder that led from the snowy ground into the back of the truck.

"Take my hand," Hans offered.

"Sit down," one of the solders said as he leveled his weapon at him. Hans raised up his hands over his shoulders as he backed away and reclaimed his seat. Another soldier pushed Werner up the ladder and he lost his footing in the back of the truck, falling face first. No one moved to assist him. Werner gathered himself. "My word," he said. The soldier tossed the ladder into the center area where two rows of men sat facing one another, slammed the tailgate into place, and pulled shut the tarp. Once again, they sat in the dark as they moved to an undisclosed location.

The Army truck rumbled to life and drove over rough terrain, jostling the men. The enclosed space warmed quickly and the odor of men who had not bathed in several days made the air pungent. The truck slowed and the men inside anticipated an end to the trip, but the truck made a sharp u-turn and dislodged several men from the bench seat along one side of the truck. While trying to gain their feet, the truck came to an abrupt stop and threw them off balance again. The gears of the transmission ground in protest, the truck reversed direction for a few yards, and then stopped. Soldiers pulled the tarp aside, the brightness of the light made Hans, and the others squint, their eyes.

"Hand out the ladder," a soldier commanded as several others stood back, weapons held across their chests. Two guards without guns held the leashes of four attentive German Shepherds. The unwilling passengers climbed out of the truck and formed a single file line. Other trucks with human cargo arrived and began to unload. An arched sign over a gate read Fort Lincoln. Two chain link fences, both topped with barbed wire, encircled the encampment; the twenty-foot span between the two fences formed a corridor in which guards patrolled the border with dogs. Half a dozen guard towers punctuated the perimeter of the camp. The black boxes with low-sloped roofs sat perched upon spindly legs and had two square-cut portals on each side. Soldiers dressed in heavy overcoats and fur-lined hats looked down from their vantage point with their weapons aimed at the new arrivals.

Although already mid-April, snow still blanketed the ground in all directions and the cold numbed Hans' toes as he became acquainted with his new surroundings. Snowdrifts, several feet deep, covered the windward sides of buildings. As the prisoners amassed outside the main gate, they could see the American flag rippling on a large flagpole just inside the compound. It looked, at least to Hans, more like a ship's mast. Steel yardarms and cable stays anchored the thick metal pole against the relentless wind of the Great Plains.

"Welcome to Bismarck, North Dakota, you bastards," a guard hollered out. He then signaled to two of the soldiers and they marched the men through the main entrance of the compound. The same guard then said, "ABANDON ALL HOPE, YE WHO ENTER HERE."

Hans and the others were marched past the flagpole and toward a small outbuilding. A narrow porch wrapped around two sides of the hut and led to the entrance of the building. One at a time, the men entered the door.

A clerk issued clothes for the duration of their internment. Each man received two pairs of heavy denim trousers, a work shirt, three t-shirts, three pairs of briefs, two pair of wool socks, a pair of army surplus combat boots, a knit toque, and a wool blanket. All these items were placed in a canvas seaman's bag, which each internee carried on his shoulder as he exited through the backdoor of the small building.

Hans' group marched through an interior gate and toward a long row of narrow wooden barracks. The guards assigned barracks to the internees one or two at a time, so as the line of men progressed it dwindled in numbers. Werner stood just behind Hans in line, and when they assigned Hans to barrack #10, he took a moment to pat the old man on the shoulder. "Be strong," he said. Werner nodded and moved on with the group.

After he entered, it took several minutes for his eyes to adjust to the dim light of the barrack. The sour smell of men and tobacco sat atop a musty odor of decay. Along the walls on either side of the building were a dozen stacked bunks: wooden frames topped with lumpy paillasses. Hans shuffled down the center aisle, looking for a vacancy. A tall gaunt man with closely cropped hair and a cigarette dangling from his lips walked toward him. Hans readied a hello, thinking he would be welcomed into the barrack, but the man walked past Hans with nary a word, leaving only a trail of smoke in his wake. At the far end of the barrack, a group of men sat around a card table. Near them, a small potbelly stove ticked with heat; the faintest amber and orange glowed through the iron grate. The men laughed and smoked, seemingly unaware of his presence. Hans found the lone vacant bunk in the barrack and tossed his bag onto the pallet, thankful for an upper bunk. The chill of North Dakota had already crept into his bones. He climbed up onto his bunk and surveyed his surroundings. A hollow pit formed in his belly as he realized he could not remember the last regular meal he'd eaten. He lay back on the bunk, using his bag as a makeshift pillow and listened to the men. They played skat, a card game he'd learned long ago, and it reminded him of his home in Germany. Hans picked at the dirt under his nails as he thought of his wife and sons. Loneliness snuck up on his soul like a slow moving train. He was thirty-seven years old, a bit soft around the middle, and had a round face and pale blue eyes. By no means was he handsome in the traditional sense, but there had been something about him that appealed to Lucy when they first met. He didn't know what she saw in him, but something she saw in his face that first day had spurred an act of kindness. That simple generous moment, one that came toward the end of a very long day, had moved him in a way he could not put into words. She was in a drugstore with a girlfriend, sharing a soda. Her dark, chestnut-colored hair hung in loose curls and her dark brown eyes reminded him of home. Her determined chin set her face forward and created an air of confidence Hans found attractive even before she spoke. When she stood, her hipbones pushed against the plain skirt she wore, and if she had not been indulging in a treat at that moment they met, he would have thought she had been starved. Her personality flowed from her actions with a quiet assuredness that seemed uncontrived and effortless. Hans knew all this in the first moments of their meeting. Even though he could not have articulated all these assessments and judgments in those few minutes, the sense of ease he felt in her presence could not be denied, and as such, she filled his thoughts for several weeks.

Years later, he could still smell the sweet aroma inside the apothecary, a fragrance he would forever associate with his wife. The laughter from the three men playing skat punctured his dream state and brought him back to his bunk in a barracks in North Dakota, feeling all the two thousand miles separating him from his family. He looked at the ceiling of the small wooden barrack and wondered how things could have gone so wrong. This did not fit into the plan Walter had set out, and now a pall settled on his heart.

When he had left Germany he stood at the railing of the ship; a crowd of well-wishers gathered on the dock below to say goodbye to the travelers, but he recognized no one. Hans looked down at his worn shoes and the dull wooden planks of the deck. Sand had been added to the gray paint to ensure passengers did not lose their footing in wet or icy conditions. He shuffled one shoe back and forth across the grit, leaving brown specks of leather behind. His fellow passengers jostled beside him, throwing streamers and handfuls of confetti into the air while waving and screaming their goodbyes. A steam whistle blasted three short notes and then a long one. A sudden jolt made Hans stumble as the *SS Karlsrue* began to move away from the quay, separating the two worlds. The people on the dock waved handkerchiefs, cheered, and even cried. Hans noticed an old woman with a kerchief tied over her head. She had a slight stoop to her posture and reminded him of his Aunt Frieda, and so he decided to wave to her. His arm moved in a frenzy, as if he were a drowning man signaling for help. As the ship moved away from the dock, the old woman pulled the collar of her coat tight around her neck, turned away, and disappeared into the crowd.

Aside from the initial jolt, Hans did not feel the movement of the ship. Instead, it appeared as if the wharf had broken free and was set adrift. The engines on a small tug escorting the ship out of the harbor blew billows of black smoke into the air as the ship's mooring lines ran from the dock like snakes slipping into the murky waters. A small German brass band on the pier played, *Auf Wiedersehen*. The hollow sounds of the brass instruments faded quickly and became feeble against the hums and whirs of the ship and the expanding distance over the water. As they began to make their way out of the Bremerhaven harbor and into the North Sea, the sounds from shore faded like an old photograph.

Hans' journey had begun three days before in the small town of Meuselwitz, about 80 kilometers west of Dresden. He had left his father's farm and stayed with his Aunt Carla, his mother's widowed sister. "There's no hope for you here," she said. "However, I have a little something that could help you." She arranged the sponsorship necessary to immigrate to America. She handed him the papers and he read the names Walter and Justine Kratsch for the first time. "Distant cousins," Aunt Carla said. "But they will look after you."

On the ship, he wore his only suit, a pale green wool jacket and pants, the fabric thin and shiny on the knees and elbows. In his pocket he carried fifty dollars, American, the parting gift from his aunt. A single trunk contained his world: books, mementoes, and clothes, including linen shirts made of flax grown on his father's farm. Within his suit jacket, he carried the all-important affidavit that would ensure his admittance into the United States. His sponsors, Walter and Justine, lived in Rochester, New York. That was to be where Hans would make his new home. Despite the excitement of the journey, a nagging self-doubt tugged at him. How would he survive in America? After all, he did not speak English and he suspected his education as an agricultural manager would not carry much weight in his new home.

When he examined a map of New York State while onboard the ship, he noticed the name of a small town just south of Buffalo, named Friedberg. He had family who lived in Friedberg, Germany, which was a small village maybe 20 km from Munich. This bolstered his optimism, at least for a moment. He understood New York City was nothing like the English York, its namesake. New England, New Jersey, New Hampshire, all this newness left Hans unsure. After all, the new industrial age in Germany caused his departure. Hans had always felt connected to farms. The soil, the animals, the space, gave him a sense of purpose. He took great satisfaction in the raising of crops; they were his children. To sow, to tend, to harvest, allowed Hans to make sense of the world. The skies over Germany had turned from an eternal blue to lackluster orange and yellow. Industry: the word in everyone's mouth. Coalmines churned out black dusty rocks that made their way to boilers, foundries, and locomotives. There the rocks were transformed into energy that pushed steel through factories and across the countryside.

The bucolic farmland Hans loved became a place for old men and women with nothing left to live for. The young people migrated to cities like Stuttgart, Bonn, and Berlin, anywhere they could find work. Germany still needed grain, but agriculture became something quaint, an antiquated vocation. He saw himself as a plow horse no longer needed with the advent of the tractor. So he found himself on this ship, heading for a new country, leaving his family, language, and culture behind. His hopes were pinned on making a new start, and he resolved never to be on the losing side of progress again. Hans walked towards the bow, looking to the horizon and the expanse of the North Sea. Whitecaps punctuated the grey water that lay outside the harbor. The salt air tickled Hans' nostrils as he took a deep breath. The tugs led the ship to the mouth of the harbor and then released their lines, casting the ocean vessel loose. The low hum of the ship's engines buzzed as though they were whispering the future into his ears.

"Jungfrau," one of the card players yelled and the others laughed.

Hans sat up in his bunk and looked over at the men. One stood and stretched his arms above his head. The virgin, the unfortunate player left without any tricks at the end of the game of skat. With a stature more akin to a fireplug, Hans smiled at the joke the card players made.

"Feuerpause," he said as he reached for his cigarettes and walked toward the rear door of the barrack and donned a black coat and covered his bald head with a knit cap. The smoke and dankness of the barrack unsettled Hans and he decided to get some fresh air. He climbed down from his bunk and followed the man through the backdoor, only garnering a passing notice of the men at the table.

"Hallo," Hans said as he stepped down the stairs at the rear entrance. The man turned and stared at him for a moment, as though he hadn't understood what Hans had said. The man's steel blue eyes narrowed under thick gray eyebrows, and then he gave Hans the briefest nod.

"Mein Name ist Hans."

The man said nothing as he took another drag from his cigarette and stared off into the distance. Something out there held his attention, but beyond the fence and barbed wire lay nothing but miles of snow, a placid ocean of white. Hans stood next to him, trying to think what to say next. He didn't smoke, but nothing else came to mind. *"Mag ich eine Zigarette haben?"* The man nodded and withdrew his hand from his coat pocket, handing Hans a pack of cigarettes and a box of matches. "Lucky Strikes," Hans said. "My brand." Hans took one out, lit it, and returned the pack and the matches. *"Woher sind Sie?"* Hans asked as he lit the cigarette, being sure to inhale as little smoke as possible. Although he had smoked occasionally throughout his life, he did not enjoy it. The flavor it left in his mouth deadened his sense of taste, and he never cared for the dizziness or the nausea that often ensued.

"Schleswig-holstein," the man said.

"Ah yes, in the north. I sailed from Bremerhaven when I came to America." Hans said, taking another small drag from the cigarette. *"Ich bin Hans,"* he said again and held out his hand to shake.

The man shook Hans' hand and nodded. "Heinrich," was all he said.

They stood ankle-deep in the snow, smoking cigarettes, and the conversation inched forward. Heinrich had been a machinist aboard a Standard Oil tanker when he and the rest of the German crew were removed from the ship in the Port of New York and detained by the INS. After Germany declared war, the ship's crew was no longer denizens of the sea, but alien enemies, and hence exiled to a place as far away from an ocean as possible. Heinrich's answers were measured, as though he said them to himself before he spoke. Although Hans' German was fluent, there were words that seem to raise suspicion in Heinrich, as if he considered the friendly conversation as something more than what it was. While Hans thought it strange, he also realized Heinrich's guarded disposition likely grew from the treatment he'd received. Was it beyond the realm of possibility the government might put spies amongst the prisoners? Hans began to explore what he imagined Heinrich's perspective to be, and he thought perhaps that his own decision to emigrate from Germany might give Heinrich pause. Hans realized the no-man's land he occupied: too American for the Germans and too German for the Americans.

Heinrich tossed his cigarette into the snow and walked back into the barrack, stomping the snow from his feet on the top stair. Hans followed suit and watched as Heinrich returned to his seat at the card table, making no move to invite Hans into his group. Hans sighed and walked over to his bunk, his new "home," and lay down and wondered how long he would have to live in this place, and if he were ever released what would be waiting for him.

Chapter 13

After meeting Betty Brewster at the bake sale, Lucy made sure her boys got an early start each morning. Richard and Bob did not know why their mother shooed them out so early, but they listened. On Friday, part of her heart fell when she watched her boys turn onto Newton Avenue and not two moments later a tall, lumbering figure she knew at once to be Caleb came running across the front of the driveway. Her boys were out of sight, but she could not help the need to call out, to warn them of the thundering bull charging. She recognized the instinct of a predator, that innate quality of being in the right place at the right moment and felt a pang in her chest.

She stepped into the house and closed the front door, certain she heard shouting or screaming as it shut. She paused a moment, but the sound faded. She fought the urge to walk to the end of the drive, hearing Hans' voice in her head. *Don't mollycoddle the boys, Lucy.* She shook her head and wondered if she had actually heard anything in the first place. She ran her hand along the front of the skirt she wore and thought about the busy day ahead. She and the boys had brought up potatoes from the root cellar during the week and now she needed to see Gus Payne about bringing them to market. Her husband had worked with Gus at an aluminum smelter right after he came to America. She had seen pictures of him in his smelting suit. The material was silvery metallic and had a diamond-quilted pattern. He wore enormous gloves that covered his arms up to the elbows and a large domed hood with a rectangular window of dark amber. He looked like a spaceman or some mechanical alien. Hans and Gus had been good friends ever since, and they were very reliable for one another in times of crises and in business.

Gus' wife, Miriam, had slipped on an icy sidewalk two winters ago while in town Christmas shopping. She was seven months pregnant. Hans saw Mrs. Payne as her feet slid out from underneath her and rushed to her side. She held her stomach and cried in pain and horror as Hans brought her to the hospital in his car. Three days later the doctor delivered a stillborn baby. They said it could have been worse, but to the Paynes, they really could not see how things could be any worse. Miriam retreated into herself for a long time afterward. The pain on her face punctuated with every glance or word sent her way. People's need to express their condolences warred with Miriam's desire to put everything in the past, to move on. She was not a callous woman. On the contrary, because of her deep feelings she needed to distance herself. Lucy and Hans had brought food over after Miriam returned home from the hospital. They set their casserole dish amongst the numerous others that had already arrived. Gus was congenial, but Miriam hid in her bedroom. "Resting," Gus had said. After a moment of silence, she and Hans made excuses about chores and errands and apologized for not being able to stay longer. The gratitude for the food showed in Gus' eyes as they said goodbye, as did his thankfulness for understanding their desire to grieve alone.

While Lucy prepared to visit Gus, it occurred to her that she could drive the Peerless. The sedan had not moved in Hans' absence. Lucy had simply ridden her bicycle wherever she needed to go somewhere, but this trip was different. She would be negotiating and counting on the Gus' goodwill. Perhaps the car could remind him that their relationship went beyond business. She walked to the garage and ran her hand over the winged-goddess that capped the radiator. The car maintained a sense of majesty, despite being older than her oldest son.

She sat in the driver's seat and pushed the ignition switch; the car was ill tempered and refused to start. Frustrated, she slapped her hand on the steering wheel. "Start, damn you." Afterward, she took a deep breath and weighed her options. She thought about herself on the bicycle and it seemed like such a letdown. Then she noticed the choke, gave it a tug, and turned the engine over once more. It roared to life and its power and noise made her heart race. After a few moments, she pushed the choke back in and the idle settled down to a normal tone. She engaged the clutch, shifted the Peerless into gear, backed out of the garage, and drove down Newton Avenue. Their neighbor Elijah Jenkins sat atop his tractor, plowing his field that abutted the road. As she drove by, he raised his hand and waved at the automobile. In mid wave, he did a double take as he realized Lucy, not Hans, sat behind the wheel. She squeezed the horn and waved back, smiling. In the rearview mirror, she saw Jenkins stop his tractor and watch her as the Peerless disappeared in a cloud of dust.

Gus lived south of Friedberg, at least a twenty-minute trip if the roads were in good condition. Lately, the rain had been making the gravel country roads mucky messes full of ruts with some portions totally washed out. She hoped she would remember all the turns, but after a few minutes behind the wheel, Lucy felt confident. She pushed her chin forward and narrowed her eyes against the rushing wind. Gus had run the co-op for the agriculture community for the last five years. Since the beginning of the war, there had been a tremendous push to increase crop yield on every farm, so she did not foresee any trouble with the deal she had in mind.

Two heifers and a mare grazed in Gus' front pasture as she rounded the last bend that led into the co-op compound. She saw Gus' old International truck dumping a fresh load of hay into the paddock. It hadn't occurred to her that she would arrive at suppertime. Gus looked up and waved to her. She pulled the car around to the front of his barn, parked, and waited for him to finish with the horses. Gus was a squat man who had a bit of waddle when he walked. Regardless of the season, his cheeks were ruddy, and he always wore denim overalls with the cuffs turned up and a straw farm hat that looked like it could belong to Huck Finn.

Lucy got out of the car and stood next to it, resting her right foot on the running board, giving it just a bit of her weight. She could not count how many times she had seen Hans in this exact pose, and as the thought occurred to her a self-conscious twinge made her smile and adopt a more lady-like stance as she waited.

Gus shook the last bit of hay out of the bed of his truck and drove over to where Lucy stood. He touched the brim of his hat, which was as close as he ever came to doffing his farm hat, and remained seated in the truck.

"Morning, Lucy. What can I do you for?"

"The boys and I brought up about twenty bushels of potatoes that we had wintering in our root cellar this week and I—" With a suddenness that was disconcerting, Lucy lost her words. Her mouth began to move, but nothing came out.

"You want to sell 'em, I suppose?" Gus said.

Lucy nodded.

"The best I could offer right now is 35¢ a bushel, upon delivery."

Lucy was taken aback. She was sure the market could bear a bit more than Gus's offer. He sensed her reluctance and upped his offer. "Well, maybe 38¢, but not a penny more."

Lucy placed her foot up on the running board again and folded her arms across her chest. "Gus," she said. "How long have we known one another?"

Gus shifted in his seat, as if it had suddenly become uncomfortable. "Lucy, I—"

"I know you need to make a living. I'm no different."

Gus looked through the windshield of the truck, like he was driving on an open highway. His eyes moved from side to side as if he was reading, or the future was a map he had laid out in his head, and as variables presented themselves, he could apply his own calculus and determine the course of action for the desired outcome. He turned to Lucy and looked at her for a long moment, taking her in and evaluating what he saw, like she was livestock. Lucy lifted her chin and tightened her arms across her chest.

"Have 'em here first thing tomorrow and I'll go 44¢, but you're breaking me. It's a good thing Hans doesn't send you over here too often; we might not be such good friends." One corner of Gus' mouth gave the slightest twitch, and for him this qualified as a smile.

"Hans is out of town. Follow me in that fine truck of yours and we can load 'em up right now."

"No can do, Lucy." He shook his head. "Too much work around here."

"Well, then. See you in the morn." Lucy got in the Peerless and the accommodating motor started right away. She waved at Gus as she pulled onto the driveway. As she drove through the front pasture she felt relief knowing that there would be some money coming in, but she also knew that there was still a lot of work left to be done. She and the boys would have to get the potatoes in the trailer, attach it to the tractor, and then she thought about how long it would take to get back to Gus'. It added up to getting up at 4 a.m. Not too bad by farm standards.

She turned into her own driveway and stopped at the mailbox. There were two letters: one from Bangstrom's and another from Hans. She got into the car and tossed the envelopes onto the passenger seat. She drove to the end of the driveway and parked. The quiet of the motor not running was disconcerting. Without realizing it, she had been leaning against the noise, and now that it was gone, she felt an imbalance. She looked over at the letters and picked them up. Her last bill from Bangstrom's demanded payment in full on their account. This, she felt, had been rather odd considering Bangstrom, the man himself, had offered to put her groceries on account. Why, she wondered, would someone offer credit the same day he wanted you to pay up? Now this letter, sure to be a more official missive, would clearly lay out the debt and the due. She decided that Hank Bangstrom did not deserve her attention now. She opened the other letter from Hans, sat in the car, and read it.

15 May 1942

Dearest Lucy,

I have wonderful news. Men from the railroad came to camp today and said we could earn money for our families if we agreed to provide labor. Some of the men in the camp are of the mind that this is a bad thing. They ask why they should help. I do understand their point of view, but I also know that things are difficult for you and the boys, and that means more to me than anything else. So your husband, the farmer, will soon be laying track between ███ ███. They said that our pay could be sent home to our families, and that is what I'll have them do. Please let me know that you received it.

                                                      Fertile Ground

Have you gone to visit my cousin Walter yet? My hearing was delayed, but it is very important that you go to him and tell him what has happened to me. Give him a message for me. Tell him I said, *alles ist gut.* And tell him I said he should do what he can to help you. I know you and he have never seen eye to eye on things, but I know he can help you and the boys. Please tell them they are in my heart.

All my love,

Hans

Lucy folded the letter in half and tapped it with her fingers. She thought about her husband and about her boys. The news that money would soon be on its way was good, but Hans' insistence that she visit Walter troubled her. She could see the man in her mind's eye: tall, gaunt cheeks, thin wire-framed glasses he incessantly cleaned, and the spotless white lab coat that he wore as proudly as a uniform. Whenever she and Hans were around him, she noticed his furtive glances, as though he was making plans for her. And the way he almost sneered at Hans' ragged fingernails. What could this man do for them? That question sat on top of something else. Was it her pride? The thought of being more vulnerable than she already felt? Or was it the thought of having to ask someone for help, which in itself made her uneasy, but to ask for help from Walter made her stomach turn. She decided more pressing matters were at hand and regardless of what Hans wanted she had to take care of the business on the farm. She picked up Hans' letter and put it back in the envelope. Then she noticed something different. There was an INS stamp, just like the other letter, but beneath it she could make out a Bismarck, North Dakota postmark. Her eyes kept looking at the smudged purple ink. After so many weeks of not knowing where he was, of wondering if she'd get another letter, and the fear of being asked a question she could not answer, she had finally reached a place where she could point to place on a map and say, *He's here.*

She picked up Bangstrom's letter, got out of the car, and walked into the house. She tossed both letters onto the kitchen table and walked into her bedroom to change clothes. Lucy slid into her coveralls, put on her gumboots, dug out some canvas work gloves, and went outside to the barn.

Chucking potatoes was dirty work. Last fall they filled burlap sacks with the harvest and hung them on nails in the root cellar. The cool, dark, and dry conditions kept the potatoes from sprouting eyes over the winter. She and the boys had brought most of the sacks up during the week, but since the deal with Gus had been set, she had to finish the job by herself. She loaded the bed of the trailer; examining each potato to make sure it had not begun to rot. About halfway through, she saw her boys coming up the drive. Bob walked well in front of Richard, who looked like the weight of the world rested upon his shoulders. Lucy wiped the sweat from her brow and walked out of the barn to greet Bob. "How was school today, son?"

"Fine," he said. "But Richard's day was lousy." Bob walked past his mother and continued into the house. Lucy's oldest was halfway up the driveway when she noticed it. Under Richard's left eye, there was a black and blue smear, colors wholly unnatural. Lucy dropped the burlap sack and ran to her son.

Richard refused to tell her who had blackened his eye, even though she pressed. She recognized that personality trait and could hardly fault him, but at the same time her interests extended beyond her boy's pride. The potatoes had to be at the co-op first thing in the morning so she would have to drive the tractor with the trailer in tow and allow at least an hour for the trip. Then there was the issue of the boys. She tapped her fingers and thought about the best way to proceed. She decided a bit of farm work was always a good way to work off feelings that wanted to be exorcised. At the end of a long day, the fatigue of the body could easily crowd out the worries of the mind. Bob would come too. Lucy planned on rising early and bringing her two boys with her on the trek to Gus' farm. She could see them, the boys on either side of her wedged with their feet at the base of the seat and their bottoms propped on the large rear fenders, all three of them on a country road as the dawn broke.

They arrived at Gus' dusty, but the long ride had not been too arduous. Rather, the boys enjoyed the adventure and Lucy felt a sense of power behind the wheel of the machine. When she drove the Peerless the day before, she felt freedom mixed with loneliness. She could not outrun it. The car belonged to Hans and behind the wheel, she felt out of place. While driving the tractor with her sons by her side there was no underlying feeling of uneasiness. The ride was rough as they bounced along the washboard roads, but as the night sky waned and the stars began to fade into the coming dawn, a sense of peace that had been absent in her life rose with the sun. As she turned into Gus' driveway, she saw him in his truck, returning from a chore in some distant corner of his property. As they approached, he got out of the truck and leaned against the front fender, taking them in as they came up the drive. Lucy tried to read the look on the man's face. Was it amusement? Were she and her boys some kind of joke? Were they interlopers in a man's world? Since the beginning of the war many women had stepped into roles they, and the men who were too old to enlist, were unaccustomed to. She decided he was simply pleased that the deal made was being completed as agreed upon. The slightly upturned corners of her mouth made a subtle shift downward as they drove up to Gus' barn. She learned from Hans that it was never good to smile during business transactions. While both parties might be happy with the deal struck, the expression tended to breed more suspicion than goodwill.

"Morning, Lucy. Boys," Gus said as he made the vaguest gesture towards his hat.

"Here they are, Gus." Lucy turned her chin slightly, indicating the load of potatoes in the trailer. "Delivered first thing in the morning."

"Yep." Gus walked around to the rear of the trailer to inspect the load.

The boys jumped down from the tractor and crowded the man on either side.

"I'm surprised to see you two up so early. Your papa told me you both like to sleep in on Saturdays."

"We had to help mom," Richard said.

Gus nodded and looked at him and paused a moment as he noticed Richard's eye. "You get in a fight, son?"

Richard's head dropped.

Bob chimed in. "You should see the other guy."

Gus chuckled and put his arms on both boys' shoulders. "Your

mother sure is lucky to have such fine young men around to help her out."
He gave them a sold pat on their backs and walked over to Lucy, who sat on
the seat of the tractor. Gus looked up at her and cocked his hat a notch. "If
you don't mind, could you park the wagon over yonder?" The tilt of his head
indicated the doors to his root cellar.

Lucy nodded without a word, cranked up the engine, and parked the
trailer where Gus had specified. She dropped down out of the seat and went
about unhooking the trailer. Gus and the boys walked over to her as she
accomplished the task.

"Hey," he said. "Since you boys are already here, would you like to
earn a little money?"

Both boys looked at their mother as if Christmas morning had
arrived early. "Could we?" they asked in unison.

"What'd you have in mind, Gus?"

"I'll give 'em a penny a bushel to unload the wagon and to store them
taters in my root cellar."

"A penny each?" she asked.

Gus rubbed his chin and slowly shook his head. "I swear, I can't
wait to do business with Hans again. When's he coming back?"

The question should have caught her off guard, but it didn't. "I can't
say with any certainty," she said. The boys looked to her with such
expectancy, as though the story she had told them about their father's
whereabouts was ready to explode from their mouths. "But he is coming back
and I'd like to tell him what an upright fellow Gus Payne is. What a fine
gentleman you were during his absence."

Gus took a long look into Lucy's eyes. "Well," he said. "I suppose a
penny each will do."

"All right then." Lucy turned to her sons. "Boys, you listen to Mr.
Payne and do as you're told. I'll be back this afternoon to fetch you."

Lucy looked at her sons; excitement brimmed on their faces, but they
had taken her cue and acted as if it wasn't anything special. She hit the ignition
on the tractor and turned it around, giving the boys and Gus a small wave as
she headed down the drive. She wanted to turn around, to wave again, to say

behave, but she kept her head facing straight ahead and made her way along the road back home.

When she got back home, she left the tractor by the house. She went inside and sat at the table, too tired to put the kettle on for tea. There it was: Bangstrom's letter. As she suspected it was a request to settle all accounts. In her mind, she had roughly calculated what she had charged since last month. Twenty and some change, she reckoned. When she looked at the amount due, she was shocked to see she owed nearly a hundred dollars. Bangstrom had included a full invoice. There was a galvanized water tank for the goats. She knew about that, but numerous other items left her bewildered. Graduated cylinders, Erlenmeyer flasks, mortar and pestle, and dozens of other items she had no clue as to their purpose or whereabouts. She looked at the dates of purchase on most of the items and noticed they were before Hans had left. It struck her how odd that sounded. He had been taken. The FBI took Hans away. She set down Bangstrom's letter and picked it up again, looking at the itemized account in disbelief.

She walked out of the kitchen and into the yard area between the house and barn. The engine of the tractor ticked as it cooled. Lucy rested her hand on her hip and thought for a moment. Two of the goats in their pen looked at her as though they were just as pensive. She had spent a fair amount of time in the barn and had not seen anything unusual, but she decided to look again. Inside the barn, it was cool and the dim light seeped through the slats. Chickens milled about her feet, clucking and pecking at the ground, looking for the feed she had not given them. She looked into each stall. The smell of manure hung in the air, although it had been several months since they had sold the cows and the plow horse. She climbed the ladder up to the loft. The only items there were old halters and horse blankets. She climbed down and stood in the doorway of the barn. The tractor was parked next to the house, and the belt and sparkplug wires Martin Adder had replaced were starkly clean against the faded red of the rest of the machine. It was then a thought entered her mind.

She walked around to the side of the barn to the tractor shed. Hans had built it himself using the outside of the barn as one of the walls. Inside there were deep ruts in the earthen floor, grooved out by the weight of the tractor. The smell of oil, grease, and earth was heavy inside the shed, but on top of it all was the musky odor of a deer pelt hung up to dry on the back wall. Tools, old belts, paint brushes, and other items hanging on pegs on the wall. At the back of the shed, a wooden workbench with a vice stood, a work lamp hanging overhead. Tools lay scattered about as though Hans had just walked out for supper. Lucy ran her hand along the smooth wood of a ball peen hammer. The handle near the head was the color of honey and the other end, the part where Hans would grip it as he worked, was darkened with sweat and oil. She picked it up and felt the heft and a fine layer of dust that had collected in its owner's absence. Lucy set it down, just where she had picked it up.

She looked at the deer pelt. Elijah Jenkins, their neighbor to the north, took great pride in his hunting and skinning skills. If he gave you a pelt, it meant something. Hans had salted, pickled, and tanned the hide and then tacked it up to stretch. It had been left up too long and one of the haunches had pulled away from the tacks and was dangling. Lucy reached out to touch the fur. It was soft but the skin under it had dried hard. She let it fall from her hand and heard the rattle of steel against wood. She lifted the loose corner of the hide back and saw a shiny hasp and padlock. She stood there looking at the apparatus for a moment. She pulled the hide off the wall and revealed a storage closet that she didn't remember. She tugged on the padlock, but it was fastened and refused to yield. She examined the lock and slid the teardrop shaped piece of metal that protected the plug to the side. The shape of the keyhole didn't look like a fit for any of the keys in house. She released the lock and it made a hollow bang against the door. She stood there for a moment, letting the lock and the sound settle in her head, and then she walked back out into the yard. The wind had picked up a bit and cumulous clouds had billowed up in the afternoon sky, their bottom edge darkening with the threat of rain. She closed the outer door to the shed and walked back to the house.

Chapter 14

When it was time to pick up the boys, Lucy drove the tractor back to Gus's farm. Richard and Bob were by the barn, next to the empty trailer, awaiting her return. They saw the tractor and ran toward her with welcoming whoops and hollers. The edges of her mouth curled up despite her best effort to remain stone-faced. She drove up toward the barn; Richard and Bob ran alongside. Their hands and their trousers and shirts blackened with dirt from their labor, and Lucy knew this day would stick in their memories. Lucy parked the tractor next to the empty trailer and shut the engine off.

"It doesn't look like Mr. Payne worked you boys too hard. Are you sure you earned your money?"

"Look and see," Bob said, pointing to the empty trailer.

"We bagged over twenty bushels, Mom," Richard added. He held out a dime, a nickel, and several pennies in his grimy hand to show his mother.

Lucy stepped down from the tractor and brushed her hair out of her face. She looked around for Gus. "Where's Mr. Payne?" she said.

"Right here," he said as he walked out of the barn entrance just behind her. "You've got some real workhorses there, Lucy," he said, pointing to the boys with his chin.

The boys smiled and beamed and Lucy set her hands on their shoulders; her pride came to the surface and she couldn't hold back a smile. "Why thank you, Gus," she said.

Gus wiped his hands with an old rag and looked at the ground for a moment. He stuffed the rag in his back pocket and looked up at Lucy.

"Could I talk to you for a minute?"

"Boys," Lucy said. "Go play and give me and Mr. Payne a few

minutes."

Richard and Bob ran over to the empty trailer and sat in the back, comparing their coins, looking at dates, the heads of Indians, Lincoln and Mercury, laying out the money on the bed of the cart to take it all in at once.

"Lucy," Gus started. "I know you got work to take care of at your place, but I sure could use a little bit of that energy those boys bring around here." Gus paused and looked out to the horizon as if there was something else he wanted to say. He pulled the rag from his back pocket and began to wipe imaginary spots on his hand. "I'm not sure how Hans feels about giving up part of his labor force. Maybe I should talk to him about this." On the last word, his eyes met with Lucy's. Inside she felt something slip a bit. Perhaps it was her pride. She had managed everything on the farm so far with, if she had to describe it, skill. Some bills had to be put off here and there, but, with the exception of one, she was current. The animals were cared for, the fields ready to be planted. She was especially proud of the way she had negotiated prices with Gus, a skill she didn't know she possessed until it was called upon in the moment. An image of her grand-mere popped into her head. A memory of her talking with salesmen who came by her store, trying to ply their wares with serpentine smiles. Large leather valises filled with overpriced goods always accompanied with promises of great profits. Her grand-mere would let these men talk and talk, patiently waiting for the final question: "So how many should I put you down for?" At that moment, grand-mere would get the slightest grin on her face and turn these men away, sometimes with a word and other times with a tirade. She would look at Lucy and say, "The more they talk, the less they say."

Lucy met Gus' eyes. "Hans doesn't have much say, right now. As I said before, he's out of town and I'm handling things." Lucy waited to see how Gus would react to her stance. She thought for a moment that he might retreat, pull back on his offer until he could talk to the boys' father.

"I understand," he said. "Farm work waits for no one." He stuffed the rag back into his pocket. "Truth be told, Lucy," he said, "I could probably handle the work around here myself just fine."

Lucy nodded more out of instinct than acceptance of the statement, crossed her arms over her chest, and looked down at the ground.

"But having the boys around... Well, you know. There was just something about Merriam today. The way she walked out with their lunch and then just stood there watching them eat." Gus reached up and wiped something out of one of his eyes. "I haven't seen her like that in a while. So I thought, maybe." Gus trailed off and looked over at Richard and Bob. He turned suddenly, as though someone had called his name from the pasture beyond the barn. He took off his hat and ran his hand through his hair. His rag appeared again and he wiped his face, put his hat back on, and turned back to Lucy.

"Let me think it over, Gus," she said. In her mind, she saw things coming together. It would be too costly for her to bring the boys to work here every day, so she had to be sure to negotiate room and board into the deal. Merriam would like that, too. With the boys looked after she could make the trip over to Rochester to see Walter with minimal fuss. It also meant she would have to do some extra work about her own place, but she could manage and the extra income could only help, especially with that unexpected bill. "We could probably work something out, Gus. The boys only have a few weeks left in school and I think we could get the planting done before they're out. Let me think on it a bit and I'll let you know."

"Much obliged, Lucy," Gus said as he touched the brim of his hat.

"Let's go, boys. We need to hook up that wagon and get back home." Lucy walked over to the tractor and Richard, Bob, and Gus hitched up the trailer. Lucy started the engine and the boys climbed aboard, taking their places on the rear fenders. They waved to Gus and pulled out onto the drive. Lucy looked back over her shoulder. Gus walked back to his house and in the doorway, she could see Merriam's silhouette.

Richard, on her left, was riding high, his cheeks smudged with dirt but a strong sense of accomplishment shone brighter than his smile, his blackened eye all but forgotten. In his face, she saw a change. Something had happened today. When she dropped him off this morning, there was only an inkling of this joy. The work had replaced the fear and uncertainty she saw in his face just yesterday. His chin stuck out a little more, and his shoulders seemed to be straighter, but it was really in his eyes. They were focused and relaxed. She patted her oldest boy on the knee. "Good work today, son."

Richard smiled.

"And you too, Bob. Mr. Payne had only good things to say about both of you." She let this sink in for a few moments as she navigated from one road to another. "Do you think you'd like to help out Mr. Payne again some other time?"

"Yes!" Richard responded and patted the coins in his pocket. "Anytime is fine with me."

"That's good to hear," she said. Lucy nudged Bob. He looked out into the farm fields that lined the road. "Son?"

"I don't know," he said, rubbing his hands on his pant leg.

"What's the matter?"

"Nothing," he said.

Lucy let the answer go for the moment. She put her hand on Bob's back and gave him a pat. "We can talk about it later," she said.

The three arrived home late in the afternoon. Clouds streaked the sky with pink and orange as the sun sank low on the horizon. The temperature was dropping and the excitement that had filled the boys when she picked them up gave way to the fatigue of a hard day's labor. Despite Bob's reticence to talk about working again for the Paynes, she detected a sense of satisfaction in both boys. In her mind's eye she could see what her sons would become as men. Richard would thrive with hard work. He needed to keep his hands and back busy to keep the doubts in his mind at bay. Bob, although satisfied with the money he earned from labor, seemed to desire a more cerebral existence, one that interacted more with people than things.

As they turned into the driveway, Lucy slowed the tractor and then engaged the handbrake. "Richard," she said. "It looks like there's something poking out of the mailbox. Could you check it for me?" He jumped down from the tractor, ran over to the mailbox, and opened it. Then he just stood there, frozen. "What is it?"

Richard looked at his mother and brother and did not have any words to describe what he saw. He took a half step back, alternating his gaze between what was inside the box and Bob and his mother. Lucy turned the engine off and climbed down from the tractor, Bob right behind her. She walked over to her oldest son. A slight breeze blew and a swirl of black and white pinfeathers fluttered out of the mouth of the mailbox. The vacant eyes of a dead chicken stared. Its wings unnaturally splayed over its head. Someone had wrung its neck and then stuffed the bird into the mailbox rear end first. A small puddle of blood had collected under the bird's open beak.

Chapter 15

Lucy was about to tell the boys to go up to the house when she decided against it. "Get on the tractor, boys," she said as she shut the door to the mailbox.

"But what—"

"Hush. Do as I say."

She recognized the bird in the mailbox as one of the Ameraucana chickens they kept on the farm. Someone had been up to the house, found no one home, and had left the dead chicken as a calling card. The boys complied and Lucy drove the tractor up the drive while scanning the area around the house and barn for anything unusual. More feathers than normal floated about in the mild wind, and the surviving chickens were milling about the open door of the barn, seemingly oblivious to the fate of one of their own. Lucy, Richard, and Bob sat atop the tractor as it idled in the yard. Seconds seemed like minutes as the sound that had been in the background during their trek from the Payne's farm now reverberated off the house and the barn. Lucy shut the engine off and the silence was sudden. All three climbed down from the tractor with a sense of trepidation. A hoe Lucy had used in the fields earlier in the day leaned up against the side of the house. She picked it up and held it like a weapon. "You two stay here," she said.

"But Mom—"

Lucy turned to Bob, hoe in hand, and he did not finish his thought. She walked around the corner of the house, not knowing what to expect, and saw nothing. The windows were intact, the doors seemed secure and as she came around the far end of the house she saw the tractor, but Richard and Bob were nowhere in sight.

"Boys!" Lucy couldn't conceal the panic in her voice.

Bob appeared from around the corner on the far side of the barn. "Mom, come quick." He waved his arm and disappeared back behind the barn.

Lucy walked as fast as she could without running, her hands gripping the hoe so hard her knuckles turned white. As she rounded the corner, she saw her sons standing together, looking at the side of the barn that faced Newton Avenue. There were six sloppily painted white swastikas in varying sizes and orientations. The paint was still wet and dripped from the angles of the perverse crooked crosses. The paint bucket sat on its side in the dirt, and the brush lay abandoned next to it. Behind them, Lucy heard the sound of a car and saw an old blue Ford Coupe speeding down Newton, the form of the car disappeared in the dust of the road as it honked its horn.

"Damn it!" She threw the hoe down, grabbed her boys by their shoulders, and walked them to the house.

"Who do you think—"

"I don't know, Richard," she said. "But I will not stand for this." She and the boys entered the house. Lucy was more than expecting something else to be amiss. She imagined the sitting room ransacked, tables and chairs overturned, drawers emptied and papers scattered on the floor, but all was as she had left it. Still, she did not release her grip on Richard and Bob. "Come with me," she said as though they had a choice. En mass they walked through the sitting room and into the kitchen. Here too, nothing seemed out of place. "Sit," she commanded. The boys sat at the table without a word. "Stay here," she said. "And I mean it this time." Both boys looked down at their dirty hands that were resting on the table. "I'll be right back," she said.

Lucy walked through the rest of the house. Her bedroom was clean and the bed made, but she thought she smelled something. She could not put a name to the odor, and as quickly as she smelled it, it seemed to dissipate. She climbed the stairs to the boys' room and it was in its usual state of disarray. Bob's broken lamp lay on Richard's desk. There was a moment when Lucy's heart thumped when she saw it, even though she knew what had happened to his lamp. Lucy went back downstairs and her boys were exactly where she had left them. "Okay," she said. "Here's the plan." The boys looked up at her with a sense of insecurity. "You two get out of those filthy clothes and get cleaned up and ready for supper. I'm going outside to clean up the mess out there."

The boys looked at each other and then at their mother, as though they had something they wanted to say. "Let's get going," she said, clapping her hands to emphasize the need for action. Richard and Bob rose from the table and headed up the stairs. Lucy stood there for a moment with her hands on her hips. She was seething. She had seen that blue Ford Coupe somewhere before, but now could not place it. She walked out of the house over to the barn, went inside the tractor shed. Tools, lumber, tins, and small glass jars were scattered across the earthen floor. After a moment her eyes adjusted to the dim light and she saw what she'd come for. She picked up a paint bucket; the dried red drips on the side indicated the color inside. She also gathered up a brush and several rags and walked out of the shed and back to the side of the barn that had been freshly accosted.

She used the rags to wipe away the paint that was still wet, leaving pink smears and swirls. *Who would do such a thing?* The question pumped through her mind. There were times she had thought she heard things. People talked about the war. How couldn't they? It affected everyone, so it was only natural that it would come up. Nazis and krauts and Jerries would be mentioned and then the conversation would lull. A glance in her direction that could have meant nothing or something would follow. She did not know how to respond, and so she didn't. Hans had friends and family in Germany. To condemn Germany was to condemn them, too. She had followed Hans' cue and simply listened, never offering a rebuttal or affirmation, and this is what it had gotten her. Sloppy swastikas on the side of her barn. *Philistines,* she thought to herself as she worked at removing the paint.

"Mom?"

Lucy turned and her two boys stood there side by side, still in their grimy clothes.

"We—we want to help," Richard said.

Lucy took in the boys and wiped a bit of perspiration from her forehead with her forearm. They stood there looking up at their mother. Lucy glanced at the smears of white, pink, and red, and then nodded to the boys. "Take these," she said and handed them each a wad of rags. "Try to get as much of the wet paint off as possible, and I'll start painting over with the red."

The boys quickly got to work and Lucy watched them for a moment. Satisfied with the technique and effort, she took the can of red paint and a brush and set herself up in front of the first swastika she had smeared away. She realized she needed something to pry open the can and went to the tractor shed. The tools, which had been scattered across the workbench, were now strewn about the ground. As her eyes adjusted to the dim light, she searched for a screwdriver or a crowbar or anything that would work. It struck at that moment that whoever had vandalized her barn had made the same search. This thought disturbed her. The fact that she had anything in common with someone who would do such a thing irked her, but she still needed the tool. She stopped for a moment, and as distasteful as it was, she tried to put herself in the mindset of the trespasser. Toward the entrance, she saw the wooden handle of a screwdriver sticking up out of the ground. The vandal had stabbed it into the dirt once he opened the can of paint. She pulled it out and saw the slightest smear of white paint mixed with dirt on its tip. She heard her boys talking, inched closer to the door, and listened.

"I bet it was Johnny Adder," Bob said.

"Could've been," Richard agreed. "Or maybe Billy Miller."

Lucy heard a familiar sound. One of the boys was jumping up and down, grunting with effort.

She looked around the corner. Richard held a wad of rags in one hand and stretched his arm far above his head, trying to reach the top of the last two swastikas. Lucy saw this and said, "Johnny Adder couldn't reach that high."

The boys stopped and looked at their mother. At once they were ashamed that their conjecture had been overheard and that it was clearly wrong. "I think I know exactly who did this."

"Who?" the boys asked in unison.

"Don't worry about it. I'll take care of it," she said. She used a tone of voice that persuaded the boys of her seriousness; they didn't ask any other questions.

The boys, despite their long day of work at the Payne's farm, moved quickly to remove all signs left by the intruders. Bob painted the lower sections while Richard procured a crate from the barn to stand on while painting the higher sections. After her boys worked for a few moments, pride welled up, but behind it, sadness hung in her soul.

She walked into the barn, found an old burlap sack, and shook it out; the chickens flurried about, perhaps fearing another abduction. Lucy turned and walked down the drive to the mailbox. She reached in with her bare hands and extracted the dead bird. It was Greta, a good layer and extremely docile. The bird was Hans' favorite, the only named animal on the farm since Philomena and probably the reason she had been captured and wrung. Hans liked to talk to her in German as he fed her, and more than once Lucy had come across him holding the chicken in the crook of his arm as he went about doing his chores. The bird had no fear of being picked up, and so while all the others would have scattered, she had quietly submitted to her fate. Lucy placed Greta in the sack and set it down gently. Inside the mailbox, smeared with blood, was a letter, a thick one without an address or stamp. She held it in her hands and considered opening it on the spot but decided it could wait. If it was from the vandals, she'd already heard what they had to say and wasn't interested in anything else they might feel the need to express. If it was from someone else unwilling to even address the envelope, they could wait too.

She wondered if the boys had recognized the bird as Greta and hoped they hadn't. It seemed that anything around the farm that had a connection to their father was causing more problems than they were worth. She walked back up to the house, the heft of the bird in the sack was lighter than she expected, but it would be enough for three.

The sun had set before the boys had completed their baths and they did little more than move the food around on their plates. They were farm boys and knew where meat came from; it had never bothered them before and Lucy chalked up their lack of appetite to the fatigue of work and the trauma caused by the trespassers. She decided upon a hearty breakfast for them in the morning: eggs, pancakes, and maybe the chicken they had left on their plates tonight would find its way in to their breakfast.

"Okay, boys," she said as she cleared the dishes from the table. "We need to talk about some things." They both looked weary. "I walked over to the Jenkins while you two were cleaning up and made some phone calls." The boys looked at one another. "Tomorrow, Richard, you will go back to the Payne's farm. Mr. Payne needs the extra help and we could use the money." Her oldest nodded and his lips tightened. "Don't smile yet," she said. "You'll have to work more than a Sunday." Richard cocked his head to the side. Then she turned to Bob. "And you, young man, will accompany me to Rochester. Unfortunately, with the rationing we can't buy enough gas to make it there and back. Besides, we need to conserve our money." Bob looked at her with a quizzical expression. "We will be bicycling to see Uncle Walter."

Bob's mouth dropped. "That's got to be like a hundred miles."

"Closer to seventy-five," she said. Richard laughed at this and Bob remained dumbfounded. "And you will be riding Papa's bicycle." She turned back to Richard. "This also means, Richard, that you will be staying overnight at the Payne's farm for three, maybe four nights. They are more than happy to have you. And I have arranged things with your teacher, Mrs. Archer, so you can keep up with your lessons." At the mention of schoolwork, the vague smile on Richard's face disappeared altogether, but she could tell that missing school, and being called upon to help the family made him feel good. Both her boys looked at her expectantly. "What? You two are looking at me like I have two heads."

"When are we going?" Bob finally asked.

"First thing in the morning, so you two need to get your rest."

"What about the animals?"

"The Jenkins have agreed to tend the chickens and goats while we're gone." She looked at both of her boys as their faces displayed a mixture of dismay and anticipation. "Any other questions?" Bob and Richard looked at one another and their mouths tried to form words but after a few moments, they both shrugged.

"Okay then, time for bed," she said.

Chapter 16

Nothing challenged the sky in North Dakota. There were few trees and no mountains or hills, just endless flat prairie in every direction. Even the buildings were squat and timid under the vast and vaulted blue. Hans wondered why the camp had bothered to put up fences topped with barbed wire. Even if he were to escape, where would he go? Canada was to the north, an even more immense and desolate frozen place. The south offered little hope and the east and west, if one followed the railroad tracks, only hinted at the possibility of anything resembling a city a man could get lost in. Hans neatly folded up plans for escape and placed them in the recesses of his mind. He and the rest of the men passed their days trying to keep busy. Heinrich, the closest thing Hans had to a friend in his barrack, liked to play cards with his fellow shipmates but also spent much of his time building models of lighthouses. One was stone gray with tiny black windows painted where the imagined interior staircase would wind its way up to the lantern room. An octagonal one with broad red and white stripes reminded Hans of a candy cane. While he admired the craftsmanship Heinrich applied to each model, he couldn't help but wonder the purpose. They were nice to look at and the construction of them helped pass the time, but at the same time, they were reminders of where they were. The absurdity of a lighthouse in North Dakota was something he could not overlook. Other men also developed odd hobbies. One group was learning to square dance and another had become obsessed with fitness and spent hours doing CALISTHENICS; they even organized a sports day with contests in running and jumping. They lobbied Captain Charles, the camp commandant, for equipment so they could throw the javelin—they wanted to make the competition a true heptathlon—but he balked at the notion of his prisoners armed with spears. However, he did allow the men to use surplus cannon balls as shot puts. He also allowed them to drag their mattresses out into the yard and place them in a heap to provide a safe landing zone for the high jump competition. Hans watched with great amusement, but he had no inclination to participate.

Werner, the old man Hans met on the train, had become the camp tailor. He repaired ripped seams and zippers, replaced buttons with precision, and sewed patches onto the knees and elbows of clothing that had worn through. Despite being over twenty years his senior, Werner got along well with Hans, much more so than with any of the Merchant Seamen. They were a class unto themselves, and they would never accept Hans and Werner into their fraternity.

Hans had decided to spend his time behind barrack #10 doing what he knew best. He staked out a small plot, tilled the soil, and planted some vegetables. One of the guards whose family owned a farm brought in seeds for some of the Japanese prisoners. Hans approached him and was obliged with a small cache of lettuce and carrot seeds. They were only sprouts at this point, but the thin green shoots breaking through the fertile ground of the plains gave him a sense of hope and purpose. Hans worked the soil while Werner sat on the stoop mending garments and darning socks. The two men talked of family, of homes once had in Germany, and of women they had known and the ones they had married. Hans told Werner of Lucy and his boys, and Werner told Hans of his wife Gretel, who had died a year before the declaration of war. "I miss her greatly," he said. "But am happy she didn't live to see me in such a place." They had no children and both of their families, what remained at least, were still in Germany. It seemed to Hans that this lonely widower, so much older than the rest of the internees, perhaps saw him as a son he had never had.

One day a ruckus occurred that changed everything. Near one of the interior gates, a commotion brought men out of their barracks. Hans and Werner looked up from their respective labors as Felix and Earl, two camp guards, and their dogs, Shep and Hooch, hurried along the corridor between the fences that segregated the Germans from the Japanese. Hans stood and looked in the direction of the tumult. Werner set the coat he was reattaching a button to next him on the stoop and stood. From all over the camp men were drawn to the area where the interior gate led to the rows of barracks.

"Let's see what's happening," Hans said, brushing his hands clean on his pant legs. He and Werner ambled toward the gate where many others had gathered. Two soldiers in the guard tower had their rifles at the ready but didn't point them at anyone in particular. Several other guards lined the perimeter just outside the gate. Hans noticed Felix and Earl, leashes taut against the pull of the dogs. At the center of the crowd, two men stood. Captain Charles, a man of medium height and build, who was only remarkable in the sense that his appearance was unremarkable. Without his uniform and Captain's bars, he would have been a man one might pass on the street and not even notice. The other man wore a dark brown suit with pale yellow stripes spread widely apart. He was short, rotund, and had a black and gray mustache. He reminded Hans of Grover Cleveland; his vest adorned with a gold watch chain, he kept his hand in his trouser pockets as he surveyed the men who had gathered. Captain Charles raised his hands over his head in order to settle the horde. "Men," he announced. "This is Henry Dobbs of the Northern Pacific Railroad Company." The internees shuffled nervously, perhaps fearing another long train ride to some other desolate corner of the country. Captain Charles nodded to Mr. Dobbs and took a half step back.

"Good afternoon, men." He smiled, showing his yellowed teeth. "Or should I say *guten Tag*."

He pronounced *Tag* as if it were a children's game, not as something that rhymed with "fog." The internees did not respond in kind and his smile quickly disappeared. "I realize that many of you Germans have no part in this war. You were, after all, living here in America. I think that says something about your loyalty." Dobbs paused and glanced back at the Captain who nodded in approval. "I have a proposition for men who are not afraid of some hard work, men with strong backs and clear consciences."

Hans leaned into Werner's ear and said, "Something's rotten in Denmark."

Werner did not take his eyes off Dobbs, but nodded his

acknowledgement to Hans' comment.

"We need 60 men who are willing to help us lay track across this great state. The days will be long, if you try to escape you will be shot, and I can't say the victuals will be any better than what you have now. What I can promise is modest pay."

The crowd began to murmur, mostly in German. Some men were translating Dobbs' message to those who didn't speak English and others were exhibiting their dismay in German so as to avoid a reprimand from any of the guards.

Hans took a step forward and asked, "How modest is this pay you speak of?"

Several of the men who had been standing near Hans glared at him. "*Verräter*," he heard, but didn't turn to see who had called him a traitor.

"A true capitalist, I see." Dobbs laughed and shared his good humor with the Captain, who only offered the vaguest smile. "I can offer each of you three cents an hour with the promise of at least ten hour days. The Captain here has agreed to extend commissary credit over the next week to any who should sign up today. It'll be your money. You can spend it here or send it home. Makes no matter to me." Dobbs rocked on his feet a bit, seeming pleased with his magnanimity, but his smile quickly faded as the crowd began to stir. Someone yelled *sieg heil*. Then the call was taken up by others and the chant grew until dozens of men were pulsing forward, striking their arms into the air. Dobbs' jaw dropped and he stumbled while stepping back from the encroaching men. The Captain, also flummoxed, took a step back. Both men stood with mouths agape, unsure how things could have changed so quickly. Guards moved through the gate and pulled Dobbs and the Captain to safety behind the fence. Felix and Earl moved in with their dogs. Hooch and Shep barked and pulled on their leashes, lurching toward the onslaught of angry internees. Other guards with guns moved in behind them. The Merchant Marines who chanted kept moving toward the guards. Hans was transfixed. He had heard this chant from crowds broadcast on the radio, and he had seen the vast and neatly regimented sea of adherents during the 1938 Olympics in a newsreel, but this was something else entirely. The faces of these men grew red with their fervor and the frenzy of their voices was exhilarating and frightening. A torrent of energy pulled at his soul and he began to feel his body giving way to the force. A hand on his shoulder pulled him back; he flinched and tried to shake it off, but the firm grasp knocked him off balance. Hans stumbled backward and saw that it was Werner pulling him away from the melee. "Come. This is a battle they can't win," he said and held tightly onto Hans' shoulder. The two men turned and hurried away from the growing riot, looking over their shoulders as they retreated. The Merchant Seamen clashed with the guards and fell under the blows from batons, and once on the ground snarling dogs pulled at their legs and arms. Dust from the brawl stirred up a cloud. Internees in denim overalls and soldiers in uniforms blended into a screaming mass. The sound of thuds, punches and blows; screams, shouts and yelps of pain, turned the muscles in Hans' chest into a knot. A burst of automatic gunfire from the nearest guard tower ripped through the awful sounds, and soldiers and internees alike stopped in mid swing. "On the ground," a guard yelled. "Everyone down on the ground. Put your arms out!"

The guards extricated themselves from the internees and settled into their fallback position, winded, gritting their teeth, and dusting off their uniforms. Nearly fifty internees lay prone in the gravel at odd angles, like a dropped bundle of sticks.

Hans and Werner, and many others were twenty yards away, creating a wide perimeter around the rioters. Felix, Earl, and two other guards with dogs started toward this outer perimeter of men, who stood dumbfounded but eager to see what would happen next. "Back to your barracks," Earl yelled. "Go on! Back to your barracks!" The dogs and guards advanced and the internees who had no stomach for conflict turned and moved back to their assigned buildings. They tossed quick glances over their shoulders at the dogs and beyond to their fellow internees who were still face down in the dirt.

"Come," Werner said. "This is none of our concern. They're mindless lunatics."

Hans followed Werner's advice and walked back to his barrack. "Thank you," he said.

Werner stopped and looked at him for a moment.

"I'm not sure what I was feeling, but it was if I was being drawn into that—" Hans couldn't find the right word as he looked over his shoulder to the men being rounded up at the gate and led away to the cooler. "You pulled me back."

Werner nodded. "It's the frenzy. It tugs at a place deep inside," he said and then ducked into #9 without looking back.

Hans entered the nearly empty barrack #10 and lay on his bunk. He wanted to shut it all out, but his body, his heart, all his tendons and muscles wouldn't let him hide the images in his mind. There was no easy way to look at this situation. The men on the ground, those loyal to the Reich, were his barrack mates. He could not expect to stay here as someone had already branded him a traitor and he could not help but feel his question was the impetus of the riot. One had to be more thoughtful to survive and not give into the desire of simply being a pawn. This thought stuck with Hans as he turned it over in his mind.

What had only been a possibility for income just a while ago now seemed like his only option for survival. His family needed the money he could earn working on the railroad, and more importantly he could remove himself from harm's way by vacating this barrack and maybe even learn something valuable in the process. As he pondered this, a voice inside pointed out that it was his own fault. His actions had brought all this about. Not only the riot, but also his incarceration. He had a choice and made the decision about whose side to be on and how he could best serve his allegiance, and now that choice revealed its consequences. He had lived a lie for so long that he believed his own fictions. He wanted to believe he was nothing but a simple farmer from upstate New York, the role he played so well, but that word, *Verräter*, echoed in his head and made his chest ache.

Men returned to Hans' barrack sporadically as he mapped out his plan. Many of those absent from the barracks were the ones who had started the riot. He saw Heinrich bloodied by a baton and knocked to the ground. The guards led him away with his arms restrained behind his back.

When Hans finally stuck his head outside the back door of the barrack he anticipated a sharp rebuke, but nothing happened. Hans stepped out and walked over to his garden. He picked up the hoe and began tilling a new section. As he did it, he knew his actions were pointless. Someone else might take up the garden, but it seemed unlikely. The idea was to work the soil until one of the guards came close enough to hail. He knew Earl and Felix were around, but he wasn't sure how they might respond to him given what happened earlier. Still, he thought, there would be a much better chance that one of them would stop to talk to him rather than any of the others. Felix's mother had moved from Germany with her parents at the turn of the century, and so he didn't view people like Hans with too much suspicion, despite the government's accusations. Hans was hardly intimidating, which he thought should work in his favor. He continued to work the soil, turning it, breaking up clumps, and removing rocks. He moved his body around so he could keep the patrol corridor in his peripheral vision. If nothing else, he would have to be patient.

Chapter 17

Richard sat on the stairs that led up to the porch of the house. Next to him lay his Boy Scouts knapsack packed with clothes, toiletries, and a copy of *Lost Horizon*. His mother and brother were still inside, preparing for their own trip. Part of him felt a bit sad that he would not get to see his relatives in Rochester, and he thought that he might like the challenge of riding so far. He had used his father's bike before to ride all over town, but to venture out onto the highway and pedal and pedal for hours upon hours intrigued him. He was sure that his mother and Bob would be fine, but he would have felt better about their trip if he were there. Instead, he had his own adventure. He had spent nights away from home before, hiking and camping with his Boy Scout troop, but this was different. He was a hired hand on a farm, only for three or four days, but the notion appealed to him. He did not have any illusions about the work; it would be tough. He looked around the yard, taking stock of things before he left. The chickens were milling about as they did on any day, the goats were feeding on hay, and the slightest smell of fresh paint curled into his nose. He stood and walked over to the newly painted side of the barn and scanned it. The paint applied yesterday did stand out against the sun-faded red of the rest of the barn, but other than that, only the image in his head remained to attest to the crime. His mother had refused to call the police.

"What can they do?" she asked.

To Richard it seemed like the sensible thing to do. Someone committed a crime, there should be an investigation, and the police were the ones who did such things.

"And what if the newspaper gets wind of it?" she continued after a moment, her face reddening. "I don't want our barn to be anybody's headline.

Fertile Ground

People in this town gossip enough without any prompting. Can you imagine what they'd say if this got out?"

Richard nodded, but he did wonder what his father would have done. He knew his father was helping the war effort, and that other kids in school had fathers who were in the service or working in faraway plants building planes and tanks and ships, but he could not help but feel something in his stomach that made him want to move with strength and force. He heard the sound of an engine and turned away from the barn. It was Mr. Payne's International pickup truck coming down Newton Avenue, a plume of dust in its wake.

Richard ran over to the porch and opened the door. "Mr. Payne's here."

The truck pulled up in front of the house and Mr. Payne got out. "Morning, Richard. You ready to do some work?" He smiled and patted Richard on the shoulder. "We'll get some meat on these bones before we're done."

His mother came out the door, wiping her hands on her apron. "Good morning, Gus. Would you like some coffee?" She stepped down the stairs and mussed Richard's hair.

"Thank you, no. Me and this one here got a lot to do today and daylight's awasting."

"Richard," his mother said. "You listen to Mr. and Mrs. Payne and do as you're told. She paused for a moment, like she had something else to say. "Gus, thank you for doing this".

"T'aint no need for thanks. You don't know what a big help this young man will be. I got plenty that'll keep him busy." Mr. Payne and his mother stood there for an awkward moment. Richard looked at his mother and then at Mr. Payne. "Let's get going," he said.

"Sure enough," Mr. Payne said. "Chomping at the bit. I like that."

Richard grabbed his knapsack off the porch, jogged to Mr. Payne's truck, and tossed it into the bed. He opened the door and climbed into the cab as Mr. Payne waddled over to the driver's side and slid into his seat. The truck rumbled to life, Mr. Payne shifted it into gear, pulled around, and drove down the drive. Richard shot his hand out the window and waved goodbye to his mother. Mr. Payne followed suit.

The sun hung low in the dawning sky and Richard and Mr. Payne squinted as the morning light warmed their faces. They drove down Newton Avenue and Richard felt a sensation he could not name: eagerness and optimism mixed with dash of apprehension. Mr. Payne, his straw hat tilted back a bit, drove with one hand on the steering wheel and his arm resting out the open window. The air swirled around in the cab, the slightest tinge of coolness from the evening gave Richard's skin a tingle that he liked. He took a deep breath and exhaled, and felt the force of his future.

He noticed something ahead, someone actually. A figure made its way along the shoulder of Newton Avenue, ambling more than walking, as though the person was headed somewhere, but not in a particular hurry to get there. A moment later, Richard recognized the gate and the red hair of Caleb. Richard's chest tightened and he touched the bruise just beneath his eye.

"Is that a pal of yours?" Mr. Payne asked. "We could give 'em a lift if you want."

A laugh escaped his mouth before he had a chance to stifle it. Then the dam overflowed. It began with a couple of low huffs and grew into an uncontrollable guffaw. He could feel his face redden in embarrassment and amusement at the suggestion.

Mr. Payne had an uncertain look on his face.

"A ride? That's rich." He was giddy and couldn't help himself. He slapped his leg, trying to get a hold of himself.

"Are you all right, son?"

"Sorry, Mr. Payne," he chuckled and shook his head. "It's just that's the fella who gave me this." Richard pointed to his blackened eye. "Instead of a ride, how about you run him over?" Richard laughed even louder.

Mr. Payne was unsure at first, but a grin began to appear. "Well," he said. "I can see your point, but that might not be the best way to start the day." He smiled at Richard and clapped him on the knee.

The pickup passed Caleb on the roadside and left the boy in a choking cloud of dust. Richard turned and saw him wave vainly at the wake of dust. He noticed a large white streak on the side of Caleb's denim overalls, like someone had spilled paint on them. The image settled in Richard's mind. The smile left his face and something stronger replaced it.

Chapter 18

Lucy stood in the yard and watched Gus's truck pull around and head down the drive. Two arms, one on each side of the cab, waved back to her. The truck reached the end of the drive and turned onto Newton Avenue and a minute later disappeared into a cloud of dust. She sighed and stood there for a moment with her hands on her hips. Hans told her that she coddled Richard too much as a youngster and that was the reason the poor boy had such a stutter. Perhaps it was true. She didn't like being blamed for her son's speech impediment, and she also didn't like being told not to embrace her son, not showing him that he was loved. She had been raised in house were such things were absent, but had vowed to make her home different. Even if Hans' mother never kissed him as a boy, as he had sworn to numerous times, Lucy didn't see why she should deprive her sons of the affection she felt and that they deserved. As much as she wanted to respect Hans' wishes about how the boys should be raised, he was not here. And, to her mind, he, more than anyone else, held the blame for his absence. She shook her head, as though she had tasted something bitter and went inside.

"Are you ready to go, Bob?" She hollered up the stairs. There was no immediate answer. "Bob!" She waited a moment and listened intently. "Where are you?" She climbed the stairs to the boys' room and didn't find him. Back downstairs, she checked the bathroom, her and Hans' bedroom, and the kitchen. No Bob. "This is not the time to be playing hide and seek," she said, hoping her youngest would slink out from a cupboard or closet, but there was only silence. She walked through the kitchen again to the back door and out into the yard. She stood with her fists on her hips, a posture she didn't like and was becoming entirely too frequent for her taste. The chickens were pecking the ground around the open door of the barn and the goats

                                    Fertile Ground

were feeding on the hay she had feed them earlier. "Robert Olen Müller, where are you?!"

A moment later, his head popped around the corner of the barn. "Here I am."

Lucy stomped over to where her son had appeared. "Don't tell me—" She stopped as she rounded the corner. "What on earth are you doing?"

Bob was standing there with a bucket of white paint and a brush in his hand, a large crooked *U* and a portion of an equally unsteady *S* painted on the side of the barn. "I'm painting USA on the barn so everyone will know to leave it alone while we're gone." He began to finish the *S*.

"Bob, dear," his mother said. "You don't have to do that."

He finished the letter and looked at her. "Someone thinks we're Nazis, Mom. If we put USA on here they'll know we aren't." He looked up at his mother, shielding the morning sun from his eyes with his hand.

Lucy stooped down so she was face to face with her son. "Honey, we are Americans. Everyone knows that. The people who painted those things on our barn are idiots. That's all. You don't have to do this to show you're an American."

Bob blinked at his mother, looked down at the bucket and the brush, and then turned to the barn. "But if I leave it like that it's just *US*."

Lucy smiled. "Yes it is. It is just us. And there isn't a thing wrong with that." She reached her hands out and Bob reluctantly handed over the bucket and brush. "Now go get cleaned up. We need to get on the road." Bob headed back to the house and Lucy stood there for moment, looking at the letters on the side of the barn and was unable to keep a smile from her lips.

Lucy and Bob made good time on their trip. They rode east through Alden and into Alexander, where they took a break for a light lunch. Afterward, they headed north to Bethany and stopped just outside Batavia late in the afternoon. They had traveled over thirty miles and both were feeling it. They found a nice site near the shore of Horseshoe Lake and Lucy spread a blanket on the ground. She unpacked the picnic dinner she had brought. They sat in the shade of a tree and languidly ate their meal. After they finished, Lucy flattened out the map she had plotted their trek on and ran her fingers along the route she had marked with a pencil the night before. "This is where we are now," she said to Bob. He leaned in, looked at the map, and then looked out at the lake.

"It doesn't look like a horseshoe from here," he said.

Lucy nodded, happy he was not too concerned about the length of the trip in front of them. She leaned back and propped herself up on her elbows. The breeze rustled her hair and she could not ignore the beauty of the early evening and the place they had chosen to stop. She thought about Richard and imagined he would be having his supper too, perhaps out by the barn with Gus, but she thought it more likely Merriam would have insisted on treating him more like a guest rather than a hired hand, and as such, she would prepare a meal for all three of them and serve it in the house. Although she was concerned about leaving her oldest boy, the thought of him brought a sense of satisfaction and pride to her face.

Bob sat Indian style, deep in thought. In the distance, they heard a train whistle. Three sharp blasts followed by one long one. When he heard the whistle, he looked in the general direction of the railroad. Neither of them could see the train from where they were, but the chugging of the locomotive grew louder and they could feel the vibrations of the train through the ground. Bob plucked a blade of grass, situated it between his thumbs, and blew, answering the train whistle with a thin reedy sound. Lucy chuckled and Bob smiled. "I suppose we could've been hoboes and jumped the train back in Friedberg," she said. He shook his head and gave a half laugh before he blew once more through the grass whistle.

Twilight crept in and the miles they traveled stiffened their muscles. "We'd better lay out our bedrolls before it gets too late." She stood and gathered the blankets she had packed on the back of the bicycles and spread them out, making two pallets on a nice grassy patch far enough away from the water so they would not be attacked by mosquitoes. As night came upon them, they settled into their beds and looked up into the sky. Polaris appeared first, and then Lucy pointed to Venus. "You can always tell a planet from a star because planets don't flicker." The curtain of night darkened as the pinholes in it shone brightly. She looked up at the night sky and wondered if Hans was in a place where he too could look up at the night sky and see the same constellations they saw. "You see that group of stars there? The one that looks like a zig-zag? That's Cassiopeia. She was a beautiful queen who was too arrogant for her own good. She angered Poseidon by saying her daughter Andromeda was prettier than the Nereids, who were sea-nymphs. She tried to get out of his punishment by sacrificing her daughter Andromeda to a sea monster, but Perseus, who had a crush on Andromeda, came and saved her. Poseidon thought someone had to atone for the sin against him so he turned Cassiopeia into a constellation as a warning to anyone who thought about comparing themselves to the gods."

"Mom?" Bob said.

She waited to for him to say something else, and when he didn't finish the question she looked over at her son. He wasn't looking up at the stars, but rather he was gazing out toward the small lake.

"What is it, Bob?"

He met his mother's eyes. "Why did those policemen take Papa away?"

Lucy's mouth opened to answer. Perhaps she was about to perpetuate the lie that had reached a level of comfort in its repeated telling, or maybe she was about to simply tell her son the truth, at least as much of the truth as she could be certain of, but her mouth and tongue weren't able to articulate any words. She wanted to say it was all a mistake, that the police were overzealous and misguided, that their father was not a criminal, and not a spy for the Nazis. She wanted to say he and his brother should be proud of their father, that they should be proud of their country, that kids at school, and their parents for that matter, could be cruel just for the sake of amusement, and that sometimes people made mistakes and things could get out of hand so quickly that there is no time to straighten out the mess before it all explodes in your face. As she looked into her son's eyes, none of these thoughts, reasons, or explanations seemed appropriate. She felt naked under his gaze and couldn't hide her own uncertainty about the situation. Instead of answering, she wrapped her arms around her boy and held him tightly. His back stiffened against her embrace, as though his body was unwilling to accept the physical contact in lieu of an answer to his question, but she held him until she felt his muscles relax a bit and his head leaned in on her shoulder. Then she felt the gentle quakes ripple through his body as the boy began to sob. Lucy knew that not being able to answer the boy's question was an answer in itself. Lucy held her son as the anguish and disappointment and bewilderment spilled out of him. She rocked her son from side to side, the way she did when he was an infant, and although the movement provided a sense of comfort to her as it gave her the sense she was doing something to alleviate her son's pain, she could also tell that it did little for the boy. After several long minutes, she sat up and placed her hands on Bob's shoulders, taking in his reddened and wet face. "Bob," she said. "Look at me."

Bob raised his eyes to meet hers but as he did something seemed to spur on another flow of tears.

"Son, your father loves you very much. He would never do anything to harm you or his family." Lucy moved one of her hands to the boy's chin and lifted up his face. "You have to believe that. Okay?" Bob nodded slightly. "Now we are on our way to see Uncle Walter, who, I hope, will be able to help Papa. I need you to be strong and to trust me. Can you do that for me?" Lucy's thumbs smoothed away the tears from her boy's cheeks. He nodded again and she pulled him to her chest and held him tightly. "We will get through this," she said.

Chapter 19

Lucy and Bob reached Rochester late in the afternoon. The sun cast long shadows and the air had begun to cool; it tingled Lucy's skin as it blew against the thin layer of perspiration that covered her body. The weather had been temperate, but all the hours on a bicycle had been tiring. Bob had removed his shirt in the heat of the afternoon and his shoulders were pink from the sun. They glided into Walter's driveway and came to a stop in front of the two-car garage attached to his house. Walter and his wife Justine lived in a large two-story colonial painted pale yellow with black shutters. It also had two chimneys. The expansive and neatly manicured yard had a white pedestal fountain with a cherub who held an ever-pouring ewer on his shoulder. Mother and son dismounted their bicycles and parked them on their kickstands. "Put on your shirt, Robert."

He reached into the basket, put on his shirt, and buttoned it up. They heard the side door to the house open and saw Justine, a tall and solid woman with black hair swept up into a bun like a schoolmarm. The lines on her face that made her look severe bent with kindness as she walked toward them. "My goodness, I cannot believe you two rode all that way," she said and reached out to embrace Bob. "What a strong young man you must be." She waved her arm to Lucy as she steered Bob toward the house. He peeked over his shoulder at his mother. Lucy smiled and gestured with her chin to follow his aunt into the house. Lucy unstrapped the knapsacks from their bicycles and followed. When she entered, Bob was sitting at the table with a tall glass of milk and a plate of cookies. "Robert! You'll spoil your supper."

"Oh let the boy have a little treat," Justine said. "He has worked up such an appetite on the trip I'm sure he'll have no trouble finishing his dinner.

Besides, he's skin and bones. What do you feed the poor boy?"

Bob looked from his aunt and then to his mother and took another bite out of one of the cookies. "Finish that one and the milk and you can save the rest for dessert," Lucy said. She turned to Justine, who was busy peeling potatoes in the sink. "Thank you for putting us up tonight."

"Psshh," Justine said. "You're family and always welcome here." She turned toward the table. "Robert. Which do you like better? Beets or carrots?"

Bob shrugged. "Carrots, I guess."

"Carrots it is, then." Justine moved with grace across the kitchen to a pantry, extracted a bunch of carrots, and began washing them. Lucy watched, unsure what to do with her hands in someone else's kitchen.

"Can I help?" Lucy asked.

"You are a guest in my home, so sit." She hit her forehead as if she was swatting a fly. "Where are my manners? Would you like some iced tea? I imagine your trip has dried you out." Justine moved to the icebox before Lucy answered. She poured Lucy a glass and set in front of her. "And have a cookie. I thought Robert was thin, but you could use some fattening up, too."

Bob reached over to the plate and handed a cookie to his mother. "Thank you," she said and shook her head *no*. He shrugged and took a huge bite of it.

"Robert! I said to save the rest for dessert."

"He must be starving. Let him eat," Justine said without turning around.

Lucy opened her mouth to tell Justine that she was the boy's mother and that she will decide when and where and what her son will eat, but as these thoughts raced through her mind, she also knew Justine was simply trying to be hospitable, and that this trip had more at stake than her son eating cookies before supper. "Is Walter home?"

"No, not yet, but he should be soon. His shift at Bausch & Lomb ended at 6 o'clock, he normally stops for a beer at The Tavern and is home for supper by 7 sharp. Since he knows you and Bob were coming, he might forgo the beer, but don't count on that. Walter is a very precise man who loves his schedule."

Lucy sat with her son at the table watching Justine move about the kitchen as she prepared the meal. Lucy crossed and then uncrossed her legs. She felt useless just sitting there and finally stood up. "Can I help set the table?" Before Justine could answer, they heard the sound of a car as it turned into the driveway and pulled up to the side door that led into the kitchen. Walter was home.

After the meal, Bob, Lucy, and Walter sat in the living room. The room had dark, mahogany wood floors and wainscoting. Cherry blossom wallpaper covered the upper portions of the walls. Bob had snuggled up on the maroon camelback sofa with his head on Lucy's lap and had fallen asleep. Justine washed the dishes and left Lucy and Walter to talk. Walter sat across from her in a burgundy wingback chair with ball and claw feet. He was a tall man with a narrow face and a long nose that curved down at the end, which gave him an avian essence. He reminded Lucy of a hawk, and she often felt like a witless field mouse under his gaze. A vertical crease just above the bridge of his nose made him look like he was always concerned about something and this made his dark brown eyes humorless. He crossed his legs at the knee and sipped his coffee as Lucy gave an accounting of what happened to Hans and the request for assistance from Walter he had made in his letters. Her eyes darted from Walter to the kitchen, fearful that Justine might be eavesdropping.

"And he told me to tell you that 'all was well,'" Lucy said.

Walter took another sip of his coffee and set the cup on the saucer he held on his knee. "Is that exactly what he wrote?"

"Well..." Lucy thought for a moment. "Yes. I think so. He wanted me to tell you that he was all right."

"I see," he said. "All is well."

Lucy thought it strange Walter would be concerned about the particular phrasing of the message. Wasn't the important thing that his cousin was fine despite being taken away from his family and secreted off away to some camp? Then she remembered. "He actually wrote it in German," she said. "*Alles ist gut,* is what he wrote."

"Ahhh. I see," Walter said. The crease in his forehead disappeared momentarily. He repeated the phrase. *"Alles ist gut.* That is very *gut* to know." He lifted his head a bit and looked off to the side of Lucy, as though he was trying to solve a mathematical equation without a pencil and paper. Lucy stroked her son's hair as she watched Walter.

"So," Lucy finally said. "Do you think we can find an attorney to help with his case?"

"Absolutely, Lucy. That is why your husband has sent you to me. I will reach out to a very good man tomorrow. Simply leave it in my hands and your husband will be back home before you know it." Walter smiled and stood. "And now, I have to make some phone calls on his behalf, if you'll excuse me."

"But—"

"I'm sure you would like very much to be there, to meet this man I have in mind, but on this you must trust me." He placed his hand on her shoulder. "You do trust me, don't you?"

Lucy met his eyes, nodded, and then looked down to her son in her lap. "There's so much at stake," she said.

"And that, my dear Lucy, is precisely why you should leave this to me. Tomorrow Justine will take you and Robert by trolley to Irondequoit. There is a lovely beach there and you can enjoy the beauty of lake. I'm sure it will still be a bit too chilly to swim, but you will have a lovely time and a chance to rest before you return home."

With that, Walter walked out of the living room and into his study where he turned and slid the pocket doors closed. Lucy continued to look at the doors after they had been shut, trying somehow to see through them. The notion of sitting on the beach and enjoying the sun did not sit well with her. Bob stirred in her lap and she stroked his hair again, gazing upon him, seeing lines and hints of his father in the boy's face. It appeared things had been settled before she had arrived, which made her wonder about the purpose of the trip. If she were not to meet the attorney to assist with the case, why did she and her son have to pedal seventy-five miles?

Irondequoit was beautiful, just as Walter had promised. Lucy and Justine sat under a brightly striped umbrella, reclining in Adirondack chairs on the beach and gazed over Lake Ontario. There were seagulls floating on the wind overhead, calling out into the breeze. Overturned skiffs lay in the sand beyond the high tide mark on the beach, and other boats sat anchored at the waterline, lolling gently in the small waves rolling in. Bob ran along the sandy rocky beach, pausing only to skip stones on the water or pick up a piece of driftwood.

"I was so sorry to hear about Hans," Justine said.

Lucy looked out over the lake, acting as if she hadn't heard. She could not say she was comfortable with the fact that Walter had told his wife what had happened and as the thought settled in, she felt her face grow flush. She felt jealous Justine's husband trusted her with the truth. Somewhere inside she had known Hans kept things from her. Perhaps he was still keeping secrets. She didn't know for sure, and that was the problem.

"Robert seems to be taking it in stride," Justine said.

Lucy nodded, not wanting to explain the elaborate lie that had grown like a mushroom, or the questions Bob had about the story. Yes, she thought, he is taking things well. Children are resilient that way, able to be easily distracted by a smooth stone or a weatherworn stick when reality hangs over their head. Hans' situation sat in the forefront of Lucy's mind. As she lay in bed at night trying to sleep the scene unfolded itself time and again: the sound of the banging, the rattle of the loose pane of glass in the door. The worse sound of all was the thud her husband's body made as he hit the floor. As each sound of that night rang through her head, images accompanied them, the flashlights, the policeman carrying the radio under his arm like a chicken, her husband handcuffed trying to turn around as they pushed him toward the car, and Bob standing at the bottom of the stairs. She knew he saw more than she initially thought. She watched him on the beach running after sandpipers that scurried but never took flight and felt despair, knowing things would never be as they were.

"Walter said this man, the attorney he was going to talk to today, was very good with immigration issues. I'm certain he'll be able to sort all this out." Justine paused and shook her head. "If it weren't so serious it would be laughable. They really thought Hans was some sort of spy?"

Lucy shrugged. "All I know is they took him."

A little while later Bob came up to the two women. "I'm hungry."

"I'm feeling a bit peckish myself," Justine said. "I do know a hotel just a block or two from here that has a nice restaurant. May I treat you two?"

Lucy did not want to say yes. She preferred to pay for her own meals and a restaurant seemed like an unnecessary extravagance. Bob raised his eyebrows and his expectations made her give in to the suggestion. They sat on an expansive veranda of a large Victorian hotel that overlooked the beach. Built in the 1800s, the hotel boasted more than thirty rooms with a water view. The waiters stood stiffly and wore white jackets and black ties as they poured water into crystal glasses. The plates were gold trimmed, and there were more forks than Lucy knew what to do with. It was a fine meal. When the check came, Lucy reached for her handbag.

"Now I said this was my treat," Justine insisted.

Lucy began to protest but before she had a chance Justine had already settled the tab with bills and a wave to indicate the change was the tip. "It's all done," she said. "Shall we go?"

As the three left the table, Bob grabbed a dinner roll and stuffed it into his pocket. Lucy saw him and gave him a look of admonishment. With her eyes, she said *put it back*, but Bob smiled and ran to catch up to his aunt. He grabbed her hand and looked back at his mother with an impish smile. She wanted to walk up to her son, grab him by the arm, and give him a good swat on the behind. It was what he deserved, but she held back. She would bide her time and Bob would learn a thing or two about manners.

"Let's take a stroll. Shall we?" Justine said more to Bob than to Lucy. The three walked down a small lane with that had shops on both sides of the street that catered to the tourists. Only a few were open this early in the season. They stopped in one that had a large shelf full of seashells that were most definitely not from the lake. Little wooden plaques adorned with beach scenes at sunset and sandpipers hung on the wall. Small lighthouses and water globes that simulated snow when shaken were on a long and deep shelf. So many trinkets filled the store it made Lucy feel crowded.

When Bob dashed to one side of the store, Lucy was certain he would knock something over. He stood over a small bucket of pennants. They were navy blue and the bold white letters spelled Irondequoit, with the *I* twenty times the size of the *t*. He picked one out and held it up to his mother. Lucy was about to say no when Justine plucked it from his hands.

"Would you like this as a souvenir?"

"Justine," Lucy said. "You and Walter have done so much already. I couldn't ask—"

"Nonsense," she said. "The boy should have something to remember this trip by." Justine took Bob's hand and they walked to the counter to pay. Lucy thought back to the question Bob asked her at Horseshoe Lake on the ride to Rochester. She thought about the conversation she had had with Walter last night, when Bob lay in her lap with his eyes closed. He had been asleep at one point, but before they finished, she knew her son was only feigning slumber, and he had listened to every word. She was sure the boy would have plenty to remember.

As they walked back to the trolley station, Bob waved the pennant back and forth, watching the triangular piece of felt ripple in the wind. He held his aunt's hand and she looked down at the boy with a great sense of satisfaction in her eyes. She glanced at Lucy and said, "You are so lucky to have such a fine boy."

Chapter 20

Following supper that night, Bob tried to play possum on the sofa again when Lucy and Walter sat down to talk. He held his pennant in his hand and as Lucy tried to pull it away, he revealed his subterfuge. "It is time for you to go to bed, young man." He reluctantly got up and climbed the stairs to the bedroom Justine had made up for him. "Get some good rest. We have a long day tomorrow." Bob climbed the stairs as if they were Mount Kilimanjaro. Once Lucy was certain her son had closed his bedroom door, she turned to Walter, who was reading the newspaper. "So, what did this lawyer of yours have to say today?"

Walter looked over the top of the paper at Lucy and took a quick glance in the direction of the kitchen. He dropped the paper in his lap and sighed. "Well. It seems things are a bit more complicated than I first suspected."

Lucy moved forward a bit on the sofa. "How complicated?" she asked.

"Richard is staying with friends, right?"

Lucy nodded.

"Do you think he could stay with them for a few days more?"

Lucy thought about it for a moment. The way Merriam fawned over her boys surely meant that she would not mind, but Gus was an able-bodied man having to pay someone for work he was capable of doing. She was hesitant to ask him to continue the arrangement any longer than the initial agreement. "Is it absolutely necessary?"

Walter nodded. "We have to make a trip downstate tomorrow. There are papers that have to be signed by you and they have to be witnessed in a United States District Court. The closest one is in Albany."

Lucy put her hand to her mouth.

"It's nothing to be concerned with," Walter said. "It's just the way Immigration and Naturalization does things. Robert can stay here with Justine and me. He'll be fine."

Lucy barely nodded. Yesterday, she was miffed with Walter for the way he wanted to handle things without her, but now that she would have to go to a Federal courthouse and sign papers a feeling of dread settled upon her heart like heavy morning dew. "Albany," she said. Walter nodded. "Well I suppose we will have to do whatever is necessary."

"It's all set then," Walter said. "Manny Horwitz will pick you up in the morning and if everything goes according to plan you'll be back tomorrow evening."

"Horwitz? Is he Jewish?"

"Of course. All the best lawyers are Jewish. Does it matter?"

"It's just that Hans—"

"You have to trust me on this. We both want the same thing. Right?"

Lucy nodded even though she was unsure of the answer. She knew what she wanted. She wanted her husband home. Her boys wanted their father home. But did Walter want the same thing? "Hans could've hired a Jewish attorney in Bismarck."

Walter laughed. "Just because he's Jewish doesn't mean he's good. However, if he is good you can be assured he is Jewish. I don't know this fellow in Bismarck, but Manny, I can vouch for him." Walter uncrossed his legs and leaned in to Lucy. "You did, after all, come to me for help. And wasn't it Hans who sent you to me?"

Lucy crossed her arms and dropped her head, then nodded.

"Well then, trust me." He stood up and took out a cigarette case. He popped it open and offered it to Lucy. She shook her head. He pulled a cigarette out, tapped it on the closed case, and paused. "You know," he said. "I always thought Hans was a smart man, too smart to be a common farmer. But we have choices in our lives and he made his." Walter pulled a lighter from his pocket, lit his cigarette, and blew the smoke toward the ceiling. "All I'm saying is that Hans got himself in a bind and you came to me for help.

Here I am. If you want, I can call Manny and tell him the entire matter is no longer of concern to him. You and Robert can ride your bicycles home and wait for the wheels of justice to grind your family under."

He took a drag of his cigarette and glanced over his shoulder toward the kitchen. "And if that is your choice, I'm sure I could still help you in other ways. We could come to a mutually beneficial arrangement." Walter sat down in his chair and tapped his cigarette on the ashtray. "You're an attractive woman with two young boys to take care of and I— well I have needs too." He leaned in to make sure Lucy understood his point.

Lucy's back stiffened. She lifted her chin and crossed her legs at the ankle. "What time will Mr. Horwitz be here in the morning? I'm eager to have my husband back."

Walter leaned back in his chair, took a long drag off his cigarette, and gave her a look that begrudgingly accepted her rebuff. "Manny said he'd be here before 8:00. It's a long drive to Albany and of course you'll have to make your way back after the deposition."

Lucy stood. "Well I had better turn in then. It seems like it is going to be a long day. And Walter," Lucy said. "I truly want to thank you for all your help in this matter. I'm not sure what I would've done without you. I'll be sure to tell Hans what a *gem* you've been."

In the morning, Lucy woke early and didn't feel as though she'd slept at all. She was anxious about meeting Mr. Horwitz. While she appreciated Walter's efforts, his advances the night before left her unsettled and perturbed, and the apprehension about leaving Bob in the care of Justine also bothered her. She and Walter never had children, although Justine dearly wanted them. She knew her son would be well cared for, but she could not put the feeling of uneasiness to rest.

When she entered the kitchen, Justine stood cooking at the stove and Bob sat at the table eating a bowl of oatmeal. "Good morning," she said.

Justine turned and smiled and Bob nodded as he spooned a bite of oatmeal into his mouth.

"Bob," Lucy said. "I have to go to Albany today."

"Okay." He spooned in another bite.

"You're going to stay here with Uncle Walter and Aunt Justine. Is that all right with you?"

Bob shrugged.

"We'll be fine, Lucy," Justine said. "You take care of what you have to do in Albany and I'll take care of that young man of yours." Justine brought over a plate of eggs and set it in front of Lucy. "Now you better eat something before you're off."

"I don't know how to thank you," she said.

"It's just eggs, Lucy." Justine smiled and winked at her.

Lucy had barely taken two bites when a car pulled into the driveway and tooted its horn. She took another quick bite, grabbed her purse, and kissed Bob on the head as he spooned more oatmeal into his mouth. "Be good," she said. "I'll be back tonight." She gave a quick wave to Justine and left through the side door where a long forest green DeSoto automobile waited. A man with horn-rimmed glasses and a brown fedora sat behind the wheel. He gave her a quick wave and then motioned to her to get in. As she opened the door, she noticed a red and white sticker with a C in the bottom corner of the windshield. She sat in the passenger seat and introduced herself, extending her hand as she did. "I'm Lucy Müller," she said.

"Manny Horwitz," the man said as he shook her hand. Manny sat atop a pillow, but could barely see over the steering wheel of the car. He wore a brown suit that matched his hat and had large ears; a nest of black and grey hairs had formed in the deepest recess of them. His face was rounded and had a gentle look, and he smiled easily. Not what Lucy would've expected from a lawyer.

"Walter has filled me on most of the details, and I think we have a good chance of getting your husband out of the hoosegow." He smiled when he said this but it gave Lucy a sense of unease; she wanted to correct him. Her husband, she thought, was not in jail. He was in an internment camp half a country away. This was not a simple matter of posting bail. "Well let's get going. We've got quite a drive." He put the car in reverse and they were on their way.

Driving through town, Lucy thought about how smooth this car drove. Unlike the bouncy ride of the Peerless, this car felt as though it floated above the ground, immune to inconsistencies of the road, and it settled her nervousness a bit. "This is a fine automobile," she said.

Manny nodded. "It's my brother's. He's a physician. Since the gas rationing started this car has become very popular in my family." He pointed to the sticker in the corner of the windshield. "That type of decal isn't easy to come by."

"Before we get on the highway, could we run by Western Union? I need to send a telegram to let my son know our trip has been extended a bit. He was expecting us back today."

"Sure thing," Manny said. "How old is your boy?"

"He's just about to turn fifteen. He's working for a friend of the family while we're gone and I want to make sure his staying over isn't an imposition." Lucy wasn't sure why, but she found talking to Manny very easy. He was amiable and relaxed and the apprehension she had felt earlier melted away. It occurred to her that she'd never spoken to a Jew before. The Nazi propaganda that had poured out of Hans' radio had described the race as something horrid, the vermin of society. She remembered being told as a child by her grand-mere that Jews had horns like a goat. Although this man wore a hat and there was the slightest possibility that he might be hiding horns under it, she realized in a moment what nonsense it all had been.

"Do you have children, Mr. Horwitz?" she asked.

"Call me Manny. Everyone does." He reached into his jacket pocket, pulled out a leather billfold, flipped it open, and showed her a photograph. "I've got three: two boys and a girl."

In the picture, there were three dark haired children with broad smiles. The two boys wore cuffed shorts and button down short-sleeved shirts, both with narrow bowties. The girl, obviously the youngest, sat at the center of the photograph and had her long dark hair held back on either side with barrettes. She wore a white dress with short puffy sleeves and a laced collar. "They're beautiful," Lucy said.

Manny smiled, closed his billfold, and returned it to his jacket pocket. A moment of silence hung between the two of them. Lucy realized she didn't have a picture of her sons to share. A camera was something she and Hans had never considered spending money on, and the thought of a paying a photographer, even though there had been several who traveled through Friedberg, was also not considered a wise use of what little money they had. She had accepted these thoughts as her own, but as they rolled through her mind, she recalled Hans thought a camera was an extravagance.

Manny turned into a parking lot and pointed to a sign over a small storefront. "Western-Union," he said. "I'll wait here, if that's all right. I've got a few briefs I need to go over before we get to Albany."

"Of course," Lucy said. She walked into the shop and began to fill out the form for her message to Richard. She held the pencil to her lips as she tried to decide the best way to phrase everything she needed to say. There were questions she wanted to ask, assurances she wanted to give, but she knew she could not write all those things. She boiled it down to the essentials:

1942 MAY 25 AM 8 55
RICHARD MULLER C/O GUS PAYNE
FRIEDBERG NY
RETURN DELAYED STOP INFORM JENKINS AND ARCHER STOP
WE ARE FINE HOPE YOU ARE TOO STOP WILL UPDATE SOON
STOP THANK PAYNES FOR ME
MOM

Lucy looked at the missive and felt it vague, but the limitation of twenty-five words necessitated such brevity. She brought the form to the telegraph operator and put 15¢ on the counter. The short balding man with glasses and a visor gave the form a brief glance, took Lucy's money, and nodded. "It'll be out within the hour."

Lucy nodded and walked back to the car. Manny sat behind the wheel with his open briefcase in his lap and papers scattered about the front seat. Lucy opened the door and startled him. "Sorry," she said.

"Oh. It's nothing. Let me clean this up." He picked up the papers and roughly stacked them together and stuffed them back into the briefcase.

"I can only imagine what your desk looks like." Lucy smiled. Manny kept his face down as he arranged a few more things before he put the briefcase in the backseat. "Sorry. I was just joking," she said.

Manny looked at her with a gravity in his eyes that she had not seen before. This was the look of a lawyer, she thought. "Is everything all right?" He started the car and pulled out of the parking lot without a word. Lucy was concerned but didn't know how to approach this man she suddenly didn't know. They drove for a few miles in silence and then Manny looked at her.

"You know, I've got family over there."

Lucy leaned in, waiting for him to say something else. He took a handkerchief out of his pocket and wiped a thin layer of sweat that had developed on his forehead. He looked pale. "Are you feeling all right, Mr. Horwitz?"

He glanced over at Lucy with a strange look on his face. "Damn it," he said and pulled the car over to the shoulder of the highway and put the car in park. He turned in his seat and faced Lucy. "I have to know something before we go one mile farther."

"Of course, Mr. Horwitz. I'll tell you whatever you need to know."

He looked away and wiped his mouth with his hand. "I just read the FBI report while you were in there sending your telegram. It says he had a shortwave radio and they believed he was coordinating with someone offshore."

Lucy's jaw dropped at what he was saying.

"I have to know if this is true. I haven't heard from anyone in my family over there for three years. I don't know what the hell is going on, but I know it's not good. If your husband is tied up with these Nazis, I'm not lifting a finger to help. He can rot wherever the hell he is as far as I'm concerned."

"Mr. Horwitz. You have to believe me. I bought him that radio as a Christmas present. Yes, it was a shortwave, but it only received. My husband is a farmer who is home every night. He left Germany because he couldn't find work and because of the Brown Shirts. He saw what was happening and came here to get away from it." Tears began to well up in her eyes as she felt possibilities slipping away. "Please, Mr. Horwitz. You have to believe me. I've known the man since I was seventeen and I've never heard him say anything good about Hitler or the Nazis."

Manny watched impatiently as Lucy made her case, shaking his head at times. "I don't know that I can do this," he said. "The stories I've heard about whole families disappearing." He shook his head.

Lucy's tears flowed but she held her head up and looked directly at Manny. "They came and took my husband away in the middle of the night. They didn't even let him put clothes on; he was in a nightshirt and a robe when they put in the back of a car and drove off, and they wouldn't even tell me where they were taking him. Please, you have to help."

Manny looked at her and it seemed the tension he felt began to subside. "Why did you buy him the radio?"

"It was a gift. I told you. He had all these newspapers about the house and I was so sick of them all. He left Germany but he didn't stop caring about it. He has family there too. He subscribed to all sorts of newspapers so he could keep up on what was going on over there. He didn't like what he read. He'd get in these awful moods, tear up the papers, and make a terrible mess. It had to stop. I thought with a radio at least he'd only hear the story once. He wouldn't keep going back to the same story. Reading and re-reading himself into a frenzy." As she made her case to the lawyer, it occurred to her these reasons were the ones Hans had presented to her. The radio sat in the display window in Miller's Emporium like a crown jewel. Hans had lusted after it and when they walked by the store one day he began to make his argument.

Manny rested his arms on the steering wheel and looked through the windshield of the car. He took off his hat and ran his hand over what little hair he had and sighed. Lucy looked at him with desperation, heaving a bit with each breath she took. Manny put his hat back on and leaned back in his seat. "It's not that I don't believe you, but I need to think about this a little more. So I'll tell you what I'm going to do. We're going to drive for a while and I'm going to see what my gut tells me. You seem nice enough, but I've never met your husband and he's the one I'd really be helping. So you just sit there quietly and let me sort things out. If by the time we get to Albany I still have a bad taste in my mouth I'm walking away from this and you can find yourself another attorney." Manny put the car in gear, checked his mirror, and pulled out onto the highway.

Chapter 21

After the first night in the railcar, Hans was rethinking his decision to work for the railroad. The overnight temperatures dropped below freezing and the blankets supplied by his new employer were hardly enough. The small potbelly stove that radiated only enough heat to keep chamber pots from freezing in the barracks would have been more than welcome. Hay covered the floor of the railcar, which offered some insulation, but cold air burst through the gaps in the boards every time the wind blew. Each night Hans and eleven other men were locked into the car. Buckets were inside to accommodate the necessary functions of life, but the stink of the waste wore upon them. The only way to keep warm during the protracted nights came from body heat shared under the blankets. The salty sour smell of body odor of men huddled together was overwhelming, but it kept them from freezing. To make matters worse, a faint orange glow of fire flickered through the ventilation grates near the ceiling. The soldiers, the ones tasked with guarding them, had the unfortunate duty of staying outside in the elements overnight, but made the most of it by building fires to keep the freezing weather from their bones. The only benefit the men inside the railcar received from the fires was the occasional incursion of smoke that allowed them to fantasize about the warmth from a fire.

During the day, conditions were not much better. The morning cold slowly ebbed on the windswept plains and the only path to warmth was hard work. Dobbs had managed to recruit sixty men from the camp and had set the quota for a day's labor at a mile. They had to remove the old rails that were insufficient for the heavy load of trains carrying coal and munitions and lay the new track that could handle the weight. Each of the heavy-duty rails weighed 250 lbs. and was 39 feet long, which translated to laying 240 rails for each mile.

As Hans worked, his mind wandered. Following the riot in the camp most of the men in his barrack ended up in the cooler. Those who weren't, but were friends with those who were, marked Hans. A few days after the melee, Hans sent a message with one of the guards to Captain Charles saying he was willing to work for the railroad. Soon afterward, Felix came to barrack #10 and escorted Hans to the Captain's quarters.

"This won't be a holiday, you know."

Hans nodded. "I need to send money home. My family—"

"We all have families, Mr. Müller. What I want you to understand is that if you try to escape you will be shot." Captain Charles met Hans' eyes as he tapped his finger on his desk. "And I'm not even sure Mr. Dobbs would want someone like you. From what I gather, he's looking for young men who can carry a load. I can't say you fit that bill."

"I've worked a farm for the last ten years," Hans said. "I'm not afraid of hard work or long hours."

Captain Charles still seemed unconvinced. He opened a file folder on his desk. From his vantage point, Hans noticed a small black and white photo of himself paper-clipped to the top corner. The Captain shuffled through the documents and then paused. "You're scheduled for a hearing with the INS in two weeks. If you take this job you'll miss it and I'm not sure when we'll be able to get them to reschedule." The Captain closed the folder and looked up at Hans. "Those federal fellows can be difficult to nail down when it comes to scheduling a visit out here." The Captain looked over at Felix. "For some reason they seem to think our fine state is a wasteland." Felix smiled but didn't say a word.

Hans pondered his dilemma. If he stayed in the camp, he might not survive until the hearing, and if he went to work, there was no telling when another hearing might be scheduled or when he might be able to return home. In the end, he decided his personal safety and the money he could send back home was the best option; he would simply have to trust Walter.

To prevent any antagonism between the internees who were willing to work for the railroad and those who saw it at as treason against the

Fatherland, Hans and others were moved to a new area outside of the barbed wire perimeter and were treated well while they awaited Mr. Dobbs' return. They ate meals in the same commissary as the guards, slept on beds with real mattresses, and even enjoyed indoor plumbing. All of these luxuries should have been an indication of what was to come, but their good fortune prevented them from looking beyond the next meal.

Dobbs himself did not return to the camp. He was merely the face the railroad put forth to persuade internees and POWs to work for Northern Pacific, the face of success and confidence meant to instill a sense of loyalty through the perceived possibility of prosperity. In his stead, a tall wiry man named Red Philips arrived to oversee the placement of the workers. Red, despite his name, had long and stringy dark brown hair that poked out from under the cowboy hat he wore in and out of doors. His horseshoe moustache hid his mouth and the only way one could be certain it actually existed was the tobacco juice he spit every few minutes. His eyes were deep-set and a crystal green. The men packed their meager belongings into the canvas seamen's bags they were issued when they arrived at the camp and gathered outside the guard's barracks. Red surveyed the group with disdain and skepticism in his eyes.

"I don't cotton to no goldbricking. You men were hired to work and by God that is what you'll do." Red looked the men over again. "If anyone wants to change his mind, now's the time."

A few of the men stirred as uncertainty rippled through them like a flag in a gale, but no one backed out. Guards loaded the men into the back of an Army truck, much like the ones that brought them from the trains when they first came to Fort Lincoln. The ride was rough and bumpy across the prairie and no one spoke. When they arrived at their destination, they were in the middle of nowhere. Two parallel lines of track separated by no more than ten feet stretched in either direction as far as the eye could see. The wind whipped through the tall grass of the prairie and made the vast landscape look like an ocean of golden waves.

On one set of tracks was a utility engine that hauled flat cars filled with cross ties and iron rails. On the other track, the one on which the rails were being replaced, there were half a dozen boxcars which were shelters during the night and off hours. As soon as the men were unloaded from the camp truck it roared to life, made a tight half circle and headed back the way it came.

The men from the camp had not made their quota the first four days of work. This irritated Red. "Each day you're short just adds more to the next day," he said. This did little to motivate Hans and the others, but as they continued to work, they found a rhythm. The forward group used long crowbars to remove spikes and then they moved the old rails off the ties and into the drainage gulley on the far side of the track. Another group of men brought the new heavy-duty rails from the flatbeds to the track. They would slide the rail across the wood of the flatbed, lift it upon their shoulders, haul it to the cess just beneath the ballast shoulder, and drop it into the soft earth. Another group used iron hooks to pick up the rails and place them on the ties. The hooks clinked against the steel, the men grunted on the lift, and finally the rail thudded against the wood of the tie. Behind them were the men who held the spikes and those who hammered them into place. The tink, tink, tink, of the hammer blows were followed by a deeper sound as the spike was set against the base plate. It became their cadence.

On the fifth day, the men made their quota. Red stood with his hands on his hips and tilted his hat back a bit. He spit and looked over the men. "I've seen a lot of workers in my time," he said. "But I gotta say this bunch has surprised me. At this rate we'll be in Fargo by the end of next month."

That evening Hans and the others were sitting in their shelters with the doors to the boxcars open, their feet dangling as they rested, and thought about the day's accomplishment. The conversation was light and for the first time since their arrival, intermittent laughter could be heard. In the distance, the men saw a horse drawn wagon and they quieted down as it pulled into their encampment. Red met the wagon and doffed his hat. Driving the buckboard was a woman and a young boy. She wore a yellow pinafore dress with ruffles on the shoulders and a bonnet that covered most of her face, but blond curls poked out of the edges. She and the boy stepped down from the wagon and waved at the internees seated in the boxcars; her high cheekbones gave her a Nordic appearance. Something stirred inside Hans, a feeling he hadn't felt in months. Others too, must have felt the allure as a low murmuring began to swell amongst the men. As though they were anticipating the worst behavior, the guards tensed up and held their rifles at the ready. "You all just stay put, fellas," one said. The woman and her son looked on as Red and a guard unloaded crates. One of the crates was shedding feathers and it was clear there were at least three chickens inside that were protesting their treatment. Hans didn't even realize it at the moment, but he'd begun to salivate.

The woman's name was Gloria Svensen and her son was Peter. They arrived every few days with provisions for the work crew. It became clear to Hans and the others that if they were able to make their quota each day the railroad company would feed them well, much better than back at Fort Lincoln. The men quickly found their work rhythm every morning and endured wind and rain and sun and cold to reach their goal.

Each time Gloria and her son arrived at the camp all activity ceased. Unlike the quiet murmuring that happened the first day she arrived, the men had grown bolder. Whistles and whoops began to occur and it clearly made her uncomfortable. It also irritated Red to no end. He would turn and glare in the direction of the noises and they would quiet down until he turned his back. Then they would start up again, like schoolboys. It seemed that this amused some of the men just as much as the sight of a pretty woman. One day Red had had enough. He threw his hat on the ground and stormed over to the idle workers. "If you want to eat, get to work." The men stood there for a moment. "Now!" Red yelled, and the men dropped their gazes and returned to their labor with reluctance.

Later that same day during an afternoon break, Red came over to Hans, who was one of the oldest men on the work crew.

"Hans," Red said, pronouncing it like hands. "These hound dogs we got here are causing me grief." His hands were on his hips as he leaned to one side and spit tobacco juice. "Our arrangement with Mrs. Svensen needs to be modified. I can't have her keep coming out here with her young son and those fools hollering at her like she's some dime whore." He spit again.

"I won't tolerate it. And neither will she."

Hans nodded, unsure why Red was telling him this.

"I've seen the way you handle yourself, Hans. You got a wife and kids, don't you?"

Hans nodded again.

"Rather than having that fine woman come out here, I've decided someone should go to her farm and pick up the provisions we've contracted for. I can't send a guard because of our contract with the Captain. I can't go because there's no telling what'll happen around here if I'm not about. It seems to me you got too much at stake to pull any shenanigans. You know you got it better here than back at the camp with those Nazi fools, and you ain't gonna run if you ever want to see your family again."

As this notion of Red's dawned on Hans, he had trouble not smiling. He did not want to seem too eager and be lumped in with the "hound dogs," but the idea of being away from the work crew, away from the armed guards that had been in his presence since March, to simply be alone, made him swell with excitement.

"Now you remember what Dobbs said? If you run, you will be shot. I will lock all these krauts up in the boxcars; damn the day's quota to hell, and me and the guards will come find you. I don't give a goddamn how hard the ground is from the frost, I'll dig a hole and put you in it." Red looked at Hans without blinking. "You get me?"

"*Ja,* I get you." Hans met Red's eyes with as much earnestness as he could muster. In that moment he realized how suspicion about him and his character had worn him down in places. Perhaps Red saw that honor in Hans' eyes. He saw something that seemed to satisfy him that his point was taken with the appropriate gravity and then he spit again.

"Okay, then. Tomorrow after the noon break you'll take a buckboard over to Mrs. Svensen's farm and pick up the supplies."

Hans nodded and reached down to pick up his crowbar.

"And one more thing," Red said. "Don't go telling anyone about this tonight. If I hear anything about it, the deal's off. You're to leave outta here quietly without anyone being the wiser. If you do good tomorrow, we can continue the arrangement. If not, well..."

"I understand, Mr. Philips," Hans said.

Red nodded, turned and spit, and walked away without another word.

After lunch the next day, Hans set off in the buckboard as planned. He followed the tracks to the east for several miles until he reached the small town of Medina. As he approached the burg, all he could see from a distance was the grain elevator situated next to the railroad track. His instructions were to turn north and keep going until he saw a large curved windbreak of trees sheltering a small apple orchard. Beyond this, he was to follow a narrow lane that had a pond on either side. Just past the pond to the east was a drive that led to the Svensen's farmhouse. Red told him he'd see a grain silo and a gray and white barn. Hans followed the directions and located what he believed to be his destination, but as he reached the end of the drive, he paused. The gouch-eared horse shook her head and snorted. Hans took a moment to survey the land and felt a sense of peace that had eluded him for months. The days, the weeks, the months had slowly built upon one another, and Hans had done little more than keep his head down and kept moving forward. All he concentrated on was the next step, and then the next one, and then the one after that. It was only in this moment that he realized what a strong gale he had been plodding against. He looked down the drive and saw all the landmarks Red had described, but he was still hesitant and unsure if this was indeed the proper farm. He took a deep breath and tried to expel the tension that crept back into his chest. He heard a door slam and the hollow clunk of boots running across a wooden porch. He saw a young boy that he recognized to be Gloria Svensen's son, waving his hat over his head as he ran down the lane. Hans raised his hand and waved, shook the reins and turned the horse and buckboard into the drive.

The boy met up with Hans halfway down the drive and pulled himself up into the seat next to him. "Howdy, Mister," he said and then pointed up the drive. "Mom says to pull the wagon up to the barn."

Hans nodded. "What's your name, son?"

"Peter," he said. "What's yours?"

"I'm Hans." He extended his hand.

Peter shook Hans' hand. "Glad to meet you."

The boy wore dungarees, a red checked shirt, and an old gray hat that was too big for his young head. He had bright blue eyes, light brown hair, and a smattering of freckles across his nose and cheeks. Hans was a bit taken aback by the boy's exuberance. The boy had been to the rails and saw Hans and the others working under the watchful eye of guards with rifles, but Peter showed no fear of him. It occurred to Hans that he suddenly felt what he had heard the other prisoners talk about. They called it *Gitterkrankheit*: the fence sickness. He had been behind barbed wire long enough that he had begun to see himself as a criminal, and this complicated things. He wore the face of an indignant citizen and pleaded his innocence when they interrogated him. Certain accusations were false and he denied them vehemently, but other charges skated so close to the truth he had to lie to himself in order to lie to his questioners. He had buried the truth so deeply that it only surfaced when he felt himself wholly accepted by this young and innocent boy.

Hans pulled the wagon up into the barn and felt the coolness of the shade; Peter jumped down and watered the horse. Hans stepped down from the buckboard and stretched out his back. The labor on the rails was taxing but it allowed him to sleep well at night, despite the difficult accommodations in the boxcars. He normally did not feel any stiffness until the end of the day, but today, having only worked the morning before taking this excursion, his back had tightened up. He heard the slap of a spring door closing and saw Gloria walking down the steps of the porch. She wore a simple calico farm dress made up of maroon, blue, and yellow squares. She wore her blond hair pulled back in a bun. Hans' posture straightened and she smiled.

"Hello," she said and extended her hand.

Hans doffed his hat and took her hand as though he was receiving a baby bird. "Hello, Mrs. Svensen."

"We have the crates over here for you." She pointed toward the barn and began walking in that direction. "You must be very trustworthy for Mr. Philips to allow you to come all this way by yourself."

Hans shrugged. "I suppose I'm the best of the worst." He smiled, hoping she would take the comment as a joke.

Gloria led Hans to the six crates containing potatoes and carrots stacked just inside the barn. Hans lifted the crates into the back of the wagon as she looked on. "Peter can ride back with you, if you need help."

"Thank you, no. I'm sure we can handle everything, but it is so nice of you to offer," Hans said.

She looked down at the hay strewn across the floor of the barn. "Please tell Mr. Philips that we will have the next order ready in two days. There will be some more potatoes, some greens, and probably some apples."

"Those are some nice hens you brought the other day. Some good layers," Hans said.

"Oh, yes they are. I have to say I'm surprised they weren't fricasseed."

"There was some discussion about that," Hans grinned. "But I think the hens overheard because they started laying eggs left and right. After the men saw that they decided an egg for each man every few days was better than one night of meat."

Gloria laughed and smoothed a stray hair back behind one of her ears.

"I'd better be getting back before Mr. Philips sends out a search party for me." Hans shut the gate on the buckboard and climb up into the seat. He doffed his hat and said, "It was a pleasure to meet you, Mrs. Svensen."

"Call me Gloria, Hans. Now be on your way. You don't want to get into any trouble."

Hans shook the reins and the horse reluctantly headed down the drive. Hans looked back and saw Peter standing next to his mother, both waving. Hans waved back and then faced forward. He couldn't help but place himself in the absent role of father and husband when he pictured Peter and Gloria in his mind. A smile crawled across his face as the fantasy expanded, but as the warmth of the sun beat down upon him on his return trip, Robert's face began to displace Peter's in the fantasy. Then as his mind returned to his family in Friedberg, he suddenly had difficulty bringing Lucy's face to the forefront of his mind, it fluttered just out of reach like an image from a dream.

He could remember the way she smelled, her laugh, and the feel of her touch, but nothing else could swim through the haze of memory. He felt an empty pit grow in his stomach and shook the reins, spurring the horse up to a trot.

Once back at the worksite, he followed Red's directions, keeping as close to the rails as possible and stopped the buckboard near the last train car, a caboose the guards and Red slept in. He knocked on the door and the camp cook opened up. "I have your provisions," Hans said, using his thumb to point to the buckboard behind him. The cook nodded and hitched up his pants.

"Okay," he said. "I'll take it from here. You better get back to work."

Hans nodded and glanced behind the man. He was surprised to see the car outfitted with wooden bunks, just like the ones in the barracks back at Fort Lincoln. A small table sat at one end of the car, and nearby sat a potbelly stove with a steaming kettle. The cook moved to come out and Hans backed up. "Go on now," he said as he shut the door to the caboose behind him.

Hans hopped down the steps, walked along the rail line, and got back to work. A couple of quizzical glances found him, but no one said anything to him about his absence. As he got back to prying spikes out of the crossties, he thought about things. What would he say if anyone were to ask him where he had been? He could say he was sick, but Red didn't seem like the kind of man who would allow sickness as an excuse for missing work. He could say he was working elsewhere on the line, which wasn't a complete falsehood. As much as he knew he needed to concoct a story for such an eventuality, he couldn't keep his mind from wandering back to the farm he'd just left. Gloria's face, her smile, and her gentle scent reminded him of a mountain iris. These things sat at the front of his mind as his hands gripped the crowbar, wedged it in under a spike, and pushed down with all his weight until the grip of the wood released the piece of steel. As his hands stayed busy his mind traveled over the North Dakota plains, through a small town, topped a gentle rise, and landed near a little farmhouse just beyond two ponds that had a little apple orchard. He saw her golden hair flutter in a gentle breeze and it made him smile.

Chapter 22

Lucy finally drew a breath of relief when she saw the *Welcome to Albany* sign. She and Manny had ridden in silence and she expected him to pull the car over and turn around at any moment, but the DeSoto didn't slow, nor did Manny flinch as they passed the sign. They drove through the northern outskirts of the capitol city, alongside the Hudson River, and made their way to the city center where the Federal courthouse was located. A stylized stone bald eagle perched over the entrance to the tall gray building. The bird's wings formed a hood over and around its body and head, like a monk's cowl. Manny pulled up to the curb and put the car in park. He sighed and looked over at Lucy. He didn't say anything for a long time and Lucy wondered if she would simply be let out on the sidewalk, left to fend for herself. Manny looked forward and a moment later turned off the ignition and tapped his fingers on the steering wheel. He turned to Lucy. "I can't say I feel good about this. Like I said before, it's not you I don't trust. You seem like a fine woman and my wife would kill me for not helping someone like you who was in need."

"Mr. Horwitz—"

"Let me finish. I've known Walter for a few years, we've done business before and he's always been a standup fellow, and while I can't say we're friends—we're never going bowling together—I can say I trust the man." Manny paused for a moment, leaned in, looked up at the courthouse, and then turned back to Lucy. "I know his wife is Polish and she's got family back there. I guess what I'm saying is that if he trusts your husband, given what he has at stake is kind of the same as me, then I suppose I should, too."

"I can't thank you enough, Mr. Horwitz."

"Now I said to call me Manny." He smiled at Lucy, but she could see only a pale comparison to the smile he had flashed when he showed her the photograph of his children. "I guess we better get going." Manny patted the steering wheel twice and pulled the keys from the ignition. As they walked up the stairs into the courthouse, Manny held his briefcase in one hand and placed his other hand at the small of Lucy's back. She felt the heat of his hand through the thin fabric of her dress. She stiffened slightly at first, but his touch was gentle and guiding and she relaxed as they entered the building that housed the mechanisms that had taken her husband away. With the skills of her attorney, she hoped to navigate the procedures and motions that might set him free and allow him to return home. They walked through the foyer of the building, across black marble tiles with jagged lines of quartz, to the bank of elevators. The brass doors slid open and she and Manny entered. "Fourth Floor, please," he said to the elevator operator.

A clerk escorted Lucy and Manny to the deposition room. A table sat at its center and there were four chairs, two on either side. In one corner of the room was a small stand with a steno machine set in front of another chair. They sat on one side of the table and Manny busied himself extracting documents from his briefcase. Lucy's foot began tapping the floor as she looked around at the drab little room. A large black Bakelite ashtray sat in the middle of the table, a box of matches next to it. The light fixture over the table was a semi-sphere of frosted glass trimmed with dark wood molding and it hung from the ceiling by three brass chains. She imagined it crashing down and shattering bits of glass across the table. Lucy felt Manny's hand on hers. "Just relax," he said. "You don't have anything to be nervous about." Lucy smiled and sighed.

"I know. It's just this room, I guess. I feel like I'm waiting for the Grand Inquisitor."

"We are merely awaiting bureaucrats." Manny laughed. "Some might say they are worse, but we have what we need." He picked up the pile of papers in front of him with both hands and held them out to her. "These are the only weapons we need." He smiled at her and she saw it was heartfelt. The tension pulling at her insides like an elastic band began to ease a bit. "All we have to do is speak the truth and give them the forms they ask for when they ask for them."

The door opened and a woman walked in. She was young, in her twenties. Her brown hair was shoulder length and was waved. She wore a peach colored blouse with a small cameo affixed at the top button and pale yellow pencil skirt and nylons. Her red high heels caught Lucy's eye. The woman didn't look at Lucy or Manny, took her seat in the corner at the steno machine, and set to checking her equipment. She had left the door open. A tall, handsome man with hair the color of hay and a smartly trimmed mustache dressed in a dark blue suit walked in. He reminded Lucy of John Barrymore. Lucy and Manny stood up as he entered and he introduced himself.　As he shook Lucy's hand, she recognized the aroma of the Brylcreem he used to dress his hair.

"I'm Peter Connolly, U.S. Attorney." He looked over his shoulder and pointed to the woman. "That's Betty." He turned the other way and leaned back a little. He saw someone outside the small room and waved for him to enter. "And I think you've met Agent Jordon from the FBI."

Lucy's heart stopped. Roger Jordon, the agent in the gray suit who had arrested Hans, came in, nodded toward Lucy, and sat down directly across from her. He had a look of smugness on his face that churned ground glass in her gut. Manny noticed her discomfort and set his hand on hers. "Is it really necessary that he's here?" Manny asked.

"From your brief I see you're contesting the detention of an enemy alien. Agent Jordon was the investigating and arresting officer," Connolly said. "It seems very appropriate to me that he's here if you plan to challenge his findings."

Manny looked over at Lucy. "Are you going to be all right?"

Agent Jordon sat back in his chair and pursed his lips. Lucy met his eyes. "It'll be fine. I'll be fine," she said.

Agent Jordon reached into his pocket and pulled out his cigarette case. "Mind if I smoke?" No one objected so he lit his cigarette and blew a cloud of smoke toward the ceiling, keeping his gaze on Lucy.

"Shall we get started?" Connolly said. He turned and nodded toward Betty. As he began reading the particulars of the deposition, the keys of the steno machine clicked away and bounced off the hard surfaces in the room.

　　　　　　　　　　　　　　　　　　Fertile Ground

Connolly's voice droned on for several minutes and Lucy's initial impression of him as handsome began to fade. His voice became more nasal than it was at first and there was something else. Lucy had the feeling that Connolly and the others were merely going through the motions, a ritual they had repeated so many times that it had lost any meaning or importance. As this occurred to Lucy she began to tremble. These were the people responsible for taking her children's father, her husband away. They were the ones who caused her so much pain and anguish over the last few months. It became clear the preceding did not matter to them. They talked, smoked, and tapped ashes into the ashtray, all simple actions that seemed to be more important to them than her family or serving the interest of justice.

Manny sat quietly and made notes as Connolly read. Afterward, Connolly asked the questions Manny had prepared Lucy to answer. Her answers were terse but succinct. Agent Jordon sat back, saying nothing and looking bored. When it came time for Manny's turn, he took a deep breath as he consulted his notes. "From what I understand the detention and internment of Mr. Hans Müller is pursuant to the provision set forth in Title 50, United States Code, sections 21-24, and also the Presidential Proclamation 2526 as it relates to German Enemy Aliens. Is that correct?"

"Yes it is," Connolly said. "I thought I clearly outlined that in my opening statements."

"You did," Manny said. "I just wanted to address that issue and I thought it best to frame the following statements with a reiteration of the accusations and the laws that relate to those charges." Manny paused and let his point settle in. "May I continue?"

Agent Jordon looked at Betty and seemed to be admiring the woman's legs.

"Are you with us, Agent Jordon?" Manny asked.

He looked at Manny and nodded.

"Good." Manny turned to Lucy and gave the slightest wink before he proceeded. "It appears to me that the crux of these charges is based on the fact that Mr. Müller is not a citizen of this country."

Connolly laughed. "That's right. He is not a citizen. That's why we call him an alien."

Manny pulled a single piece of paper from the bottom of his stack and slid it across the table. "I beg to differ."

Connolly leaned forward and reluctantly picked up the paper and read. Lucy could see the change in his continence as the meaning of the words printed on the paper became apparent. He turned to Agent Jordon. "Have you seen this?"

Jordon's sardonic expression quickly turned to confusion. "Where the hell did you get this?" He looked at Manny. The crease between his eyebrows deepened.

"As you can see, this form grants Mr. Müller permanent residence status following his marriage to Lucille Marie Benoit, a United States Citizen." Manny pulled another paper from his stack and slid it across the table. "And this form from the Immigration and Naturalization Service, dated three years and four months after their wedding date indicates Mr. Müller has been granted full citizenship." Manny sat back in his chair and smiled as the two men looked at each paper, going from one to another, seemingly trying to find some error. The noise from the stenographer stopped and the silence stood loudly in the room. Manny turned to Lucy, smiled, and turned his attention back across the table. "So you see, gentleman. You have erroneously charged Mr. Müller as an enemy alien when in fact he is a citizen." Manny pulled one more paper form his stack. "This is a motion I'll be filing with Judge Brennan for the release of Mr. Müller from federal custody."

Lucy let out a laugh and held her hands to her mouth as Jordon and Connolly glared at her. "Manny," she said. "I can't believe it!"

The two men on the other side of the table pored over the documents, each trying to find something that would mitigate Lucy's victory. Connolly turned to Jordon and said, "What in the hell, Roger?"

"Don't look at me. It was your investigator."

When Lucy and Manny entered the elevator, she could hardly stand still. "Lobby, please," Manny said. He turned to Lucy. "Now it might take a little while for the wheels to turn, but I'm pretty sure we'll win."

They left the lobby and got into Manny's car. "I just can't believe it,

Manny. Did you see the look on their faces? I think I even heard Betty laugh." Lucy sat shaking her head.

"It's not over yet," Manny said. "I'll file the motion and the judge should rule on it within the next 72 hours, but from what I've seen of their case it should be a breeze." Manny looked down at the keys in his hand and felt their weight. "And there is a chance," he said as he looked up and out the windshield. "There's a chance they could re-file charges. If they did, because we've proved he's a citizen, the charge might be treason." Lucy looked at him wide-eyed. "From what I read in the FBI file, I can't see they have much to go on." He patted her on the shoulder. "I don't know about you, but I could use a drink."

After returning to Rochester, Lucy and Bob stayed one more night before beginning their long bike ride home. Well rested, Lucy packed up their knapsacks and strapped them onto the bicycles. Justine came out to the driveway, her apron still on. "I'm sure Walter will be home soon. Are you sure you can't wait?"

"I wish we could, Justine, but it's such a long trip."

"Walter owed someone a favor and worked the night shift." She paused for a moment. "I don't think he's ever done that before."

"That must've been a pretty big favor to get that man off his schedule," Lucy said with a smile.

Justine nodded and rubbed her knuckles.

"Please tell Walter thank you for everything and that we wanted to wait for him."

"I will," she said and walked over to Robert. "It's been wonderful having you for a visit. Hopefully, you can come again with your big brother." She reached down and hugged the boy.

Lucy gave Justine a hug. "Thank you so much. I just can't say—"

"You're family. There's no need."

Lucy and Bob mounted their bicycles, pedaled down the drive, turned onto Cooke Road, and headed toward home. The little pennant Bob had gotten at Irondequoit was stuck between the basket and the handlebars. It rippled in the breeze as the two rode down the street, leaving Walter and

Justine's house behind.

After riding for several hours, they found the same spot at Horseshoe Lake where they had camped on the way up to Rochester and spent the night under the stars once again. As they lay under the night sky and the miles began to settle into their muscles, Bob looked up to the heavens. He turned to his mother. "Tell me another story about the stars."

She pointed up to the sky and said, "See those stars that form two trapezoids? And that little line of stars that angle out from where they meet in the middle?"

Robert nodded.

"That's Orion. That little line of stars is his sword. He was such a great hunter, and so fearless that when he was killed, Zeus, the king of all the gods, placed him up in the heavens as a tribute to his courage."

Robert looked into the sky and then over to his mother. "How'd he die?"

"Well, some say a giant scorpion stung him as they battled." Lucy turned to her son, "That's the story I like the best. Can you imagine fighting such a creature?"

Robert shook his head. "Giant scorpions aren't real, are they?"

"No sweetheart. It's just a story about bravery. Now it's time to get some rest." She kissed her son on his head and pulled his covers up over his shoulder.

They slept soundly that night and returned to Friedberg by midafternoon. As Bob began to recognize the landscape he pedaled faster and Lucy had difficulty keeping up with her son. When they turned onto Newton Avenue Bob was well ahead and something dropped in Lucy's stomach. She noticed a dark blue sedan parked in front of their home. Bob was already up the drive and a woman was speaking with her son when she pulled into the drive. Lucy felt a sense of relief when she didn't see a military uniform, but the rigid posture of the woman worried her. As Lucy reached the end of the driveway, the woman walked over to her as she set the kickstand on the bicycle.

"Hi. I'm Beverly Parks from the *Buffalo Evening News*."

Lucy's heart sank. She was so close to having her husband back and now it seemed everything would be splayed out in the paper. The woman's hair was auburn and she wore a double-breasted black and white hound's tooth dress, and although she was acting in a professional manner, Lucy thought she saw something soft in her eyes.

"I've been informed that you and your son rode your bicycles all the way to Rochester. Is that true?"

Lucy nodded, reluctant to say anything else about the trip. "Informed by who?" she asked.

Bob interrupted. "We went to the beach at Irondequoit while we were up there." He held up his pennant to show the woman.

"I'd like to do a story about your adventure, if that's all right."

Chapter 23

The story appeared in the paper the next day and Bob's classmate celebrated his return to school with a new nickname: Spokes. Richard came home from the Payne's farm much different from his experience too. His skin had developed a deeper tone from working outside, and when she hugged her son upon his return, she felt an unfamiliar strength. She wasn't sure, but it also appeared he'd grown taller in the days since she'd last seen him, or maybe he was just standing taller. "What did they feed you over there?" she asked. Richard shrugged and looked down at his shoes and then back to her face.

"Mr. Payne wants to know if I can work for him on weekends."

Lucy put her hand to her mouth. Whenever Richard asked for something he felt somewhat uncertain about, he would stutter. The look in his eyes and the way he spoke made her proud. She couldn't do anything but nod.

"Thanks, mom," he said and took his knapsack upstairs to his room. She sat at the table in the kitchen and looked out over the fields. There was a lot of work to be done, but she felt good and decided to write a letter to Hans. She set the kettle on the stove and thought about where to start.

The photograph that appeared with the newspaper article showed Bob and her with their bikes. Bob was bare-chested and his Irondequoit pennant proudly displayed. She knew Hans would enjoy the look of self-satisfaction on his son's face. Because gas rationing had just begun, their trip was held up as a model of patriotism, of sacrifice to the war effort that should be applauded and emulated. As the reporter interviewed Bob, Lucy held her breath, waiting for the inevitable question about his father, her husband. Beverly Parks had sharp eyes and a quick wit about her that made Lucy feel as though she would not be able to hide anything. But the question was never asked. It was not until the article appeared in the newspaper that she breathed a sigh of relief; it made no mention of Hans.

Perhaps the reporter had stepped into that question before, innocently enough, only to find out that the father or husband was MIA, or worse, KIA. As Lucy thought more about this, it became clear that it was not a carless omission, but calculated discretion. The focus was on the story of a mother and son riding seventy-five miles on bicycles to visit family. Anything that veered away from this central focus could only detract from the singular message of sacrifice for the common good. The message to leave your car in its garage and save gasoline for the police, fire trucks, and other government vehicles was a clear one that should not be diluted. The fact that they were going to visit family only added to the charm of the story that the reporter carefully wove. As she had reread the article just before putting it in the envelope, she could not help but notice the craft employed by the writer. The emphatic tone suggested the righteous nature of Lucy and Bob's trip, and the reporter's painstaking list of all the small towns that they traveled through not only broadened the appeal of the article by mentioning towns that struggle to be an afterthought, but it also implied how much courage such an endeavourer would demand. As Lucy thought these things over, she was sure Hans would only see the image of his youngest son, astride a bicycle too large for his nine-year old body, and he would smile with pride.

The next morning after the boys left for school, Lucy decided to head into town. She wanted to mail the letter to her husband and she needed to talk to Bangstrom about the bill that was now overdue. The morning was cool and as she rode, the sun shone of her face and warmed her with optimism. Before long, she pedaled onto East Main and parked her bicycle in front of Bangstrom's groceries. Her hand patted the invoice in her pocket as she took a deep breath; she hoped payment over time could be arranged. As she entered the store, she saw Liza DiMarco who instantly smiled.

"There's Friedberg's intrepid traveler," she said.

"Hi, Liza." Lucy smiled shyly.

"You're the talk of the town, Mrs. Müller. I can't believe you rode all that way. You must be sore, and yet here you are again, riding a bicycle. I never would've made it."

Lucy imagined Liza on a bicycle. "Well from what I read in the paper you brought in more at the bake sale than anyone else. So you have your own reason to be proud."

"Oh that's nothing," Liza said. She leaned in and whispered, "I bested Bangstrom's wife by a nickel." Liza glanced back at the counter where the grocer was stocking goods. "She was livid and demanded a recount." She straightened up and said, "Anyway, that's nothing compared to you and Bob."

Lucy nodded, but did not know what else to say. The accolades made her strangely uncomfortable and somewhere deep inside her chest she knew it was just a matter of time before someone would mention how proud Hans must be of his son. She would nod in agreement, but such an encounter would make her feel like she was falling through the air, certain the ground was coming.

"Oh!" Liza said. She grabbed Lucy by the arm and walked her to the far corner of the store. "You wouldn't believe what I found out about that Brewster boy." Liza looked around Lucy and down the narrow aisle, making sure no one was within earshot. She leaned in again and whispered, "His father was a Merchant Marine, and his ship sank when that convoy was attacked in the North Atlantic back in November." Liza crossed herself and then continued. "They're actually related to old Hank Bangstrom—second cousins or something. They moved here because she couldn't pay the rent anymore. That property out on Newton? It actually belongs to Hank and he's letting them stay there until they can get back on their feet."

"That's awful," Lucy said. "I can't imagine how devastated they were. I mean to lose your husband and then your home." Lucy shook her head as all the thoughts she had about the boy and his mother dangled in front of her mind. Liza stepped back, gave Lucy room to take it all in, and glanced down the aisle again. She reached up and rubbed her cross pendant between her thumb and forefinger. "I simply feel terrible," Lucy said. "We should do something for them." Liza nodded but didn't offer any suggestions. Lucy stood there for a few moments. At once, she thought she understood why

Caleb had chosen to pick on her son. She knew Richard's stammer made him seem weak, but their last name, something so obviously German must have hit a nerve connected to the loss of the boy's father. She pictured Caleb in her mind, the way he had looked at her when he came to deliver the groceries. At the time, she felt he was simply odd, but now she could see it was something else. He had looked at her as though she was the enemy and he was suddenly caught behind the lines. A mixture of panic and hatred had flashed across his face that she mistook as uncertainty one might feel in a new place. Lucy thought about the shame she felt in the way she responded to Betty after the bake sale. It also occurred to her that the woman had no clue what her son was feeling about the loss of his father and how he was retaliating in the only way he could.

"Can I help you ladies find something?" Hank Bangstrom asked.

He startled Lucy out her thoughts. "Oh, Mr. Bangstrom, I didn't see you there. Liza and I were just talking about the bake sale and what a success it was. I'm going to have to make something really special next time if I expect to keep up with Mrs. DiMarco. "

Hank nodded. "Well let me know if I can help." He wiped his hands on his white apron and ambled toward the front of the store. The two women watched as he paused and straightened a can of olives on the shelf. He glanced back at them with an arched eyebrow. Lucy waved and leaned into Liza. "Thanks for telling me about the Brewsters. I've got to go to the post office and take care of a few other errands." She squeezed Liza's hand and walked to the front of the store where Mr. Bangstrom had settled on his stool behind the counter and was reading a newspaper. Lucy glanced over her shoulder back towards where she left Liza and then cleared her throat. Hank Bangstrom looked up and put the paper down. "Yes, Mrs. Müller?"

Lucy's gaze dropped to the counter as she pulled the invoice from her pocket. "Mr. Bangstrom," she said. "I was wondering if it would be possible to arrange installments for this account?" She handed the bill to the man and he put on his reading glasses and held the paper at arm's length. He scratched his chin as he read over the bill. "My wife normally handles these things, Mrs. Müller, but I'm sure we can make arrangements." He folded the bill and tucked it into his pocket. "Hans told me he might need a little time on this purchase; I guess I forgot to mention it to Sally." Hank winked as and removed his glasses.

"Trust me, I understand that completely. Hans didn't tell me a thing either."

Hank chuckled and nodded.

Lucy couldn't recall ever having seen Hank Bangstrom laugh before.

"I was just reading about you and your boy in the paper," he said. "Quite an adventure you two had."

Lucy nodded. "It certainly was. I have to admit, though, I wasn't too excited about riding the bicycle into town today. My legs feel like rubber."

Hank nodded. "Okay, Mrs. Müller. I will talk to Sally and we'll work something out for you and Hans."

Lucy thanked the grocer and left the store, and waved to Liza through the window as she walked down the sidewalk. She headed toward the post office, eager to send the letter to Hans containing the good news from the hearing and the newspaper clipping detailing the trip to Rochester. Lucy carefully navigated the questions from the reporter and skillfully neglected to mention her trip down to Albany in a car, which would have spoiled the gist of the story. It also allowed her to avoid all the questions about the purpose of the trip. A billow of pride began to lighten her steps, but then she had the odd feeling that eyes were following her as she walked down the street. She glanced around and didn't see anyone specifically looking in her direction, but she couldn't shake the feeling.

As she approached the door to the post office, she ran into Marjorie Wright and Dora Brown. Dread washed over her like cool water, and the letter in her hand quickly became a source of shame as she tucked it into the pocket of her skirt.

"Mrs. Müller, what a pleasant surprise," Dora said.

Lucy thought about it and couldn't remember the mayor's wife ever directly addressing her. They had been in the same room numerous times, and of course, Lucy knew who she was, but the suddenness of the greeting brought about an equally sudden epiphany. Lucy had never been worth her time. This thought must have played across her face with utter transparency.

"I do know who you are, Lucy," she said. "I just read all about you in the newspaper."

Lucy smiled and tried to cover her shock. "Of course, Mrs. Brown. It's just you were the last person I expected to see at the post office. Not that there is anything wrong with the post office, or that you shouldn't be here... Goodness, I am making a mess of it all aren't I?"

"Lucy," Dora said. "Marjorie and I were speaking of you just a few moments ago."

"We were?" Marjorie said.

Dora patted her on the arm. "Yes we were."

Marjorie nodded.

"And we decided, didn't we Marjorie, that we should invite you to our luncheon at the Daughters of the American Revolution next week. We, as I'm sure you know, are members of the Abigail Fillmore chapter in Buffalo, and we'd simply be delighted to have you as our guest." Dora turned to Marjorie. "Wouldn't we?"

"Well yes, yes of course. We'd be...delighted."

Lucy looked at the two women. "Which day next week?"

"Thursday, my dear. Luncheons are always on the first Thursday of each month," Dora said, as if Lucy should have known such a detail.

"I'll have to check my schedule," Lucy said. A breeze blew and ruffled her skirt and the corner of the envelope in her pocket poked her thigh. "I'm sure I can, but I do need to make sure I don't have any other obligations that day."

"Absolutely, dear Lucy," Dora said, glancing at Marjorie with a slightly raised eyebrow. "Just let me know for sure by Monday."

Lucy nodded. "Absolutely, Dora." The name felt foreign in her mouth. She gave a quick wave to the women and moved toward the door, hoping she had followed the proper decorum in releasing herself from the engagement of the conversation. As she pushed her way through the door, she looked back over her shoulder and watched Dora and Marjorie chat as they walked away. Neither turned and caught her looking, but she could not help but notice the tension apparent in Marjorie's body language.

The door of the post office closed behind Lucy and she expected relief. Instead, she was confronted with the same postal clerk that she dealt with the last time she mailed a letter to Hans. She pulled the letter from her pocket, placed in on the counter, and requested a nickel stamp.

The clerk looked at her, gave her quick smile while he affixed the stamp, and asked, "Will there be anything else, Mrs. Müller?"

"No, thank you," she said and walked out of the building. As she made her way back to her bicycle, Lucy noticed how the women on the street nodded in her direction and the men touched the brim of their hats as they passed. She felt as though she was in a parade and everyone was admiring her as if she was Miss Buffalo of 1942. The unexpected attention was both pleasant and disconcerting. She felt the scrutiny before, but it was simply a feeling. Now, no doubt rested between her and her perceptions. People were looking at her, acknowledging her as they passed her on the street, as they served her at stores or the post office. She felt naked under the eyes of the community. Rather than shrink, however, Lucy raised her chin a bit and straightened her back, and walked with purpose. Anonymity, which had grown into a comfortable cocoon, had been shorn away and it felt good. Her pride lifted her above the troughs of despair that had overwhelmed her over the last few months. She had seen a future, like a skier who sees an avalanche before being enveloped by the snow, rocks, and ice, and did her best to escape the suspicion and accusations. Unbelievably, it had worked. Her husband would be home soon and the boys would have their father back. Things were looking up and no one in town would be wise to the secret she had kept. She got on her bicycle and rode home, smiling, waving, and ringing the bell mounted on the handlebars at people she passed. The sun hung high in the sky and her shadow all but disappeared.

Chapter 24

A week after she mailed the letter to Hans, the farm was eerily quiet. Both boys were in school and the early June weather was mild. A light breeze blew in from the lake, the sky's hue was a deep azure, and the cumulous clouds floated overhead, soft and white. Lucy plowed a field and readied it for the summer planting of onions and chard. The soil turned easily and it gave Lucy hope for a good harvest by the end of the summer. The spring had been a wet one, normally a good sign for summer crops. Unfortunately, it also tended to indicate an early and brutal winter. She thought of the letter she had written to her husband, how many hands it might pass through before he received it, how long it would take to get there, and how many times he would read and reread the letter and the article. She imagined him pinning it up next to where he slept and seeing her and his son every night before he went to sleep. The anticipation of waiting to hear from Manny and the court was tortuous, but the hope she held close to her heart made the waiting a bit easier.

She pulled the tractor into the barn and released the harrow she used for the plowing. The boys would move it into its place against the wall when they came home from school. Lucy drove the tractor out of the barn and to its shed, moving slowly into the darkness. Lucy shut off the motor and sat in the seat for a moment, smelling a mixture of oil and gasoline tinged with the smell of turpentine and paint. The shed smelled the way a workshop in a barn should smell, including the stink of the wild. As her eyes adjusted to the dimness of the shed, the deerskin tacked up on the wall hiding the storage closet caught her eye. She thought it was possible that Hans hung it there because that was the only space big enough to accommodate the pelt, but she recalled the shiny hasp and the lock hidden behind the skin. It was too

          Fertile Ground

deliberate. She climbed down from the tractor, walked over to the pelt, and yanked it off the wall. She grasped the lock and pulled on it. She knew it would be locked, and she wasn't sure she wanted to know what was in the closet, but after a moment decided remaining ignorant was not a choice.

She grabbed the hammer, felt its weight in her hand, glanced at the lock, and knew she would need more than brute force. The tools lay scattered across the workbench: she selected an awl. Hans used it for punching holes in the leather harnesses around the farm, and she thought it could be put to another purpose. Lucy ignored the imposing lock. The heft and the dozen or so rivets that held it together seemed too fortified. Rather, she focused on the hinge of the hasp. She moved a wooden crate and stood on it for a better angle. She placed the awl at the center of the hinge pin and gave it a solid whack with the hammer. The effort left a small indentation. She struck repeatedly and the awl sank deeper into the metal with each blow. After several minutes and much effort, the shaft of the awl penetrated deep into the hinge pin. In the dim light, Lucy could see where the axle was separating from the retainer cap. She stepped down from the crate and replaced the awl with a sturdy screwdriver. After three strong blows, the cap came off and she was able to push the hinge pin out. The door came forward a bit, just ajar as Lucy stood there for a moment realizing her efforts were suddenly successful.

She opened the storage closet door. Inside on the shelf at eye level she saw a wire rack holding dozens of test tubes. Next to them were cone shaped glass containers with white measuring numbers on the side and rubber stops plugging the openings; pale blue and amber liquids were in them. She reached out to touch one, but her hand stopped. On lower shelves sat other items that she had only seen in monster movies with mad scientists. Rubber hoses, long glass tubes that looked like straws, a stand that had a black metal base and a long metal shaft that rose perpendicular from the base. Halfway up was a thick steel ring four inches across, blackened from soot and held in place on the shaft with a wing nut.

Lucy crouched down. On the bottom shelf sat several containers that looked like paint cans. Plain white labels with black printing indicated their contents: nitrobenzene, hydrogen sulfide, diethylstilbestrol, and many others

Lucy couldn't begin to pronounce. She stood and took a step back from the closet. On the top shelf there was a long white cardboard tube. She reached in and pulled it down. There was a cluster of stamps and a Rochester postmark; it was addressed to Hans. At the end of the tube was a tin cap that she pried off. Inside she saw a large piece of paper rolled up to fit inside. She pulled it out and unfurled it on Hans' workbench, pushing tools to the floor in the process. It was a map. She weighed down the corners with tools and took a close look. It showed the western half of New York State, from Syracuse to Buffalo. Someone had drawn on it with a grease pencil. Lucy's heart began to beat quickly as she tried to figure out why Hans locked away the map in a storage closet with chemicals. She knew Hans had been discussing a proposition with Gus Payne about starting a business that tested feed for livestock. There were local stores that were selling Purina and other packaged products and the owners wanted to convince the local farmers of the area that their feed was cheaper and better for their animals. Farming was a difficult living, and the idea appealed to both Hans and Gus, and the dealers who were selling the products. As she looked at all the chemistry equipment, she wondered why he would've kept it all a secret.

She looked more closely at the area that had been marked. It was north of them in Depew and noted by a star with a G at its middle. Leading east from the starred G was a line that followed the railroad. Lucy traced her finger along it until she came to an X and the line stopped. It appeared that the train tracks crossed a small creek at that point, just outside Attica. She stood there for a moment, trying not to believe what she was seeing. Her hands began to shake as she looked back to the origin of the tracks where the star with the G in the middle was marked. Lucy leaned in closer and tried to make out street names in the area. The only one she could make out was Transit Road. Suddenly, she heard a noise behind her, like tires in gravel. She rolled up the map quickly, stuffed it back in the tube, tossed it into the storage closet, and shut the door. It would not stay closed so she propped the crate she had been standing against the door. She turned around quickly and smoothed her slacks, as though she had spilled crumbs on them and walked out of the shed. The sunlight made it difficult for her to see and she raised her hand to shield the sun from her eyes as she rounded the corner of the barn.

"Mom!" Bob was on his father's bike. Since the ride to Rochester, he had appropriated it as transportation to school. "Richard's in a fight with Caleb Brewster again."

Chapter 25

It was the last day of school, and given his preference, Richard would have finished the week the way he had completed his assignments while his brother and mother were in Rochester. He had discovered something about himself while working on the Payne's farm. It had little to do with the actual work, as he was accustomed to many of the chores he performed for Gus and his wife. He fed chickens, brushed out the horses, led the cattle in from pasture at the end of the day, cleaned out stalls in the barn, and even did some minor carpentry work and painting. The difference was how the Paynes treated him. His father, when around, kept a close eye on every move and quickly corrected every misstep. At Gus's, he told the boy what to do, he did it, Gus would look over the work and nod, and maybe even say "good job." His abilities were valued and appreciated, and he discovered he knew more than he thought he knew. He had also realized he enjoyed the sense of satisfaction found working with his hands. At home, he preferred to work on his studies or read a book. These activities he viewed as his way off the farm. He loved his parents, but he didn't want the life that they had chosen to live. Getting up each morning before the sun and working in the fields until it set, never having enough money for the wants in life, and sometimes not enough for the needs, held no appeal, but things changed.

Gus treated him like a man. No one came in to wake him in the morning, to tell him to get dressed, to eat, to bathe. The first day at the Payne's farm, he stayed in bed even though he heard Gus and his wife in the kitchen, bustling about, readying for the day. When things quieted down, he got up and walked into the kitchen. He expected to find a plate of food left behind for him, but the kitchen was spotless. He peeked out the window and saw the two of them by the barn. Mrs. Payne was hitching a team to a wagon, preparing to go into town. Gus was busy shoveling manure he'd collected from the stalls into the back of his pickup truck. As he watched the two work, he felt a twinge deep within his chest. He went back to his room and sat on the bed. He wanted to resent the feeling he labeled as guilt. As long as he could remember, he had worked when others worked and so in that moment, sitting idle, he was cutting against the grain of his life. He couldn't, in good conscience, blame the Paynes. They had offered to watch after him and didn't demand anything in return. Immediately his thoughts turned to his mother and father. He could not attach blame to them either. They worked to survive, to feed Bob and him, to give them clothes and shelter. And so he was at a loss, and in that moment found himself. He realized that the expectations of others no longer mattered. He dressed, poured himself a glass of milk, walked out to the barn, surveyed the tasks before him, and put in a full day's work. In the work, he felt self-satisfaction. Over supper that evening, he wasn't complimented on his initiative or the quality of work he performed. Gus and his wife talked about the price of commodities, the weather, the new foal, and only a vague mention of the war in relation to the good prices the government was paying. The next morning Richard awoke and dressed before the others. He led the cows out to pasture after milking them, collected eggs from the hens and brought them into the kitchen as Mrs. Payne was brewing the coffee. "Set those over there and have a seat," she said. She cooked him breakfast and smiled as he ate it.

Since he returned to school, he felt like he had taken a huge step backward. During the last week, Mrs. Archer stood over him as he worked on his composition, reading the sentences before he completed them. It made him feel closed in, as if his clothes were too small. The end of each day could not come quickly enough for him, and as he made his way home, it occurred to him that he'd rather go to the Payne's farm. He looked ahead to the future: school ended for the year and starting next weekend he would begin working for Gus, making his own money. The thought pleased him.

As he walked down the road that led to Newton, Bob came up behind him on their father's bicycle and pedaled past him, tossing him a grin over his shoulder. The feelings of resentment he'd had toward his little brother still lingered deep somewhere inside, and he could hear them cry out as Bob rode by and kicked up the dust of the road, but now they were easy to ignore. He raised his hand and waved the cloud of dust and dirt away, then saw something change in Bob's face.

"Whe-whe-whe- Where you going, Richie?"

Richard turned. It was Caleb Brewster loping toward him; his red hair had grown long and shaggy. "Po-po-po-poor Richie looks so sad." Johnny Adder, one of Caleb's disciples who had egged him on when Richard's eye was blackened, followed closely behind.

Richard stopped, dropped his books, and waited for the two boys to reach him. He heard Bob ride up behind him. He hollered, "You better leave my brother alone or I'll tell."

Caleb and Johnny thought this hilarious. "Yeah, go ahead. Go tell your mommy," Johnny said.

"No, Johnny. I couldn't face Richie's mommy. Sh- sh- sh- She might..." Caleb stopped and turned to Johnny with a wide-eyed expression on his face. And then it broke. "Oh, yeah. That's right. She couldn't do anything. She's probably chicken just like her little Richie here."

"That's it," Bob said. "I'm going to get my mom." He turned the bicycle around and pedaled down the road. "You're gonna get it!" he yelled over his shoulder.

Caleb walked up, stood inches away from Richard, and looked down on him. "I guess that's what I expected from you. Who else but a chicken would stand around and wait for his mommy? Isn't that right, chicken?" He pushed Richard and he stumbled back a few steps. "See?" he said to Johnny. "Just a big chicken. A big black and white chicken that don't know any better." Caleb and Johnny laughed.

"Hey, carrot top," Richard said.

Johnny and Caleb stopped laughing and turned toward Richard. "What'd you say?" Caleb said as he walked up to Richard. "I know this chicken didn't just call me—"

Richard's fist landed on Caleb's jaw and cut his words short. He stumbled backward and fell into Johnny Adder, knocking them both to the ground. Richard stepped forward and held his fist up, thinking he was Jack

Dempsey. "You want some more of this?"

Caleb held his jaw, a thin line of blood trickled from the corner of his mouth. He stood up and brushed the dust from his overalls. "All right you pecker." Caleb put up his fists and the two boys squared up.

Richard didn't see the fist that knocked him out, but he vaguely remembered seeing Caleb stand over him as he lay on his back in the road. His head felt like it was inside the church bell, all loud, thick, and dull at the same time. He looked up into the sky and saw Caleb's face hang above his, and then it was joined by Johnny Adder. He felt like an ant under a magnifying glass. Caleb and Johnny looked at one another, laughed, and then their mouths moved into a pucker and warm hocks of spit landed on Richard's face. He tried to sit up, but it felt like he was strapped to the world, feeling it spin under him. He closed his eyes and when he opened them again Bob's face had replaced Caleb and Johnny, and then his mother appeared. The ringing in his ears had quit and he could hear the birds, the wind rustling the trees, and finally his mother's voice.

"Are you okay?"

He nodded and felt little rocks dig into the back of his head.

His mother and Bob helped him stand; he looked down and saw the mess on his shirt. His hand went to his face and touched the dried blood and mucus that had caked on his lips and chin, and when he felt his nose, the throbbing turned into a sharp pain.

Bob pulled a handkerchief from his pocket and handed it to his brother."You got something up here," he said, pointing to his forehead.

Richard wiped the spit away and then attempted to clean his face. The blood was dark and thick, and he wondered how long he had been lying in the road. He looked around and saw his books had been kicked into the ditch; his fists clenched, and his heart beat like he'd just run a mile. He flexed his hand and felt a little stiffness in his knuckles from where he had landed a punch on Caleb's jaw. A wry grin appeared.

"What so funny?" Bob asked.

Richard inclined his head toward his books. "Grab those for me, would you, Bob?

He picked up Richard's books and dusted them off. Lucy put her arm around his shoulder and asked him again, "Are you sure you're all right?"

Richard nodded and from the look on her face, he knew things were bad. "I'm okay." He took a few steps toward home, the road seemed to tilt one way, and then the other, but he managed to keep a straight line and shrugged his mother's arm from his shoulders. "I'm okay."

He made slow progress on Newton, each step thought rather than felt. His mother matched his steps, seemingly waiting for him to toddle over, and Bob walked the bicycle. As they neared their house, Richard listened to the buzzing of cicadas in the warm afternoon and watched them flit through the tall grass.

Farther down the street, they saw someone on a bicycle. The rider wore a dark blue uniform with a black leather belt and a billed cap with goggles. Brass twinkled from his collar. It was a telegraph boy. Lucy, Bob, and Richard watched as he pedaled into their drive.

Chapter 26

After the evening meal, Hans tended to the horse Gloria Svensen had lent to the railroad as part of her contract to provide provisions for the work crew. The horse was an old mare, speckled grey with black points. The June evenings were mild, but she still needed an overnight blanket. Hans was fastening the strap that went just behind her forelegs when she got skittish. "Hold there," he said and patted her neck. "There's a girl. It's all right." His voice calmed her and he got the blanket set. He took the rein, led her out to the field on the far side of the railroad, and hobbled her. He removed the bit so she could eat and as soon as he did, she began to graze. Hans walked back to the caboose where the guards slept near the parked wagon. In the twilight, Hans saw a shadow on the rear platform and the orange glow of a cigarette. As he got closer, he saw Red. Hans walked to the back of the wagon and tossed in the tack.

"You sure know your way around horses," Red said.

"*Ja*. Nice animals, but so stupid sometimes."

"Aren't we all," Red said and took a drag of his cigarette; the cherry glowed bright. The ever present cowboy hat had been left inside the caboose and Hans could see the narrow shape of the man's head.

"I wanted to let you know that I appreciate the job you've done trucking the provisions in from the Svensen farm." Red shook his head. "Sad thing to happen to a woman like that."

"What sad thing?"

"All those times out there and she never told ya?"

Hans thought Red might be playing a game with him. "She's told me lots of things. Some sad, some not."

"I reckon she didn't tell you about the boy's father then. Mr. Svensen."

"No. I just figured he was in the service."

"Yep. He was." Red took another drag from his cigarette and tossed it out onto the track behind the caboose. "Anyway. Wanted to let you know that tomorrow will be the last load we get from the Svensen's farm so the boy will ride back with you and take the wagon and the roan home."

Hans didn't say anything, but he didn't move either. He tried to read Red's face in the darkness, to see something, to try to understand. Red must've been able to see the expression on Hans' face.

"You and the fellas are making real progress and the trek to her farm is too far away now. Day after tomorrow we start a new contract with a family called Kismet who live outside Jamestown."

Hans looked down at the ground and put his hands in the pockets of his overalls.

"Don't look so sad there, Hans. You'll get a chance to say goodbye tomorrow." Red gave a little huff of a laugh. "'Bout time to turn in. I'll see you in the morning."

"*Gute Nacht,*" Hans said and began to walk toward the car he slept in. He walked slowly with his head down, thinking about Gloria. Too beautiful to be a widow, he thought. And what of the boy? No boy should grow up without a father. He heard the steel sound of the sliding door closing on the boxcar and the metal clank of the latch quickly afterward. He stood still in the shadows as he watched the guards walk down to the next car and perform the same operation. He inhaled, ready to speak loudly enough to catch their attention, to let them know he needed to be in there before they shut it up for the night. As he began to speak, something made him stop. They had been working the rails for more than three weeks and the guards had become relaxed in their duties. During the first week one had to move slowly because the guards were so jumpy with their rifles, but as the days passed and no one made any move to escape they began to loosen up. Now the nightly roll call had gone by the wayside. Hans stood still in the dark and watched as the two guards made their way to the last boxcar and shut it closed. A small campfire, just off the tracks, burned about 100 yards in front

　　　　　　　　　　　　　　　　　　　　Fertile Ground

of where Hans stood. The guards made their way to the fire, sat down on stools, and warmed their hands. He heard them talking but couldn't make out any words. Hans took a step backward, his eyes trained on the two shadows by the fire. He took another and then another and before long he stood just outside the caboose. Inside he heard Red and the cook having a good-natured argument about something, probably a card game. Hans crouched down close to the ground and moved swiftly out to where he'd left the mare to graze. He spooked her a bit, but the hobble kept her from bolting. He soothed her with whispers and strokes. When she calmed, he bent down, removed the straps from her ankles, slipped one end under the halter, tied a loose knot, and did the same on the other side. He led the roan away from the tracks with the makeshift rein until he felt they were far enough away. He held onto the rein, took two quick steps, and mounted the horse. The mare skittered a bit, as it seemed it had been a while since she'd been ridden bare back. He turned the horse toward Medina and took things slowly in the dark.

The moon was nearly full and loomed over the prairie like a watchful eye. Hans picked his way across fields and roads and found his way back to the Svensen farm. It was late by the time he got there. A single golden light shone through one window of the house. He didn't know for sure, but he imagined it was Gloria's room, that she was in bed reading with her hair in a kerchief. He paused as he reached the end of the drive. The roan snorted, probably curious why Hans had decided to stop so close to the end of the trek. She shook her head and took a step or two, either inadvertently or purposely announcing their presence in the yard. A figure came to the window and blocked most of the light. She was a silhouette, her hair loose and flowing. She lifted the sash. "Who's that out there?" she said in a loud whisper.

The horse shifted again, seemingly telling Hans it was time to get down. He dismounted. "It's Hans," he said and took a cautious step toward the window. She took a step back, stood still for a moment, and moved away from the window. Hans looked around. The roan snorted at him. "Well it was your idea I should get down," he said to the horse. The front door to the house opened and Gloria came out. Her nightgown was covered with a blanket wrapped around her shoulders that she held in place in the middle of her chest. She looked down the drive, to the horse, and then back at Hans.

"What are you doing here?" She stepped toward Hans who stood in the middle of the yard.

He took a step or two toward her and whispered. "I had to see you."

"This is foolish. They will find you. Then what will happen to you? You'll be put in a prison or back in that camp you like so much." She flinched at every noise of the night and looked back to the house. "Put Gertrude in the barn and come into the house."

Hans nodded and took the horse by the halter. "Gertrude, eh?" He walked the animal into the barn and shut her in one of the stalls. She snorted and nuzzled the hay on the floor. "Thank you, my lady." Hans bowed to the horse. The door to the house was ajar and he stuck his head in before he entered. Gloria was by the stove putting a kettle on. "Is Peter asleep?"

Gloria waved Hans in with one hand and then hurried behind him to the door and took a quick peek outside before shutting it. He had never stood so close to her before. He held his hat in his hand as he looked into her eyes. He could smell the lingering scent of soap on her skin and the image of her bathing made his legs feel unsteady. He longed to touch her hair, to feel it in his hand, on his skin.

"You must be mad coming here."

"They don't know I'm gone," he said. He told her about how he had been locked out of the boxcar and what Red had said about tomorrow being the last day of the contract. "I didn't know what else to do. I had to see you, to speak to you. I knew tomorrow we would be rushed, that Peter would be around, and I wasn't sure I'd have a chance..."

Gloria cinched the blanket together at her chest and tilted her head slightly. "Have a chance for what?" she said as she inched closer.

Hans set his hat down on the table next to the door and turned back to her. "I wanted to say," he began and then looked down at the floor. Gloria stepped closer. She reached out and smoothed the hair behind one of his ears.

"What is it you wanted to say, Hans?"

He met her eyes and, unable to find the words, shook his head slightly. He leaned in and felt her heat, could smell her breath as he brought her body close to his and kissed her. Her hand that held the blanket released it and let it fell to the floor. She moved into his body and wrapped her arms around him in a way that made him feel something he couldn't name. His fingers swam through her golden hair as he held her head next to his chest.

"I can feel your heart beating," she said.

"I feel...I don't know what. I've never felt this before." Hans kissed her and his hand dropped to her shoulders. She looked into his eyes, took him by the hand, and led him to her room.

"We have to be quiet; Peter's sleeping," she said and closed the door to her bedroom. "Sit down on the bed." She walked over to the window, drew the sash, turned to Hans, and looked at him. The golden light in the room made her eyes sparkle and glisten as she stood before him. She undid the buttons on her nightdress slowly, watching Hans' reaction with each one. The gown slid off one shoulder and after the next fastener released it dropped to the floor and she stood before him. Hans began to stand. "No," she said. "Stay right where you are." She sauntered over to him and rested her hands on his shoulder. "Do you like what you see?"

Hans nodded. "Yes." His hands slid up her bare back and pulled her close. He kissed her chest, working his way down from her collarbone to her breasts. Her legs were on either side of his and he smelled her scent. His hands flowed down her back and then she stepped back.

"Not so fast," she said. She pushed Hans' shoulders and he lay back across the bed. She climbed on top, straddling him and she undid the snaps on his denim work shirt. She ran her hands up and down his bare chest and then leaned in and kissed his neck. Hans heaved with excitement as he felt her weight settle on his pud. "Steady," she said and her hips moved forward and back on him and she kissed his neck and ear.

"I—"

"Shhhh," we have to be quiet. Remember?" She slid off him and undid his trousers and let them bunch around his ankles and work boots. She knelt in front of him and teased him with her hands and then her lips and tongue until his breath raced. She stood, clasped his hands, and pulled him up from the bed and led him over to a small throw rug that lay in front of a rocker and where her sewing sat. She knelt and then laid back on the rug and the wooden floor beneath her creaked. "The springs on the bed and the frame," she said, inclining her head towards Peter's bedroom.

Hans removed his boots and trousers and lay down next to her. "I have a w—"

"Don't speak," she said and pulled him onto her.

Hans startled Gertrude when he came back into the barn. She must have thought her chores were done for the night. Hans led her out into the yard, and the moon was setting and the darkness was getting deeper. Gloria stood by the porch as Hans mounted the reluctant mare. They waved to one another as he walked the roan down the drive and then spurred her on to a trot. He knew dawn would be breaking soon and if he were to avoid trouble, he would have to get back to the worksite as quickly as possible.

As he neared the railroad, the indigo sky was quickly paling with streaks of pink, yellow, and orange. The lights in the caboose were out and the campfire along the rails had died down to smoldering embers. Two shadows near the fire were still and appeared to be sleeping. Hans slid off Gertrude's far side, placing her between him and the train cars. He slipped the makeshift rein off her halter and hobbled her, even though he knew she was too tired to go anywhere. Afterward, he crouched down in the tall grass. He only made it a few steps when Gertrude shook her head and snorted. "Shh" Hans whispered back at her. She looked at him with her big brown eyes for a moment and then turned and began grazing. He made his way as quietly as possible to the edge of the tall prairie grass. From his vantage point, he could see the two guards by the campfire were dozing, and he stepped gingerly across the ballast stones and was steps away from one of the boxcars when he heard the backdoor of the caboose open. He dashed between two of the boxcars and made it down the other side of the train cars to the one he was supposed to be in. He crouched down by the wheels and waited.

"Hey, you sonofabitches," Red hollered as he kicked the stool out from underneath one of the guards. "You two are supposed to be guarding these krauts, not napping away."

The guards scrambled to their feet bleary-eyed, reacting instinctively like they would to a drill sergeant, even though Red wasn't in the service and had no real authority over the men. "Come on, now. Daylight's a wasting. Let's get Fritz to work."

As Red walked back toward the caboose, the two guards cursed him under their breath. Hans peered under the car he was hiding behind and watched as the two guards walked to the last car, undid the latch and slid open the door. "All right, you kraut bastards, time to get to work." They banged on the side of the car with the butt of their rifles and the sound echoed inside. They moved down the line, performing the same actions with slight variations in the profanity. They got to Hans' car and did their routine as Hans watched under the middle of the car until he saw the men drop out of the open door to the ground. Then he climbed under the car and stood up right in front of the open door. He stretched his arms over his head. "One morning, I'd like to sleep in," he said to no one in particular. Those around him grunted their approval of the idea.

The day warmed up quickly and Hans felt the lack of sleep, but the images that lingered in his head allowed his hands and body to work with an energy he hadn't felt in years. As he pulled the spikes out of the crossties, he considered scenarios where he and Gloria might excuse themselves from Peter's presence. Maybe there was an errand he could send the boy on that wouldn't take too long, but long enough. How long could he stretch out his visit without raising any concerns with Red? He thought about the way Gloria's hair splashed down on her bare shoulders, the tenderness of her lips, the way she moved under him, the feel of her hands on his skin. More than anything else, Hans was taken with the way her eyes held him. There was so much heat he thought he might start burning from the inside. He worked and worked, trying not to think about the time. The anticipation of taking the wagon out to her farm that afternoon was too much to keep in the forefront of his mind. As long as he kept his hands busy, time would pass and the magical hour would arrive. As he worked, other thoughts wormed in: Lucy, Robert, and Richard. He had pushed his family into the deepest recesses of his mind, and now they surfaced and eyed him like specters he couldn't escape. The harder he worked, the more vivid they became.

"Hey! Hans! Hans Müller!"

Hans didn't hear his name at first, but when Müller hit his ears it penetrated his thoughts. He turned and looked up the rail line, wiping the sweat from his forehead. Red was walking toward him with a piece of paper in his hands. He figured it was some kind of paperwork that Gloria would need so she could get paid. As that thought occurred to him he also realized that he'd kept his head down and kept busy long enough for the magical hour to arrive.

"What you so happy about, Hans?" Red said. "I've seen you working like a maniac when everyone else is dragging and you're smiling like a weasel in a henhouse."

Hans shrugged. "I don't know. Maybe I thought it was time for the lunch break."

Red laughed. "No, it's barely half past ten."

Hans' smile faded and he wiped the perspiration from his forehead and leaned on his crowbar. "Oh. Well I guess I don't have anything to be happy about then."

"I wouldn't say that, Mr. Hans Müller." Red held up the piece of paper in his hand. "I think this right here might put a smile on your face."

"What's that?"

Red cleared his throat and read the paper in a sarcastically official tone. "Effective immediately, Hans Joachim—" Red looked up at Hans. "What the hell kind of name is Joachim?"

Hans shook his head and turned his palms skyward.

"Anyway, 'Effective immediately, Hans Joachim Müller is hereby released from the custody of Immigration and Naturalization Service and is to be returned to his lawful residence in Friedberg, New York." Red looked at Hans. "Well, grab your stuff." He pointed over his shoulder with his thumb to two North Dakota State policemen. "These fellas are taking you back to Ft. Lincoln so you can be processed out."

Hans looked at the policemen and then back at Red. "Is this a joke?"

"No joke, Fritz. Now come on. Grab your stuff out your boxcar.

Before you know it you'll be riding the rails rather than working them."

Hans looked at the crowbar in his hands and didn't know what to do with it.

"You can just leave your tools where they are, Hans." Red walked over to him. "You all right?" Red rested his hand on Hans' shoulder. "I'm sure this is a shock to you and all, but you're free. You think any of these other krauts would take more than two seconds to clear out of here?"

"No. I guess not. It's just—"

"I know. You get so used to how things are and when they change on a dime it's kind of hard to know how to react. I gotta tell you something." He leaned in. "I hated my wife for twenty years and one day she finally up and left me." Red spit. "I just stood there in the kitchen for a good while. I should've been happy, but at that moment I didn't know how to exist without that hate. It was a wall I'd been leaning against for so long I didn't know what to do when it was gone."

Hans looked into Red's eyes. He wanted to explain that it wasn't that way at all. He wanted to say he had just found a shelter, warmth he'd never known, and it was being stripped away before he had a chance to—

"Come on, Hans," Red steered Hans off his spot and walked him over to the boxcar. "The government's kind of funny about their stuff. They want it back. So climb in there and grab your things. I reckon these officers would like to get outta this heat."

Hans' body obeyed the directions Red gave him and before he knew it, he was in the back of a police cruiser driving away from the tracks. In the field, he saw Gertrude grazing, still wearing the hobbles. The police car turned and everything behind them disappeared.

Chapter 27

When Lucy and her sons arrived at the end of the drive leading to their home, the telegram boy was standing on their front porch. Richard whistled and the boy looked over his shoulder at the three of them coming up the drive. He paused for a moment and looked down at the paper in his hand and then rolled it into a tube and stuck it between the knob and door jam. He scampered down the steps and got onto his bicycle. "Telegram for you," he said as he rode by the three of them. "I left it by the front door. No reply was requested." He waved and pedaled on.

Lucy couldn't blame him for not wanting to stick around. So many of the telegrams they now delivered were bad news, it must wear on a person after a while, she thought. Bob pedaled up the drive with as much speed as he could muster. Lucy wanted to stop him, but she didn't. She and Richard walked up the drive at the same pace they had walked down Newton Avenue, steady, but not languid. Her oldest son had turned 15 years-old at the end of May and since the winter, he'd grown more than she thought possible. As she walked her bicycle next to him, she could see the man he would become. There were still elements of his youth he had yet to outgrow, but his shoulders were sturdy and his hands had a sudden grace and strength she had not recognized before.

Bob ran back down the drive, holding the yellow telegram over his head. Her heart felt like a stone beating against her ribcage. Unsure if her son had read it already, she tried to gauge things by his face, but as he reached her and handed her the telegram she could see his excitement was born of anticipation rather than any sort of knowledge.

Lucy took a deep breath and unfurled the message.

1942 JUNE 21 PM 1 15
LUCILLE MULLER
FRIEDBERG NY
RELEASED FROM FORT LINCOLN STOP LEAVING SOON VIA
BISMARCK MINNEAPOLIS CHICAGO CLEVELAND BUFFALO
STOP MEET TRAIN AT STATION ON JUNE 24
HANS

Lucy folded the telegram. "Your father will be home the day after tomorrow; he's already on his way." The boys smiled but didn't react the way she expected. "Aren't you excited?" she asked.

Richard nodded but looked down at his feet rather than meeting his mother's eyes. Bob gazed out over the fields without a word or any kind of response to the question, all the animation that filled him moments ago had seeped out. "What's the matter?"

"The war isn't over yet."

"Yes. So?"

"Was he wounded?" Richard asked.

Lucy understood. She had portrayed their father as someone who did important work for the defense of the country, just like the fathers of so many of their classmates, and now that he was due to come home that image would change. Before Richard could articulate what he felt, Lucy saw the shame on his face. Other fathers were giving everything, fighting until they couldn't fight anymore. Lucy put her hand on Richard's shoulder. "Your father has contributed to the war effort in a very special way." Her stomach tightened as the fiction spilled from her lips. "We can't talk about what he's done while he was gone, but you both should know he was exactly where the government wanted him to be, and he was doing exactly what they wanted while he was there."

"He really did his part?"

It sounded like a slogan from a poster or radio broadcast, but she saw how earnest Richard's eyes were and she nodded. "Yes he did. And now he gets to come home."

Richard held her eyes for a long moment, almost asking a second time. He turned and walked toward the house, seemingly satisfied with the answer. Bob, on the other hand, had wandered over to the field where Lucy had planted the beets. The green leaves of the crop had poked out of the soil and the red petioles at their center looked like little flames. Bob plucked one and mindlessly shredded it. Lucy walked over to him. "Are you all right?"

Bob nodded but did not look up at his mother.

"I must be crazy, but I thought you two would be happy to have your Papa back."

He looked up at her and tilted his head a bit. "So they're letting him go?"

"You read the telegram?" Lucy said it in a way that it might sound like a question or a statement. "Regardless of everything else, he's your father."

Bob looked out over the field and tossed the rest of the leaf he had been tearing up into the wind and the pieces fluttered to the ground. He put his hands in his back pockets and walked toward his mother. She put her hand on his shoulder and they walked back to the house. "I know it's difficult to understand, but what they did wasn't right. Your Papa's been cleared and he's coming home."

The next day was spent sprucing things up around the farm. During the last three months, Lucy had spent more time in the fields and the barn than in the house. A not so thin layer of dust had settled on everything in the sitting room, and no one had sat in Hans' chair, turned on his lamp, or even set foot in the room since March. As she cleaned the room, she thought about that night, the banging on the door, Hans lying face down on the floor as she came down the stairs. She also remembered the arrogance of Agent Jordon as he turned and spoke to her on the porch. She felt again the anger and confusion she had felt that night, but what overshadowed it all was the memory of the ache in her chest as she watched the car drive away with her husband in the backseat, trying to turn to look out the back window, unable to wave goodbye because of handcuffs.

Later in the day, she directed her attention to the cleaning of the kitchen. Papers and missives had piled up in a way that was uncharacteristic. A war was going on; things were not normal. While going through some papers she saw an envelope she had forgotten about. The copper brown streaks across it brought back the day Greta the chicken had been killed and unceremoniously stuffed into the mailbox. The letter had been under the hen and with everything else that happened that day it was cast aside. She held it in her hand now, and did not recall the heft, the thickness of the envelope. The dried chicken blood obscured the writing scrawled across the front of the envelope. All she could read was Müller and Friedberg, New York. Lucy opened the letter and pulled out what seemed to be a stack of something wrapped in plain white paper. She unfolded the outside sheet and more currency than she had ever seen fell onto the table. Dozens of portraits of Alexander Hamilton stared up at her. She stood there for a moment, unsure what to do, and then she counted it. There was $300 in ten-dollar bills. She heard a noise upstairs, undoubtedly the boys were doing as instructed and straightening their room, but the sound made her jump and she collected the money quickly and held it in her hands, still disbelieving it was real. She opened the pantry and took an old coffee can down, the same one that she collected Christmas money in during the year and put all of the bills inside. After she safely concealed the money, she picked up the sheet of paper it had been wrapped in and examined it. Nothing, not a word. She looked inside the envelope and there was nothing there either to indicate the identity of the sender.

The boys rumbled overhead again and a bolt of anxiety rippled through her. She folded the envelope over and stashed it in her skirt pocket. She walked outside and across the yard to the barn. As she rounded the corner, she glanced up to the dormer window that let light into Richard and Bob's room. She hoped that they didn't see her, but she couldn't be sure. Inside the shed, she squeezed by the tractor and made her way to the storage closet. She removed the crate sitting in front of the closet and the door slung lazily ajar. She opened it all the way and quickly got the tube down that contained the maps she'd looked at before. She examined the map again, not only looking at the site that had been marked near their home, but also noticing there were numerous other places on the map that had X's in the same grease pencil. Near Rochester, she saw a circle with an S at its center and a line that followed another railroad track. Lucy rolled up the map and stuffed it back into the tube. She knew it was mailed from Rochester, and she assumed that it came from Walter, though there was no return address. She stood in the dark tractor shed for a few long minutes weighing her options and trying to keep another part of her mind at bay. She could return the tube back to where she found it, but that wouldn't do. She could not un-see what she just saw. To ignore the map was simply out of the question. She could give it to the FBI, perhaps anonymously. Then she looked at the closet, the damage she'd done when she opened it. Too delicate she thought.

Lucy kicked the crate over that had kept the door closed and placed all the test tubes, glass containers and tin containers of chemicals into the crate. She put the tube with the map on top and carried it to the door of the shed. She looked around for her boys and didn't see anyone. She went back inside and stood for a moment with her hands on her hips, her heart beating with such force she thought it might explode. Against the wall leaned a post-hole digger. She picked it up by the wooden handles and walked over to the padlock that remained secured. She raised the implement over her head and smashed down on the lock, repeatedly. Each time letting out a small cry, giving voice to the pent-up frustration that had seethed for months. On the fourth blow, the lock yielded and hung limply with the broken hasp behind it. The damage to the closet spoke of rage and urgency; it hung open like a black gaping wound. She wiped the sweat from her forehead, then took the lock, and walked over to the crate that contained everything else she had collected. She dropped the padlock in with the rest of the items and closed the lid and secured it with some bailing wire, and carried it around the barn to the Peerless.

Lucy had just placed the crate in the car when she heard the sound of a furious motor coming up the drive. Lucy walked out of the garage as a blue Ford Coupe with Betty Brewster behind the wheel drove up to the house and stopped abruptly, raising a dust cloud. The woman's mouth was a grimace and her eyes were alit with indignation. Lucy remembered what Liza had told her about Betty losing her husband in the North Atlantic and could see the presence of that pain and anger, but that moment of empathy quickly evaporated as Betty got out of the car and slammed the door. "Mrs. Müller! We need to have a conversation about your boy."

Lucy placed her hands on her hips. "Oh. Do we now?" She walked over to Betty's car and looked at it. Any doubts she had had about who had killed Greta and vandalized the barn were erased. "Any *conversation* about my boy should include one about yours too."

"Did you know your son punched Caleb in the face?"

"Yes I do." Lucy stood her ground, raising her chin a bit.

"And what do you plan on doing about it?"

Lucy smirked. "Absolutely nothing."

Betty's mouth opened like she wanted to say something but the words had gotten caught in her throat. "I don't know how you Yankees—"

"Let me stop you right there, Miss Southern Belle. Did your darling Caleb happen to mention he blackened my son's eye two weeks ago?" Lucy took a step forward. "And that he borrowed your car to come over here and paint swastikas on my barn?" She took another step toward Betty. "And did he say anything to you about killing one of our chickens and stuffing it in our mailbox?"

"Surely there must be a mistake."

"I'm absolutely certain I saw this car drive away with your son behind the wheel."

"So you didn't see him—"

"You haven't noticed a white paint stain on your son's overalls?" Lucy could see in her eyes that she had. "And yesterday, *your* son picked a fight with him by calling him a chicken."

"Well that doesn't—"

"A black and white chicken." Lucy pointed to the hens pecking at the ground in the yard, all with black and white plumage. "Seems pretty specific, if you ask me."

"I don't know what to say. Caleb has always been kind and gentle."

"Your son is a bully. Now I have chores to do so if you'll excuse me—" Lucy crossed her arms over her chest and waited for Betty to move.

"I'm sure there's an explanation," she began to say. Her eyes pleaded for understanding. Lucy thought about the post-hole digger that lay on the other side of the barn. One good whack over the head and Betty's worries would be over. She took a deep breath and felt much of the anger she felt flow out of her like a great purge.

"I understand you and your son have had a rough go of it the last few months, but that doesn't give you or your son the right to make *our* lives any tougher than they already are." Lucy glared at the woman. "Now why don't you get the hell out of here before I lose my temper and do something I might regret."

Betty retreated to her car. "I have an errand I need to run. We can talk about this later when you've calmed down." She shut the door before Lucy had a chance to retort.

Lucy felt the urge to get in the Peerless, chase her down, and drive her off the road. She felt eyes upon her and she looked up. Richard and Bob were wide-eyed. They had been watching the entire scene from their bedroom window. "Aren't you two supposed to be cleaning your room?" The faces disappeared and Lucy walked back to the garage. "What a piece of work," she said under her breath. She rested her trembling hands on the hood of the car. She thought about going inside and telling the boys a story about where she was going, but decided she had already told them enough stories. She got in the car, pulled out the choke, turned the ignition, and the automobile started right away. She put the car in gear and drove out onto Newton Avenue.

She kept her eyes ahead of her; she wasn't sure what would happen if she were to look back and see her sons calling or running after the car. She simply drove down one road after another, taking so many turns that she eventually lost herself in the countryside. She pulled to the side of the road and stopped the car. Her chest began to heave, unable to stop the tears that followed. She beat the steering wheel, pounding out her anger until her hand throbbed. So many emotions poured out of her at once she couldn't distinguish rage from pity, or fear from love, or pride from shame.

A steady breeze rippled the alfalfa in the field next to the Peerless. All the individual plants came together under the force of the wind, like a green ocean with specks of purple floating on its surface. Not far from the road, a small murky pond sat at the bottom of two hills. The brown water reflected the clouds in the sky. Lucy got out of the car, removed the crate from the passenger seat, and carried it through the alfalfa field to the pond. As she got close, her shoes sank into the marshy soil, each step felt thick and treacherous. When she was very young, two horses became mired in a marshy section of a farmer's tract. She had been on her way home with her grand-mere, riding in a buggy when they heard the horses scream as they thrashed about and became even more entrenched. The horses' necks strained with each belabored breath and eventually blood began to flow from their flared nostrils. Two farm hands tried to lasso them, like cowboys, to no avail. No one could get near them. The whiteness that surrounded the deep chestnut color of their eyes haunted her ever since that day. Witnessing the struggle of the beasts, their tortured spirits, the sulfurous smell of the swamp, and the muscles of the horses straining against the relentless pull of the muck. Worst of all was the blast and smell of gunpowder as the farmer's rifle put an end to the suffering.

She stopped a few feet from the water's edge and caught her breath for a moment. A crow cawed in a nearby tree. She twisted her body and heaved the crate as far as she could. It landed with a muddy splash and bobbed for a moment on the surface. It began to sink and Lucy felt a sense of relief, but then its progress toward oblivion halted and the top third of the crate remained above the surface of the murky water.

"Damn it!"

The crow cawed again in response and flew away on its dark wings. Lucy reached down, gathered her dress in one hand, and waded into the pond. When she reached the crate, she was knee deep in muck and pushed one side of the crate, rolling it toward the center of the pond. After two or three times the water was thigh-high and the crate was fully submerged. She stood there, in the middle of the pond looking up at the sky, mud dripping from her arms and her dress wicking the water up to her belly. She wanted to scream in triumph, but the wind gusted and goose bumps covered her flesh.

She made her way back to the car barefoot, the sticky muck having claimed her shoes. The gravel on the side of the road hurt her feet, but there was something satisfying about the pain. She started the car and drove off, trying to recall the turns that would lead her home.

Dusk had fallen by the time she found her house. She parked the car and checked herself in the mirror. She was a mess. No story or explanation could account for her condition. Then she noticed the white tube that contained the map. It had fallen to the floor in front of the passenger seat. Her shoulders sank and her head dropped to the steering wheel. She wasn't sure how long she stayed that way, and probably would've stayed there longer if it weren't for Bob.

"Are you okay, Mom?" He stood next to the driver's side window.

Lucy looked up at her son and nodded without hesitation. "I had to run an errand, and I'm just so tired I wanted to stay here and rest for a bit."

Bob shifted from one foot to another and then looked back at the house. "Okay," he said. "Well Richard and I cooked supper. We can eat whenever you're ready."

Lucy nodded and her son walked back to the house without another word. Tears teased the corner of her eyes as she tried to hold them back. Her dress was a mess and her feet and legs were stiff with the dried mud. She took a deep breath and got out of the car. She grabbed the damn tube, walked over to the burn barrel, and jammed it under the trash until none of its whiteness showed. She went into the barn. Under the coat Hans kept on a nail in the barn was a pair of stained coveralls. Lucy put them on, rolling up her dress to the waist to get her legs in. She buttoned up the coveralls. On another nearby nail was a hurricane lantern, a small box of wooden matches were jammed between the frame and the glass chimney. She shook the lantern and heard the slosh of kerosene. She walked out to the barrel, poured the fuel on the trash, and struck a match. The rubbish blazed as she stood there, watching the flames in their slow orange dance as they consumed everything. She stood there and watched until she saw nothing but ashes. As tired as she felt, a sense of relief filled her, knowing everything that could damn Hans had been destroyed. The money in the coffee can would be her secret, her security.

The boys must've been surprised: the coveralls she wore, her bare feet, the dirt still clinging to her forearms, the smell of smoke, kerosene and pond water, but neither said a word while they sat at the table and ate their supper. Afterwards, the boys cleared the dishes and went upstairs without a word. She went into her room, shut the door, and cleaned herself up. Hans was due home tomorrow.

Chapter 28

Lucy, Richard, and Bob, stood on the train platform waiting. It was Sunday and they looked as though they had just come from church. Lucy wore a white dress and the boys were in jackets and ties. A few people were milling about, chatting, reading papers, but the station was largely empty. Lucy had a boy on either side as she stood waiting, like a battleship with two destroyers flanking her. Richard and Bob were restless, either uncomfortable in their formal clothes or with the prospect of facing their father. Lucy wanted to believe the clothes were the culprit, but she knew Bob's feelings about his father were tarnished and Richard feared regressing to how things were before his father left. Lucy had her own apprehension about her husband's return. They could see the train coming from far off and as it grew closer all three fidgeted with their hands. The locomotive was sleek and modern, like a painted bullet with deep blue on top, a white stripe at its midpoint, and gray on the bottom. The platform vibrated under their feet as the slowing train passed them. One Pullman car after another rolled by until the train came to a stop. Porters hopped down onto the platform, placing wooden blocks under the steel steps for passengers disembarking the train.

The boys shifted from one foot to another as travelers began to get off the train. Lucy wanted to hold onto them, to keep a tight rein, but her own nervousness consumed her. Their father emerged from one of the cars. He wore denim pants, a blue work shirt, boots, and had a seaman's duffle on his shoulder. He looked like he belonged on a ship rather than a train. The two boys moved towards him in at a deliberate pace, not a run, nor an amble. "Papa!" Bob said as he reached out to be picked up. Richard stood aside and waited his turn. Lucy followed and watched as her husband greeted the boys. He dropped the duffle and hugged and kissed his sons, more affection than she had ever seen him display. He looked trim and fit. His face was red from the sun and his head bare, just as it was the first time she saw him on the streets of Buffalo. As she neared, he released the boys and came to her, his arms wide. He embraced her tightly and buried his face in the nape of her neck. She felt his tears and could not stop her eyes from welling. She wrapped her arms over his shoulders and kissed his head.

"Oh, Lucy," he said into her neck. "You don't know—"

"It doesn't matter. Nothing matters now that you are home. You're home." She squeezed him as hard as she could, pushing her body into his. They stood like that until the crowd around them had all but disappeared. Lucy released Hans and held him at arm's length. "I can't believe you're home. Look at you."

He put his arm around her shoulder and began walking. He looked over his shoulder at the boys. "Robert, grab my duffle. Come, let's go home."

When they reached the parking lot, Hans stopped. "Ah! There she is." He walked over to the Peerless, ran his hand along the fender, and got into the driver's seat. "All aboard! This train is leaving the station." The boys smiled and climbed into the rumble seat and Lucy took her old seat on the passenger side. The engine roared to life and Hans smiled broadly. He put the car in gear and drove his family home.

Later that night, after the boys had gone to bed Lucy and Hans sat in the sitting room and had a cup of tea. He looked naked sitting there, no papers, no radio, and smaller somehow. A silence hung between them, the kind that only exists when there is too much to say, to ask, and no one knows where to start. When they had come home earlier in the day, he walked out into the beet field and crouched down in the middle of the rows. He dug into the soil with his hand and sifted it through his fingers, felt the leafy greens of the plants, and looked up and smiled at Lucy. "You've done a fine job," he said. "I must've taught you well." He chuckled. He also inspected the barn and found everything to his satisfaction. When he went into the shed Lucy held her arms crossed over her chest and kept her distance. She could hear him moving things around in there and it took him longer to come out than she expected. "You've been painting?" he asked, walking out with a brush in his hand.

"One side of the barn needed to be touched up."

He held up the brush. "Someone forgot to clean it. Now it's ruined."

Lucy nodded.

"When those men came," he began. He looked down at the ground and then out over one of the fields, and back into Lucy's eyes. "Did they come back after?"

"After?" She knew what he was driving at, but wanted to hear him say it.

"After they took me away, did those men come back and search our things?"

"We did have some uninvited guests."

"I see." He walked away from her and to the burn barrel and tossed the brush in. He stood there for a moment, looking into the ashes as though he were looking for something. After a moment, he walked into the house, leaving Lucy standing out in the yard.

Now, as he sat across from her, she in the settee and he in his favorite chair, she still felt that way, as if he had walked away.

"So what are your plans?" she asked.

Hans seemed surprised by the question. "My plans? To finish the planting and bring in the next harvest. The same as before..." He trailed off, as though the words at the end of the thought were something he didn't want to approach. He looked around the room. He gazed at the family photos on the mantle, the table where his radio once sat, and then at the lamp he had always read his newspapers under. "It all feels so strange." His hand swept across, indicating everything, including Lucy. "I know these are my possessions, things I coveted and enjoyed, but I feel so..." He struggled for the right word.

Lucy leaned in. "Distant," she said.

"*Ja.* That's it exactly. Everything is ordinary, but it doesn't feel that way anymore. It's all exactly the same. It's me. I'm what's changed." He nodded, having heard himself say something that rung true on the inside. He took a sip of his tea and grimaced. "It's grown cold."

"You've had a long day, Hans. Why don't you go to bed and get some rest. You'll feel better sleeping in your own bed and you'll see, tomorrow things will be better."

Hans nodded but didn't stir from his seat. "My chair doesn't feel right. It's like it was replaced with one that looks exactly the same, but feels different." He stood up, turned and looked at the chair, like he expected to find some evidence that it was not the chair he'd left behind in that very spot.

"Hans," Lucy said.

He turned. "*Ja?*"

"Go to bed. You're exhausted."

He turned back to the chair, taking another, closer look. Lucy stood up, took him by the arm, and led him to the bedroom. She turned down the sheets and fluffed his pillows. "Settle in and I'll be in shortly."

She walked out of the bedroom and pulled the door closed. She stood there for a moment and then heard the floor creak as he began moving about in the bedroom. She collected the cups and saucers from the sitting room and as she did, she paused and looked at Hans' chair. There was a worn indentation in the seat, a place molded to his rear-end over the years, and now it seemed as though it would never be filled in just the same way. She brought the dishes to the kitchen and rinsed them out, deciding to wash them out tomorrow. When she walked back into the bedroom, the lights were off and she could see her husband's form under the covers. His breathing was slow and steady and she thought he had fallen asleep already.

She had missed sharing her bed with him. When they were younger, he was passionate with her, touching her places that she dare not mention, even in her own mind. He had the power to make her feel free, like she was a feather floating on the breeze. Other times he would get her so tightly wound that she was sure her bones would snap under the pressure. As time passed, the distance between those moments grew longer. She had learned to settle for the simple comfort of his warmth in the bed next to her. As she climbed into bed and moved next to him, feeling his body heat, she wondered if it would ever be enough for her again. Hans wasn't the only one who had changed, she realized. She lay there under the sheets, staring at the ceiling of their bedroom. The shadow from the tree outside the window swayed as the wind blew, and she felt a stranger next to her.

Chapter 29

Hans awoke early the next morning, before everyone else. He sat in his car and started the engine. This, he thought, feels the same. He put the car into gear and looked up through the windshield. Lucy stood in front of the car with her arms crossed, dressed only in her nightgown and robe. Their eyes met and he turned off the engine. She walked up to the driver's side of the car.

"Where are you going?" she asked.

Hans shrugged. "I don't know. I just felt like a drive." Lucy looked at him in a way that made her seem different. There had always been softness to her, a generosity that one could see in her eyes, and when she and the boys met him at the station, he noticed something had changed, but he wasn't sure then. Now, he was sure it was gone. She stood next to the car with her arms folded and Hans finally averted his eyes. "I need some time to think," he said. "You don't know what I've been through."

Lucy tilted her head. "You don't know what I had to go through while you were gone."

Hans nodded. He had wondered how long it would take for the resentment to fully surface. In her letters, she had blamed the police, the FBI, the government for his internment, but now it seemed she was beginning to see he, too, was to blame. Perhaps it had been a mistake to come back home. He could have gotten off the train in Fargo and found his way back to Gloria and Peter. She needed a husband and Peter needed a father. In doing so he could have walked away from the entanglements he had become enmeshed in, but he was drawn back home. There were responsibilities he had to honor. As intriguing as a new life in North Dakota might have been, he could not walk away from his family or the others to which he was beholden. He was born at the wrong time in Germany. Being a farmer no longer mattered to the industrial machine that had taken over his country, and so he came to America to work with the soil, to have a farm. Now, the same type of industrial machine was taking over this country. It had brought nothing but death, and it was why Germany declared war on America, a country that had no business being in Europe. That's what they had shown him. He had a chance to help stop it before his arrest but did not, and now he had to figure out what to do next.

"You're right. I don't know the troubles you endured. We both need time to..." He didn't know the word to use. The biggest decisions in his life had been made for him for so many years, and now he had a moment where he could change the course of his life or follow through with what was expected of him.

"What were you hiding, Hans?" she said.

"I wasn't hiding anything. What are you talking about?"

"You don't owe him anything, Hans. You already gave up three months of your life. And what about your sons and me? We didn't agree to anything."

Hans could see a storm brewing in his wife. She was starting to tremble.

"It was me," she said. "Not the FBI. If they had found what I found you'd still be in North Dakota, or worse."

"I don't—"

"Don't lie to me. The closet behind the deer pelt, the one with all those chemicals and maps? I got rid of all of it.."

Hans wanted to speak, to say something that would show her he had come back for her and the boys; he wanted to say how thankful he was for all she did in gaining his release, but each time a sentence formed in his mind it sounded disingenuous. He wasn't sure he would be able to complete anything before she'd jump in and call his bluff. He had to keep it simple. "I love you, Lucy." He looked her in the eyes but only saw skepticism.

"Before, they thought you were an Alien Enemy. I helped prove you're a citizen, and now if they arrest you again the charge will be treason.

You *know* what they do to traitors." Lucy slammed her hand on the roof of the car. "And what about your sons? Should they have to suffer a father who betrays his country?"

"Lucy," Hans said.

"Don't say another word to me." She turned away with her hands on her hips and half looked over her shoulder. "Go!" she said. "Go for your drive. If you come back all that nonsense that Walter put you up to is over. If it's not, don't come back." She walked away and was back in the house before Hans had a chance to say anything in response. He sat behind the wheel for a long time and thought. All he could say that he knew for sure was that he wanted to drive, to feel the wind in his hair and the steering wheel in his hands, the steel and rubber all at his command. He started the car and as he turned onto Newton Avenue and felt eyes follow him. Whose eyes he could not say, but he felt hollowness spread inside his chest. He tried to fill up the emptiness by driving too fast on the dirt roads. He drove far out into the countryside, followed roads without signs, and looked over fields of wheat, alfalfa, and rye. The sun was golden and low. As the roads dipped, the sun hid behind hills and then as he crested them it would appear again, like small dawns he that repeated over and over. It made him feel strong and weak at the same time.

He reached a crossroads. The east arrow, the one pointing into the rising sun, read Attica, a town with a prison and a railroad bridge that crossed Tonawanda Creek, a town he'd have to cross through to reach Rochester. The other arrow, the one pointing west, read Buffalo. He thought of the railway station there, and the one in Cleveland, Chicago, Minneapolis, and Fargo, and then his mind continued to drift over the Plains to a secret refuge, a place where he could simply disappear and become part of the land. He sat there for a long moment while the engine idled. To the east was a day in a life that he wasn't sure belonged to him anymore. To the west, was the promise of something new—but at what price?

Overhead he heard Canadian Geese. They formed a V in the sky; all following the one at the point. He envied the leader and the followers: one for its confidence and the others for their blind obedience. If only he had the courage to choose to be one or the other.

Lucy heard the stairs thunder, the front door slam and shouting in the front yard. She hurried from the kitchen to the picture window in the sitting room in time to see her youngest son running after the Peerless as it turned on to Newton Avenue. Bob waved his arms and screamed *Papa*, but Hans must not have seen nor heard him. The automobile didn't hesitate as it drove away, its form lost in a cloud of road dust. Bob ran to the end of the driveway and stopped, his chest heaving hard from running, but put forth one last yell for his father who was too far away to hear or see. Lucy's jaw clenched, as did the muscles in her arms. Her hands became fists and the urge to punch through the glass that separated her from her son grew loud in her soul. Her son stood at the end of the drive, staring off into the distance of the road, and then his shoulders fell and his head dropped down as he turned up the drive and plodded back toward the house. Like a jumble of bees, her temper let loose. She pushed Hans' chair over and it crashed into the side table; it and the lamp that sat atop toppled and smashed into the floor, and glass shattered across the floor.

"Is he gone?" Richard asked, standing halfway down the stairs.

Lucy turned, "He just went for a drive." Richard's chin stiffened a bit and he reminded her of herself as he glanced over at the sudden mess she'd made in the sitting room. She'd seen the same expression on his face the night before at the supper table when Richard told his father about the work he'd been doing for Gus Payne and how he wanted him to work on their farm on the weekends.

"Absolutely not," his father had said. "We need you here."

The work at the Payne's farm had not only become a source of pride with the money he had brought into the household, but he had learned to see himself in a different way, as one who was capable, strong, and sure. Richard's chin had set forward and his eyes narrowed in response to his father's imperative, just as it had set now in response to Lucy's lie.

"I don't know," she said and dropped her head as she walked back into the kitchen. She came back a moment later with a broom and dustpan and saw Richard had righted his father's chair and sat in it, his posture stiff, as though the chair were a throne. Lucy paused and looked at her son and took him in as he lifted his head and met her gaze.

"So what now?" he asked.

Lucy handed him the broom. "You help me clean up this mess."

He nodded and rose from his father's chair and took the broom. Lucy straightened the side table and checked it for damage. Richard picked up the base of the lamp, unplugged the cord, wrapped it around the broken lamp, and set it on the table. He swept the glass that had skittered across the floor into a loose pile and Lucy held the dustpan for him as he pushed to broken pieces into it.

The front door opened and Bob walked through, looking as though he'd lost the world. Richard and Lucy glanced over at him as he began up the stairs as if they were the thirteen steps of a gallows. As he neared the top, he looked over and saw his mother and brother bending over the pile of broken glass. He paused for a moment and said, "Richard, did you break another lamp?"

Richard smiled and inclined his head toward his mother.

"At this rate we won't have to worry about the blackouts," Bob said with a wry smile and then walked into his room.

"He's going to be okay," Richard said.

Lucy nodded. "I think so too." She walked into the kitchen and emptied the dustpan and the glass clattered in the bottom of the can. Richard came in and handed her the broom and she stored it and the dustpan on a nail sticking out of the wall.

"Is there anything else I can do?"

She put her hand on Richard's shoulder and felt the muscles he had developed over the last few weeks of labor and smiled at her son. "The beet field needs weeding and the east field has to be turned and readied for the squash and melons." She expected Richard to balk and make an excuse about other things he needed to take care of, but instead he nodded.

"Which do you want done first?"

"Let's hitch the disc plow to the tractor and you can turn the field, if you're feeling up to it."

Richard nodded and his chin stuck out just a bit as he walked out the door. "I'm up to it."

Lucy smiled as she watched her oldest son walk out to the barn with the pace and gait of a man. He pulled work gloves from his back pocket, put them on, and clapped his hands together as he disappeared around the corner of the barn. The familiar sound of the tractor's engine came to life and a moment later, she saw him atop the machine, maneuvering it deftly through the open doors of the barn. He set the brake, banged it once with an open hand to make sure it was truly set, just the way his father had always done, and then jumped down and went into the barn, emerging a moment later walking the disc implement to the rear of the machine. He hitched it on, climbed back up on the tractor, and released the brake. The machine rolled forward and the chickens scattered out of his way as he engaged the gears and steered it toward the field. He turned in his seat, raised the implement, and then caught his mother watching him. He straightened in his seat and waved to her as he drove by the kitchen window and toward the east field. At the edge of the field, he checked his alignment, dropped the discs, and moved forward. The dark fertile ground turned under the discs like a slow black wake as the tractor moved across the field in a straight and simple line, furrowing deep rows for the summer planting.

Conspirator who helped the 8 Saboteurs of June 1942 Indicted On Charges of Being Spy Aide

WASHINGTON, July. 20 -- Indictments charging Walter Emil Kratsch of 264 Cooke Road, Rochester, N.Y., with conspiracy to aid the eight Nazi saboteurs of June, 1942, were handed down in Albany today by Attorney General Aramis Bindle.

Shortly after midnight on the morning of June 13, 1942, four men landed on a beach from a German submarine and brought ashore explosives, primers, and incendiaries devices.

The four men, led by George John Dasch, age 39, landed on a beach near Amagansett, Long Island, New York, about 12:10 a.m., June 26, 1942. Accompanying Dasch were Ernest Peter Burger, 36; Heinrich Harm Heinck, 35; and Richard Quirin, 34.

The saboteurs were instructed in chemistry, incendiaries, explosives, timing devices, secret writing, and concealment of identity by blending in as Americans. During their training the saboteurs were familiarized with the vital points and vulnerabilities of aluminum and magnesium plants, railroad shops and bridges, canals, locks, and other facilities they planned to attack.

Upon apprehension, a total of $174,588 was recovered by the FBI from the saboteurs.

Kratsch was active in a [pro-Nazi] German-American Bund and made several efforts to propagandize and win adherents for Nazism among German Americans and German immigrants in America.

After Dasch's arrest by the FBI he quickly revealed to his interrogators that Kratsch was a vital resource for the planned operations, supplying intelligence, money, and additional materials and personnel necessary for their missions.

During the initial investigation, Kratsch denied any involvement with the saboteurs. However, after being implicated in the sabotage plots by Dasch he was arrested and charged with conspiracy.

Subsequent to his arrest, a search of Kratsch's residence resulted in the discovery of maps indicating American targets. The maps were annotated with the spots where railroads could be most effectively disabled, the principal aluminum, magnesium, and steel plants in New York state, and important canals, waterways, and locks.

Of particular interest, according to the maps, were the Symington-Gould plants, one located in Rochester, N.Y., which supplies steel and hulls to the Charlestown shipyard outside Boston, Massachusetts, and the other located outside of Buffalo, N.Y. in Depew, which also supplies vital components to the United States Navy.

Security details at these and other targets on the maps have been increased since Kratsch's arrest.

Attorney General Bindle also indicated that there is an ongoing investigation into Kratsch's work as a technician at the Bausch & Lomb plant located in Rochester. Bausch & Lomb is a major supplier of high-grade optics to the United States Navy.

Bindle says his office continues to investigate the conspiracy and fully expects to make more arrests as more information becomes available through the interrogation of the saboteurs, Kratsch, and anonymous sources.

Kratsch's wife, Justine Misslewitz Kratsch, has denied any knowledge of her husband's treasonous activities.